T

W9-BZL-409

The Hearts
of
Horses

**Center Point
Large Print**

**This Large Print Book carries the
Seal of Approval of N.A.V.H.**

The Hearts
of
Horses

Molly Gloss

CENTER POINT PUBLISHING
THORNDIKE, MAINE

This Center Point Large Print edition
is published in the year 2008 by arrangement with
Houghton Mifflin Company.

Copyright © 2008 by Molly Gloss.

All rights reserved.

The text of this Large Print edition is unabridged. In other
aspects, this book may vary from the original edition.
Printed in the United States of America.
Set in 16-point Times New Roman type.

ISBN: 978-1-60285-171-9

Library of Congress Cataloging-in-Publication Data

Gloss, Molly.
    The hearts of horses / Molly Gloss.--Center Point large print ed.
    p. cm.
    ISBN 978-1-60285-171-9 (lib. bdg. : alk. paper)
    1. Young women--Fiction. 2. Horses--Training--Fiction. 3. Country life--Oregon--Fiction.
4. Large type books. I. Title.

PS3557.L65H43 2008
813'.54--dc22

2007050020

For Ed, this last gift

1

I N THOSE DAYS, even before the war had swept up all the young men from the ranches, there were girls who came through the country breaking horses. They traveled from ranch to ranch with two or three horses they were taking home to break or with horses they had picked up in trade for work they'd done. Of course most outfits had fifty or sixty horses back then so there was plenty of work, and when the war came on, no men to get it done. Those girls could break horses as well as any man but they had their own ways of doing it, not such a bucking Wild West show. They went about it so quiet and deliberate, children would get tired of watching and go off to do something else. They were usually alone, those girls, but it wasn't like in the moving pictures or the gunslinger novels, the female always in peril. If they were in peril it wasn't from outlaws or crooked sheriffs, it was from the usual things that can happen with ranch work—breaking bones, freezing your fingers off—the kinds of things that can happen whether you're a man or a woman.

In November in that first winter of the war a girl named Martha Lessen rode down through the Ipsoot Pass into Elwha County looking for horses that needed breaking out. She was riding a badly scarred mare she called Dolly and she had a couple of other horses towing behind her, which she had brought along just because she didn't feel she could leave them behind.

At the upper end of the valley where the road first drops down along Graves Creek she saw a man out in a big fenced stubble field feeding about thirty cows and half a dozen horses and a pair of white mules. She called to him from the road, "Hello," and he stopped what he was doing and looked over at her. "If you've got any horses need breaking to saddle, I'll break them for you," she told him.

The daylight was thin, a cold and wintry light, and it pulled all the color out of the man's face. He stood up straight. The winter before, there had been a string of about a hundred days when the temperature never rose above freezing and some counties—Elwha, Umatilla, Grant—had piled up seven feet of snow. Deer had been driven down into the towns, and cougar had come into the pastures with the cattle. Starving horses had wandered into people's houses. But this particular winter, the winter of 1917 and 1918, would be an open one, and the day Martha Lessen rode down out of the Ipsoot Pass there wasn't any snow on the ground at all, although the stubble field the man was working in had been grazed off and the skimpy leavings were dark from frost-kill. He was feeding from a wagon drawn by a pair of black Percherons.

"Maybe I do," he said. "There's a couple could use working." He looked her over. "I guess you ain't no Land Girl." This past summer a lot of men from the ranches had gone into the army and quite a few town and city girls had come out to the countryside to fill in where they were needed—"Land Girls" the newspapers had begun to call them. Some of them had come to Elwha County with the idea of being cowboys, though mostly the work that needed doing was getting in the hay crop and the wheat. Martha Lessen was the first girl he had seen advertising herself as a bronco-buster.

"No I'm not," she said. "I've been riding and doing ranch work since I could walk. I can break horses."

He smiled and said, "I just bet you can," which was a remark about the way she was built, big and solid as a man and five-eleven in her boots. Or he meant something about her old-fashioned cowboy trappings, the fringed batwing chaps well scratched up and her showy big platter of a hat much stained along the high crown and the rolled edge of the brim. Then he said, not with serious misgiving but as if he had discovered something slightly amusing, "Breaking to saddle, so I guess that means you're not interested in breaking horses to harness."

She could have found plenty of work around Pendleton, where she had come from, if she had wanted to break horses to drive, so she said stubbornly, "I'd just rather train a stock horse than a wagon horse if I'm able to choose."

He considered this. "Well, go on up to the house and I'll be up shortly and we'll see about it." He went back to feeding hay.

She followed a line of telephone poles from the road back to the ranch house, which was a paintless tall box with skinny windows set among a scattering of barns

9

and sheds and bunkhouses built variously of lumber and pine logs. A yellow dog scrambled out from under the porch of the house and barked once and then walked up and smelled of the girl's boot. "Hey there," she said, which satisfied him, and he walked off and flopped down in the hard dirt at the edge of the porch steps.

Elwha County was more than two-thirds taken up by the Clarks Range and the Whitehorn Mountains, with the towns and most of the ranches lying in the swale between. This house stood on the first moderately flat ground at the foot of the Clarks, its front windows facing south across the valley toward the Whitehorns. The girl wondered what sort of view could be seen from those windows, and she turned in the saddle to look. There had been a little cold rain earlier in the day and the clouds were moving southeast now, dragging low across the pointy tops of the lodgepole and yellow pine stands in the far distance; there was no telling whether the serrate line of the Whitehorns might show in better weather. By the time she turned back toward the house a woman had come out on the porch and was wiping her hands on her apron. She was just about exactly the age of the man who'd been feeding cows, which was fifty, and she stood there in black high-top shoes and a long dress and a sweater with the sleeves rolled up to the elbows, stood there wiping her hands and squinting at the girl.

Martha said, "I'm here to see about some work breaking horses. The man feeding cows in that field by the road said I ought to wait here till he came in to talk to me about it."

"Well it's cold," the woman said. "You can put up those horses in the barn and then come in and have a cup of coffee. He'll be a while." She went back inside the house.

Martha watered her horses and led them over to the barn but she didn't put them up. She left them standing saddled in the open runway, out of the wind, then walked back to the house. The dog met her again and smelled of her boots and her chaps up to the knees and she patted him on the head and went past him onto the porch. When she rapped lightly on the door the woman inside called out, "You'd better just come on in." She tucked her gloves into her belt, scraped her boots as well as she could on the porch boards and stepped inside. The dim front room ran the width of the house and was furnished more elaborately than Martha was used to, with upholstered chairs, carved end tables, Turkish rugs, kerosene lamps with elaborate glass shades. Thick draperies closed off the windows, which might have been to keep the heat inside; but Martha felt if there was any chance of seeing the mountains she'd have left the windows open to the view.

She crossed the room and went through a doorway into the kitchen where the woman was pouring coffee into heavy china cups. This room was bare of the fussy furnishings at the front of the house. The long pine table and chairs and two kitchen cupboards were painted white, and the windows were tall and narrow

11

and curtainless. The day's gray brightness flooding through those panes of glass made the room seem clean and cold. From this side of the house you could see some trees, but the house was too close to the Clarks to get a view of their snowy peaks. The girl took off her hat and held it in her hands.

"What's your name, dear?" the woman said.

"It's Martha Lessen."

"Well my goodness, I have a sister and a cousin both named Martha, so that's a name that will come easy to my lips."

She put the coffee cups and a pitcher of cream on the kitchen table and sat down in a chair.

"If I was to pay you for it," the girl said to her, "I wonder if I could later on give my horses a little bit of your hay."

The woman made a dismissive gesture with one hand. "Oh heavens," she said, as if that was just the most outrageous idea. "You help yourself. A horse has got to have something to eat. Sit down now and drink your coffee." Martha sat in a kitchen chair and put her big hat in her lap and poured as much cream into her coffee as the cup would hold.

"You talked to George, did you?"

"I didn't get his name. He had on overalls and a brown coat."

This amused her. "Well of course every man in this part of the world is wearing overalls and an old brown coat," she said, "but I guess it was George Bliss who is my husband and I am Louise Bliss."

She then started right in telling Martha how they were Old Oregonians, both she and her husband, children of first comers, and how this house they were sitting in had been built from trees cut and milled right here on the ranch by her husband's daddy right after the Indians were driven off, and how her own granddaddy had fought in the Civil War and then come up to Oregon with one of the first big trail drives out of Texas and bought half a dozen cows with his wages, and by the time he died owned almost two hundred head of cattle and eight hundred acres of Baker Valley pastureland. She spoke as if the girl had asked for every bit of their family history but it was just that she had immediately taken Martha Lessen for a certain kind of ranch girl, the kind that followed the seasonal work traipsing from ranch to ranch; and Louise had known such girls to be shy as the dickens and indisposed to talk. She felt it would be up to her to fill the silence, and Martha's old-time cowboy trappings seemed to make her a perfect audience for romantic pioneer stories.

When George Bliss came in through the back porch he poured himself some coffee and stood there drinking it without sitting down at the kitchen table. His wife wasn't saying anything he didn't already know. She and George had brought four children into the world, she was telling Martha, and one had died shortly after being born but they had a boy who was now in Kansas preparing to fight in France and another who was at college up in Pullman, Washington, with the intent to learn veterinary medicine, and a girl, Miriam, who was married and living with her husband's family on a ranch up around Pilot Rock. George stood there drinking his coffee quietly and letting Louise go on talking without interrupting her, and it was the telephone that finally broke the thread of her story and made all three of them jump. It wasn't the Blisses' ring—theirs was two longs and a short, this was three long jangles—but Mrs. Bliss went to the telephone anyway. In those days there were seven ranches on the party line at that end of the valley and they listened in on each other's calls without a bit of apology.

George took his opening to say to Martha, "I've got a couple of likely-looking three-year-olds, or I guess they're four-year-olds now, that haven't never been broke. They're halter-broke more or less, and I suppose I could get a saddle on them if I was determined about it, and I suppose if I was truly determined I could stick on and ride them out. But they ain't been finished and I haven't got the time to do it now that my son has gone off to fight. I've got just two hands I've been able to keep this winter. Henry Frazer, who was my foreman, has left me and gone over to help out the Woodruff sisters since all their hands joined up, and one of the two I got left is a kid who I expect will be joined up as soon as he turns eighteen and anyway ain't had much experience bucking out horses. I hired him mostly as a ditch walker and for moving the gates on my dams and so forth in the summer, and I'm trying to teach him cowboying but he's not the best hand I ever had in the world; and the other is a fellow with a bum arm that keeps him out of the army and also keeps him from doing any kind of roping, and which is a disadvantage, I guess you know, if you're trying to break broncs."

The usual method of broncobusters in those days was to forefoot a horse with a catch rope, which brought him right to his knees, and then wrestle a saddle onto him while he was on the ground, climb on and buck him near to death. Martha Lessen was a terrible hand with a lariat and horses hardly ever bucked when she rode them the first time but she didn't say any of this to George Bliss. "I'd like to break them out for you," she said. "I can gentle most anything that has four feet and a tail."

"What would you want for the two of them?"

"I could do them for ten dollars apiece."

He lifted his eyebrows. "Ten to get them started or will that get them finished?"

Since this was the first time she'd been asked to name a price, she was easily warned off. She'd been helping out her dad since she was old enough to sit her own horse, and she'd been about thirteen the first time anybody hired her to move cattle or gather horses off the open range or round up a runaway team. She'd been breaking horses since she was fifteen but it had always been something she'd done in her spare time while she was working summers on one ranch or another and not something she'd been paid separately for. "I expect I can get them close to finished for ten dollars," she said, looking down into her coffee. She knew the hard part wasn't climbing onto a horse for the first time and a decent working horse might take a year or two to truly finish, and she thought George Bliss must know this too. But she could get a horse pretty well along in a few weeks, and after that it would be a matter of the horse gaining experience. She waited and when nothing more was said, she added, "If you aren't happy with the way they turn out, you don't have to pay me."

Mr. Bliss looked at his wife, who had by now hung up the telephone and come back to the table. Martha wanted to know what sort of look Louise Bliss was giving back to him but she deliberately kept from acting interested: she turned the coffee cup in her two hands and looked down at her thumbs rubbing along the rolled rim of the china.

"That was the hardware store over in Bingham," Louise said, because George's questioning look had been about the telephone and not at all to do with Martha Lessen. "The nails and wire have come in, and after all this time, I should hope so." George knew whose nails and wire she meant, and merely nodded at his coffee. Then Louise said suddenly, "Do you know? This girl sitting here is named Martha?" as if she expected the news to amaze him.

George said, "Is that so," with no more than mild interest. "Well Miss Martha, let's go out and take a look at them broncs and you tell me do you think you

16

can make them into cow ponies." He winked at her without smiling and set his coffee down and went out through the back porch into the yard.

"Thanks for the coffee," she told Louise Bliss and followed the man outside.

His two white mules were standing there tied to the porch rails; George Bliss had saddled them before he had come inside the house. He climbed onto one of them and when she realized what was expected of her Martha got up on the other and they rode out to find the horses. The yellow dog ran to get ahead because it was his habit to take the lead, a habit that had resulted in his acquiring the name Pilot.

The war had encouraged George Bliss to plow up a big stretch of his deeded pastureland to plant wheat, so his wheat fields, fenced and cross-fenced and edged with irrigation ditches and diversion dams, took up most of the flattish ground to the east and the south near the homeplace. George led Martha the back way, north through a gate into the grass and bitterbrush foothills. After forty minutes or so they went up through another gate into the scattered timber of the Clarks Range. Those mountains had been part of Teddy Roosevelt's freshly minted Blue Mountain Forest Reserve back in '06, then were split off into their own reserve about 1912. The Taylor Grazing Act and all the rules and rigamarole of leasing from the government were a good fifteen years off at that point and George was still using the mountains as pasture for his livestock, was still wintering his horses and some of his cattle in the grassy canyons inside the reserve. He and Martha began scouring the creek bottoms one after the other, looking for the horses he wanted to show her.

She had a cowboy's disregard for mules—a mule lacked the dignity and honorableness of a horse was one of the things she believed. But this belief wasn't in any way based on experience and it was a surprise to her to discover that the white mule had a nice swinging walk and a sure foot and a look in his eye that struck her as entirely dignified. When they had been riding in silence for a while, she finally worked up the nerve to say a few words to George Bliss about the mule's gait and his sure-footedness. He told her, "Well, a mule is no good for working cattle, I guess you know, but I've always been partial to them for packing or if I'm going up into broken ground. They never put their foot wrong is my experience. My daddy used to raise mules for the army, which is how I got interested in them. They've got a lot of good sense. A mule won't put up with a lopsided load; he'll walk right up to a tree and scrape it off. I guess if I was smart I ought to go to raising them again, with the war and all, and there being a lot of call for mules."

The girl's showy rodeo costume had caused him to saddle the mules out of amused contrariness—he intended to surprise and upend her. But now that she had spoken well of the mules he was coming to a slightly different opinion of her, and he began looking for a way to feel out her knowledge. After he'd thought about it he said, "These mules come out of a mare, Tulip, that I wish I had a dozen more just like her. She was half-Shire, and her mule colts was good big work animals. People say it's the stud, but when it comes to mules my money's on the mare."

Even farm girls in those days were modest and circumspect when it came to talking to men about the details and mechanics of stock breeding, so George didn't say anything further along those lines; but all the time they were riding he went on talking in the same indirect way about matters to do with horses, especially anything to do with their breaking. He was mildly trying to provoke an opinion out of Martha Lessen without ever directly asking her anything. "I guess you know a mule is just about nothing to break," he told her. "You can climb up on a mule and he'll raise his back once or twice and then settle down to work, that easy." And later on he said, "I don't know what the difference is, or why horses have got to be so hard about it."

She had opinions and might have stated them; it was just from natural shyness and a failure to realize what he was fishing for that she didn't say much. But as he kept on with it, she finally figured out what George was after and began to speak up, and once she got going she had plenty to say. She told him, for instance, about her preference for a McClelland saddle when she was breaking a horse, because those old cavalry saddles were light in the stirrup leathers and she liked how they let her feel the horse, and the horse feel her. She told him she liked to use her own homemade basal hackamore as long as possible on a green colt and after that a snaffle bit; and that she didn't have much use for a spade bit. She told him when a horse misbehaved she figured it was for one of two reasons: either he didn't understand what you wanted or the bad behavior hadn't ever been corrected in the past. She said that in her experience horses weren't mean unless some man made them that way; but some horses, once they'd been made mean, just weren't worth the time it took to break them. "Like people," she said, glancing at George. "Some people just belong in prison and some horses just belong in the rodeo."

They made a full swing along the timbered breaks of the foothills, passing through several small bunches of cows and steers, and three different bands of horses. In one bunch of fifteen or twenty mares, George pointed out a young buckskin stud horse he said was half-Arab that he'd bought to improve his herd. Martha said appreciatively, "He's got an awfully nice-looking head," and after watching him a moment—he was tossing his head, kicking and rearing and whinnying, showing off for George and Martha in front of his wives—she also said, "Those young horses sure like to make a big show," without saying what had come into her mind, which was a young stallion she knew of who'd been put into pasture all one summer with half a dozen experienced brood mares without producing a single foal. Those mares had just been disgusted by his adolescent male lordliness, and they hadn't ever let him cover them.

He showed her maybe forty horses altogether, and among the last band the four-year-olds he wanted to have broken to saddle, a bay and a chestnut, both of them geldings. The chestnut, when he moved, had an odd action, a kind of conspicuous engagement of the hips, which Martha thought might make for a smooth trot. They were in their long winter coats and looked pretty rough, almost wild. She doubted they had much memory of being halter-broke, but if they'd been broken out in the usual way then not remembering was good news as far as she was concerned. She told George Bliss her opinion about the chestnut, the way he lifted his hips, and George gave the horse a close look in silence and then said, "Well, it do look different," without saying whether he thought she was right about the horse having a smooth gait.

When they got back to the house it was late in the afternoon, the daylight already failing, and it had grown pretty cold. They put up the saddles and turned the mules loose in the stubble field by the road and stood watching them trot off to rejoin the other animals. The cows in that field were all of a type, short horns and short-coupled bodies and red-brown hides spotted rarely with white. "Those is Louise's cows," George said. "I hate those pure breeds, all that extra work trying to keep them separate, and all the paper filing and so forth. Her daddy give her two registered ones when we was married and she was just dumb enough to like it." Martha would have taken this at face value if it had been her own dad saying it. She didn't know how to take George Bliss, who sounded only cheerfully long-suffering.

"Well, let's go eat," he said to her, and slapped his palms on the top rail of the fence. She had expected George Bliss to say yes or no while they were standing there looking over his animals, and he hadn't given her the word either way. She had a sleeping bag and tent with her and some sandwiches and cheese, and had more or less imagined that if she had trouble finding work she'd sleep in fields or sheds and make do with her own groceries. She didn't know if George Bliss's invitation to supper constituted an unspoken offer of employment. If she thought she was hired, she'd have wanted to put up her horses before going in to eat; but there was no way to know if Mr. Bliss had just forgotten about her animals standing saddled in his barn or if he hadn't yet made up his mind whether to hire her on.

She followed him across the shadowy yard and around to the back door, onto the closed-in porch where they kept the wash basin and a towel. He let Martha have first turn at the water, which may have been a concession to her femaleness. She was used to elbowing a turn with her brothers and her dad, used to dirty towels and brown water, but sometimes when she'd worked on other ranches the men would put her at the head of the line. She didn't mind being singled out for such things but liked it better when the men seemed to forget she was a girl. Once some women relatives of the boss, women dressed in linen suits and delicate shoes, had come out to watch a branding crew where Martha was helping out, and some of the men had grumbled about it. "When there's women hanging around it sure takes your mind off what we're doing, don't it?" one of them had said to her seriously.

She washed her hands and stepped into the kitchen, where George's wife was turning out sourdough biscuits from a pan. A man with a graying handlebar mustache was sitting at the table drinking coffee and he gave her a curious look. He was about forty, with a falling-away jaw and thinning brown hair and old pockmark scars on his cheeks. Martha nodded to him and took off her hat and stood holding it and waiting, without knowing whether she ought to help Louise Bliss bring the soup and biscuits to the table, which was something some ranches would have expected a hired girl to do, or whether to sit down with the hired man. When George Bliss came into the kitchen she saw he had hung his hat on a peg on the back porch and so she stepped back out and found a peg for her own hat there. The Blisses were both sitting by then, and she took one of the remaining chairs. She wished she had had sense enough to take off her chaps and leave them outside—the old-fashioned batwings took up a lot of room under the table—but it was too late to do anything about that now.

"Dear Lord bless this food and the horses and cows and the other animals and our children and all the boys in France and all the little Flanders children who are hungry," Louise Bliss said with closed eyes while her husband and the hired man looked down into their laps with identical expressions of seriousness.

"Amen," they said quietly when Louise had come to the end of her prayer.

As the food began to be passed, George said to Martha, "This here is Ellery Bayard but don't never call him that, he goes by El. El, this here is Martha Lessen who is a broncobuster."

El Bayard said, "Is that right?" matter-of-factly without seeming to be amused by the spectacle of a girl bronc rider; and this, together with his family name, immediately put him in a good light with Martha: Bayard was the name of a legendary horse she had read of who had outraced the army of Charlemagne while carrying four men on his back. El's right arm was fixed or nearly fixed in a half-bent position as if it had been broken once and poorly set. He made deft use of it lifting and passing plates and bowls but it was a puzzle to Martha how he would ever manage to get a saddle onto a horse or shovel out a hole or tighten a fence wire. Martha was left-handed and had been made to feel self-conscious about it, especially when she was with new people, but El Bayard's frozen arm seemed in some way to mitigate her shyness as she spooned her soup with the wrong hand.

They had eaten their dinner earlier in the day and supper was therefore pretty light. There was turnip and carrot in the soup and a chicken may have run through the pot on its way to somewhere else, or more likely this was one of the meatless days that had become patriotic in the last few months. Given that there wasn't much to eat, Martha minded her appetite, though the only food she had had all day was a breakfast of toast and buttermilk, and a sandwich eaten while in the saddle riding down from the Ipsoot Pass. When Louise Bliss encouraged her to eat up the last biscuit, she allowed herself to be persuaded.

Talk at the supper table was devoted to the war. In the afternoon newspaper had come more news of the fighting around Passchendaele, finally taken by the Canadians after months of bloody battle. In the midst of something the men were saying about soldiers who had drowned in the deep mud of the trenches, Louise Bliss stood up from the table and said in a tired voice, "I just can't bear to think about it." As she clattered dishes and stepped back and forth from table to sink, her husband gave his hired man a silencing look. Then he pushed his chair back and said to Martha, "Let's go turn out those horses you brung with you. I guess I forgot entirely about that."

They walked out to the barn in a damp cold. The yellow dog Pilot, who didn't ever like being left behind, scuttled out from his place under the porch and ran ahead of them. George brought along a lamp from the kitchen and stood by in the broad runway while Martha unloaded her gear and stripped the saddles from all three of her horses. She'd been riding Dolly on a good California stock saddle, and she'd put the old McClelland army saddle on T.M.; Rory was carrying a saddle with a wide flat seat, which she'd borrowed from her brother Tim, in case she ran into a horse who was big in the barrel like Rory. Tim and one of her other brothers, Davey, had both gone into the army, which meant Tim wouldn't be needing the saddle for a while. When she had finished stripping the tack off her horses, George unwired and pushed back the gate that let into the stubble field and stood by while she waved the animals through. The Bliss mules and horses, clear out by the road, lifted their heads and spoke and came trotting over stiff-legged. Martha watched them become acquainted, a ritual of snorting and low nickering and mutual inspection of flanks. It appeared that a bright chestnut mare was the lead horse in that bunch and Martha watched her with Dolly to be sure there wouldn't be any trouble between them, though she didn't think there would be. Dolly was old enough and had been through enough troubles in her life that she liked to keep to herself, and other horses usually let her go her own way.

"You can put up in the daughter's room is what I think," George Bliss said. "We don't keep the bed made up since she was married but I guess you can just shake out your blankets on the mattress."

"I wasn't expecting to be put up in the house."

He gave her a look. "Well, that's sure up to you. I guess there's the barn. My hired men are living in the bunkhouse so I expect Mrs. Bliss wouldn't listen to you sleeping out there."

"I don't mind the barn," she said.

"It'll be cold, I'll guarantee you that."

"All right," she said.

He laughed. "All right you'll take the barn? Or all right you'll come into the house?"

"All right the barn."

Her eyes were on the dark shapes of the animals moving off now toward the far side of the field. George Bliss looked out there too. "How did that sorrel mare of yours come to get scarred like that?" he asked her.

"She was scorched in a fire."

"Was she, now? That's a shame. I bet she was a good-looking horse before that."

"I don't know. She was already scarred when I got her."

"Are you breaking her for somebody?"

"No sir, she's mine, I got her off a man who thought she was spoiled. She was only scorched, but he figured she was spoiled and he sold her to me awful cheap."

George Bliss gave her a look.

"She's an awful good horse," Martha told him.

He nodded skeptically. "Well I guess it don't matter what a stock horse looks like if she's got good sense." He offered her the lamp. "As long as we're speaking of fire, my wife worries a lot more about kerosene than about anything else—her family was burnt out when she was young, and it was a kerosene lamp that did it—so there's candles and matches in the barn, I believe, and you go ahead and keep this here lamp with you for now but I'd appreciate it if you'd turn it out when you get good and settled and a candle lit and so forth. You can make yourself comfortable in the tack room and if you need another blanket you come over to the house and get one. My other hand has a girl he's spooning and that's why he wasn't at the table tonight but he'll be at breakfast, and you come on over to the house tomorrow too and have breakfast, come around to the back door and walk right in but don't come before daylight. We're getting old enough we don't like to roll out until the sun is up." He winked at her solemnly and walked off across the dark yard. The dog considered the question of who he ought to stay with and finally trotted off to get out in front of George. It occurred to Martha that the rancher still hadn't, strictly speaking, said she was hired.

On one side of the barn runway six stalls were laid out on either side of a tack room. The other half of the barn had been left open to shelter machinery, and she made out a set of harrows, a cultivator, a stoneboat, pipe for irrigation, parts for a homemade buck rake. There was a haymow above, but she wouldn't have wanted to sleep up there on account of the dust, and anyway George had said to make herself comfortable in the tack room. It was small and crowded, half a dozen saddles on wall trees and twenty or more bridles and halters and hackamores, as well as collars and rope and harness pieces hanging on pegs or slung over the half-walls that divided the room from the stalls. There was barely space to turn around between the wooden boxes spilling over with tools and black-smithing equipage. She lit a candle she found standing inside a sooty glass chimney on a shelf crowded with veterinary gear and turned out the kerosene lamp. She went back to where she'd left her things and carried her saddles in one at a time and slung them up onto the half-walls of the stalls, then carried the rest of her gear into the tack room and shifted some things around a bit so she could make her bed in the cramped space on the floor. After shucking her chaps and walking out in the darkness to use the privy, she came back and stripped down to her long underwear and crawled into the sleeping bag.

On ranches she'd worked for, it was never expected she would sleep in the bunkhouse with the men, so when she was too far from home to sleep in her own bed she had often been put up in the ranch house, and she'd slept in some pretty poor conditions, one time for several weeks sharing with two children on a bed with no mattress, just a spring with gunnysacks filled with straw, and a couple of wooden fruit boxes under the spring so it wouldn't sag down to the floor. She had gotten in the habit of asking for the barn, which at least was likely to be quieter and more private. This year, before heading out on her own, she'd sewn together a sleeping bag made from a wool blanket and a piece of felt and an old fur rug. In the newspapers she had read that the British soldiers in France were sleeping in mud and had only a couple of thin blankets to keep them from pneumonia, so she didn't think she had any grounds for complaint.

The candle cast a high shadow, but it was enough

light to read by. She was making her slow way through *Black Beauty*, a page or two at a time, too tired most nights to read for very long. Tonight, coming to the part where Beauty meets his old friend Ginger, in terrible condition from bad treatment as a cab horse, she shut the book and blew out the candle and then went on lying awake looking out into the darkness. Gradually the saddles and the other things took dim shape around her, and the smells of the fur rug and saddle soap, leather and hay, the warm, clean, fecund smell of horses, arose out of the cold darkness and were a comfort against a yearning that was not homesickness.

2

THE BLISSES' OTHER hired hand was Will Wright. That winter he was a lanky boy not yet filled out, with buckteeth and a crop of pimples but a smile that came easily. When they were introduced he flashed Martha one of those easy smiles and then returned his attention to the breakfast on his plate; El Bayard, who gave her no more than a brief look, scooted his chair a couple of inches to one side to make room for her at the table. They behaved just as if she had been coming to meals in the house for years, and that served to put her at ease. It was a relief to see ample food on the platters and gallons of hot coffee; she sat quietly and tucked into her biscuits and sausage gravy.

People were mostly silent over their breakfast. The men exchanged a few muttered words about the day's work—something about the fence above Dewey Creek, something about moving some heifers into the Ax Handle pasture—but otherwise there was little conversation. Louise Bliss passed silently from stove to table, refilling coffee cups and bringing fresh plates of biscuits, eating her own breakfast in brief spells of sitting. Once she made an exasperated sound and went out through the back porch and came back a bit later with a wet jar of butter retrieved from the cellar under the house. Her face, thrown into relief by the slant of the early light, seemed to Martha somewhat aged and mournful, which would have surprised Louise had she known of it. There were plenty of women back then who thought they were old at fifty and women who made a practice of unhappiness, but Louise Bliss wasn't one of them.

When George had finished mopping the last bit of gravy from his plate, he sat back and fished out his Bull Durham and made a cigarette and smoked it and squinted out the window into the pink sky. "You figure you can find those horses again, do you?" This was evidently directed at Martha, although he never looked toward her. "I expect you'll want to bring them down here to use some of these pens. You need help getting that done?"

She divined from this question that she was hired. "No sir, I don't need any help, but when I go up there I wonder if it would be all right if I left the gate open, the one along the section line between your place and the reserve?" When she brought the horses down, they would naturally be looking for a way to stay ahead of her, and when they found the hole in the fence she hoped they'd go through to the ranch.

George seemed to know this was what she meant. He nodded and said, "Just close it, after them broncs go through."

"And if it doesn't matter to you," she said after a moment, "I think I'd want to use those old pens you've got, the ones over back of the bunkhouse."

He winked at her, which wasn't the first time, and which she had already begun to realize had no meaning beyond a mild sort of amusement. "I thought you might. My daddy built those corrals when he first come here in the eighties. They ain't been kept up as well as they should and those gates are sagging pretty good but I guess you saw one of them has a snubbing pole. When he was raising mules Daddy used those corrals for breaking them out. That's mostly still what we use them for—broncobusting. They're too small for branding."

She had never made much use of snubbing poles— she had seen more than one horse wind his rope around the post until he strangled—but she didn't tell George Bliss that. She said, "I don't mind if they're small, but I like that they're kind of out of the way of things and they're good and high so a horse can't climb over, and the rails are near-solid so a horse can't be looking around at other interesting things when I'm working with him."

He didn't wink again but he might as well have, his

expression saying clearly he was amused. "I'll leave you to it, then," he said. He shoved back his chair and stood, and as he moved away he gave his wife's shoulder a light pat. She reached up absently and touched his hand as it trailed from her. El Bayard and Will Wright followed the boss. They made considerable noise of it, standing on the back porch buckling on chaps and spurs, slapping the dry mud off their hats, dragging boot heels across the board floor. When they had gone out, a sudden quiet struck the whole house. Martha didn't know Louise Bliss at all yet and was leery of getting caught up in conversation with her. She put away the last of her breakfast quickly, stood, and went to the porch for her coat and hat. Then she stuck her head back into the kitchen. "Would I find a crimper and a hammer out in the barn, in case those pens need shoring up?" She had seen hammer and nails and a couple of crimpers in a box in the tack room, so she was roundabout asking permission to take them, which she'd meant to ask of George Bliss but the words had found her too late. She had already seen yesterday that the gates to the old pens were sagging and needful of repair.

Louise was gathering up the dishes. "Oh heavens, you take whatever you need," she said without once looking up.

The corrals Martha had in mind were a pair built kissing each other along one side with a connecting gate in that wall and a short gap left in the lower rails so a big sheet-metal washtub standing on the ground there could water stock in both corrals. They were made from heavy pine logs, the kind you hardly saw anymore, all the posts and rails from old trees a good foot through. Put up in the eighties without the bark skinned off, they'd spent the last thirty years and more shedding their coats in long brown scabs that littered the ground. The rails were stacked eight feet high and so close together a thick daub of caulk might have been enough to turn them into walls.

Martha tightened up the sagging gates and stood the gate open on the pen that didn't have the snubbing pole. She wedged the uprights until they were tight and toenailed the loose rails. She walked around and picked up all the stones and limbs and pieces of bark and kicked at the ruts in the dirt until the ground inside both corrals was more or less level and then she spent half an hour carrying water over from the pump, filling the big washtub to its brim.

It was a cold morning but yesterday's rain had blown off to the southeast and the sky was clearing. When she called Dolly in from the field the mare waded to her through plumes of ground mist. She leaned against the horse's shoulder in order to tie on her big chaps, which were awkward to get in and out of. Dolly wouldn't stand for spurs so she left them off. Then she tacked up the horse and rode off in the direction she had taken the day before with George Bliss, north and west into the grass and bitterbrush of the foothills and then up into the timber on the Clarks Reserve. The sky was beginning to lighten toward blue by then, striate with white silk thread. The leaves and empty seed cases on the alder trees shivered slightly, though the air felt still.

She was a couple of hours hunting down the right band, which had gone higher up into one of the narrow draws and was spread out along a little creek that ran through there. She drove the horses gently ahead of her down the draw. In the mouth of the canyon at the edge of a stand of yellow pine and spruce there was a big old corral with a chute trailing from it, which George Bliss's father, and now George, had used for branding and roundup of cattle. These horses were familiar with the place without being afraid of it, and some of them wandered into the corral and snuffled around and then fell to grazing the high clumps of grass that had sprung up along the edges of the fence. If Martha could have figured out a way to get the bay and the chestnut to go in there, she might have been able to shut the gate and save herself a lot of trouble; but as soon as she singled them out they understood what she was about and they broke from the rest of the band and dodged back through the trees, cracking through low dead branches and jumping fallen wood and brush with grunts and low squeals.

A horse hates to be separated from his fellows, and any grazing animal dislikes being moved off his familiar range. Martha and Dolly had to work hard to get those two ponies loose of the trees and headed downhill, but the horses had each other, which con-soled them, and whenever they tried to circle back to the band Martha kept them turning and turning until they wound up moving downhill again. She mostly gave them a lot of room—those horses hardly knew they were being driven—but at every little creek they crossed she pressed them hard and wouldn't let them stand to water. They struck the section-line fence about a quarter of a mile above the open gate and turned downhill along the fence and then went neatly through the opening as if they had asked Martha what she wanted them to do.

When the Bliss buildings came in sight Martha and Dolly hung back and gave the horses plenty of room to make up their minds. They were familiar with the place, having been driven down here with the Bliss herd at least twice a year since they were colts, and they were tired enough and thirsty enough she hoped they wouldn't make a real run for it. If the horses wouldn't go into the corral on their own she'd have to shake out a loop in her catch rope and try to lasso them. She was a terrible hand with a lariat. Once she and Dolly had chased a sick cow for more than an hour, dodging back and forth through brush and trees, and she had made half a dozen miscasts, dragging in her empty loop over and over until she and Dolly and the cow had all worked themselves into an exhausted lather. Dolly had been disgusted with her, the ragged stubs of her burned ears twitching irritably. "Don't give me that look," Martha had said to the horse in despair. "If you could throw a rope, I'd let you do it."

But now, as the bay and chestnut circled once and

then came toward the buildings a second time, the chestnut went right through the open gate and drank water from the washtub. It looked as if the bay horse was veering off but then at the last minute he went in too, not liking the idea of being separated from the other horse.

Martha rode up at a slow walk so as not to startle them into bolting, and she leaned down from the saddle to close the gate on the pen and then climbed up on a rail where she could look down at the horses. It was by now late morning and the day had warmed enough she could open her coat. The horses had been drinking, but when they saw her they pushed away from her as far as they could get. Those horses figured she was a species of bear or mountain lion, or they were remembering which creature it was that had castrated and branded them. After a while she walked off to the outhouse and while she was sitting in it relieving herself she heard the horses come up to the water again.

3

I N THOSE DAYS a lot of cowboys figured a horse wasn't broken until he'd had the spirit entirely beaten out of him. It wouldn't have been out of the ordinary for six or seven men to throw ropes at a horse from all directions with a view to lassoing him, which the horse would understand as men trying to kill him. He might pull three or four men over on the ground before they could bring him down and wrestle a saddle onto him, after which one of them would climb on and spur him until he quit bucking or until he was crippled or dead from ramming into a fence or throwing himself over backward.

Some girls must have done it that way too, just to show off they had the same gumption as the men; and Martha Lessen was big and strong enough she might have turned out a bronco twister like any man except she didn't have the nature for it. She'd learned what not to do by watching her dad, who liked to break a horse by trussing him up in a Scotch hobble, pulling the hind leg clear up to the brisket and tying off the end of the rope to a post so the horse couldn't lie down or ease off the pain in the hip joint. He'd leave him standing that way, trembling on three legs, and come back hours later when the horse was half in shock, dripping under a blanket of sweat, foaming around the gums. Once, when Martha freed a horse from the hobble—she was nine or ten years old and the horse had been left to stand under a blistering sun for half a day—her dad beat her with a belt and then tied the horse up again and walked off and left him standing overnight. In the morning the horse was dead on the ground, strangled in his hobble. "I guess he won't never try that again," was all her dad said, and which was meant for Martha.

When she was fourteen she began working summers for the L Bar L, and the boss put her with Roy Barrow, who was their old wrangler and horseshoer. Of course this was in the days before all the whispering got started, but Roy had come up crippled with arthritis after breaking his hip and had figured out how to outsmart his horses instead of bucking them to a standstill. It was Roy who showed Martha that a Scotch hobble wouldn't harm a horse if it was used right, the hind leg never drawn clear up to the belly but raised just barely off the ground and the horse given his foot as soon as he quit raising a lot of dust. Another thing Roy liked to do was send Martha out on a good quiet strong horse, with a raw horse tied to the saddle horn: after traveling ten miles like that without enough halter rope to get his head down to buck, that unbroke horse would usually be halfway to tame.

Martha had an inborn horse sense, which Roy had seen right away, and he let her work out her own methods of making a horse less scared of the whole thing and more agreeable to be ridden. One of the things she tried was to walk out in the middle of a corral and just stand there with her head down and her hands in her pockets, blowing air out through her nose, making kind of a low snort as if she was a horse, which was the way horses investigated each other when they were first getting acquainted. Sometimes she wouldn't have to stand there very long before the horse would edge up to her and smell the air she was blowing and then blow his own air into her nose, and before long they'd be getting along fine.

But she was always looking for ways that didn't involve so much waiting around, ways that didn't depend on a horse having an inordinate amount of curiosity about the human species, ways that would work for just about any horse that hadn't already been mistreated and ruined. By the time she took work breaking horses for George Bliss, her method was to come into the corral with a little buggy whip and brandish it—she almost never had to touch a horse with it, the noise of the thing whipping through the air and the flicking motion being enough to get him started, make him jump and run, racing around the pen looking for a way out. At the same time, Martha always acted as if there was nothing to get excited about, figuring the horse would eventually get the same idea; so she'd begin singing to him quietly or talking all the time she was making him run, and she'd keep up the quiet talking and the whip-snapping until she figured he was good and tired of running around or just tired of being scared of her, at which point she'd stop all that business with the whip and walk off into a corner as if she'd gotten tired of it herself.

Sometimes at this point a horse would be so glad to quit running, so damned relieved and grateful for it, he'd walk right up to her to thank her—at least that was what she imagined was going on. And if he did, she'd turn to him quietly and talk to him, tell him what a good old horse he was; and now and then a horse might be ready for her to put out her hand and touch him. Even if he didn't walk up to her, he'd at least stand there facing her with his four legs planted and his sides heaving and he'd look at her as if to say,

What's next? And as soon as he turned his head to her she'd put the whip under her arm and step toward him and go on talking to him in a steady, quiet way, acting as if a horse and a human getting acquainted was the most ordinary thing in the world. Usually it wouldn't take more than a few tries—making him run and then letting him stop—before he'd get to that thankful place, and he'd let her come up to him, or he'd come up to her himself and bump his head against her arm to get away from the whip. Or she might hold out the butt end of the switch and let him touch it, examine it with his muzzle, and after that she would start scratching his withers with it and shortening her grip on the thing until finally she'd be scratching him with her bare hand. And it wouldn't be long before the horse would let her scratch under his chin and high on his forehead and behind his withers and along his neck, which is where horses like to groom each other. As soon as he was all right with that, she would go on to touch his mane, his muzzle, and his poll. And after that it would be a simple thing to slide a halter onto him.

And this was all in the first short while—an hour or two, generally.

So after Martha Lessen had hazed the chestnut through the connecting gate into the other corral, she began working the bay gelding in this way. She had found it to be a surprisingly easy thing to break a three- or four-year-old range horse, a horse that had been living almost wild but among older horses who regularly took up with human beings as an ordinary part of life. Those young ones were afraid of humans in a general way but not deeply so, and they didn't lay back their ears and come at you like a horse that had been manhandled, badly treated and consequently made stubborn or vicious; and though it was different for each horse, it wasn't uncommon for her to be saddling and riding a horse by the second day, and some of the agreeable ones within a couple of hours of being introduced.

The bay was pretty agreeable.

When the Blisses' ranch hand Will Wright climbed up on the corral rails across the way, she was at the point of beginning to teach the bay what it might feel like to be ridden. She had brought him close to the fence where she could step onto the lower rail and boost herself up, and she was leaning part of her weight onto him just below the withers, with her left hand on his halter and her right hand on his back, and she was quietly telling him a story out of *Black Beauty*, the part about Beauty's life as a hired horse in a livery stable. The bay tossed his head and took a couple of nervous steps sideways when he saw the boy, but Martha said "Whoa" and went on leaning across his back and continuing to talk to him as if nothing untoward had occurred, and after a moment the horse believed her and went on with his business of learning what it felt like to have something up there that wasn't a big cat or a bear out to kill him. Will Wright watched her a minute and when Martha leaned back from the horse again he said, "I was sent to fetch you in to dinner before it gets cold on the table." He flashed her his big-toothed smile and dropped down from the fence.

The men had ridden in while she was getting the bay used to being touched on the legs and under his belly and brisket. She had heard their horses first and then their low voices and laughter, and through the narrow gaps in the rails of the corral had seen them look over toward her, all three of them, though afterward they turned their horses into the barn lot and went into the house and none of them came out to watch her work, which was a relief to her. Now she spoke quietly to the bay and offered him a carrot, which he examined before taking it gingerly into his mouth, and she left him to seek counsel with the chestnut, who hadn't had a turn yet. She followed the hired boy to the house. Pilot came halfway across the yard to say hello and then went back to where he'd been lying by the house. She hadn't seen him all day and figured he must have gone out with the men and now was resting up from his morning's work.

On the porch Will was washing his hands. Martha stood behind him and waited. Through the doorway she could see George Bliss sitting at the kitchen table leaning his chair on two hind legs and reading the afternoon newspaper, and Louise going back and forth between the stove and the table. When George looked up and saw her there on the porch he called out, "Have you got those horses ready for me to ride yet?" and Louise said, "George, for heaven's sake."

"Well, I was just asking her," he said cheerfully.

After dinner she went back out to work the bay a little more before starting the chestnut. She was scratching him along his withers, letting him get reacquainted with her before she put her weight on him again, and talking to him about what she'd had for dinner and the war news that people had talked about at the table, when George Bliss climbed partway up the high fence and rested his arms on the top rail. She whispered to the bay, "Don't be scared now, he's just the boss," and then began to hum softly "Hinky Dinky," which was a song everybody was singing that winter.

After a minute, when it was clear that George Bliss had settled in to watch her, she went on with what she had planned to do. She hoisted herself across the bay's withers on her belly and slipped one leg across his back and lay straddled a moment with her head down along his shoulder, patting his neck and humming in his ear, before sliding off again; and she went on doing this over and over, staying a little longer each time and sitting up just a bit straighter. A horse knows that anything coming at him from above is something that could kill him, so she took her time acquainting him with glimpses of her body looming over his back, and whenever he tossed his head and half-reared, rolling his eyes to see what was up there, she would stop the whole business for a minute and spend a while just talking to him and leading him around the corral before starting again. She expected George Bliss to ask her a question or make a remark about the way she was going about things, but he watched her quietly, a cigarette dangling from his chapped lips. He didn't brag about how many horses he'd rode to a stop or broke in two, which is something plenty of men and one or two women had said to her while watching her work a horse. He didn't say anything at all to her, he just watched her a while and then lowered himself off the rail and walked away. He had shucked his chaps and spurs. In his overalls he looked like a farmer.

She got both horses through the first day's work, or as much of it as they seemed able to tolerate after that long morning being driven down from the mountains. She didn't think the bay was in the mood to get acquainted with a saddle, and the chestnut was nowhere near as agreeable as that. She brought them each an armload of hay and left them to commiserate with each other through the gaps in the log pens. Then, because she didn't see anybody around and it appeared it wasn't time for supper yet, she went to the barn and got her book and perched in the chilly late afternoon sunlight on a rail of the pasture fence and read a few pages, looking out every little while to her horse standing with the Bliss animals investigating scraps of hay left from the morning feeding and the Whitehorns now lifting their saw-edge against the peacock blue sky.

Louise Bliss startled her, walking up quietly and placing a hand on one of her boot heels. Martha didn't drop the book but she fumbled it a little.

"Dear, I had to come out and see what you were reading."

She climbed down from the fence and said, "It's just *Black Beauty*," putting it like that in case Louise might think *Black Beauty* was a child's book, or too sentimental toward horses.

"Oh my goodness, I've read that three or four times," Louise said, "and I cry every time." She took the book in her own hands and opened it, smoothing the page with her palm. "I just can't stand it when Beauty is sold away from that taxi man, the one with the children, I forget his name." She went on looking down into the open page of the book, her eyes unfocused, seeing Beauty and the taxi driver, whose name Martha knew was Jerry though she didn't volunteer it.

"I love to read, and now my children are grown I've got more time for it," Louise said. She looked at Martha and handed the book back to her with a laugh. "You'd better read now while you can. Once you're married and those babies come along you'll hardly have a moment's peace."

It was Martha's intention never to marry or have children but she didn't say this to Louise Bliss. Other women, she had learned, took it as a personal affront and a challenge, and once they'd gotten over their dismay they always launched into arguments of persuasion. She had discovered there was never any point in trying to argue back, to say that she didn't want to give up her life working outdoors with horses. There was never any way to say *My mother had six babies in six years and I don't know why anybody would want that kind of life.* So she cast around for a topic of conversation that would get Louise Bliss away from marriage. "Whenever I'm not working I've got to have something to read, but I guess it's a bad habit. I guess too much reading is bad for your eyes." This was what her granddad had always complained of—that she'd go blind from too much reading, and moreover that reading was a goddamned waste of time. He had been old before she was born, a dour and unsparing and bitter old man hated by his only son. Martha guessed her dad had let her have books—had said little about the time she spent reading—purely as a way to spite his own father.

"Oh, I think that's an exaggeration, people saying reading is bad for your eyes. You go ahead and read all you want is what I think." Until now the two women hadn't stood toe to toe. Louise was tall, taller than her husband, very nearly as tall as Martha, which unaccountably cheered Louise when she realized it. She put her hands in the pockets of her apron and looked out at the stubble field and the animals. "George said that horse of yours was burnt in a fire."

Martha looked over at Dolly. "It was a barn fire, I guess. She didn't belong to me when it happened so I don't know the whole story."

Louise went on looking out at the horses and cows and after a few moments she said, "I was in a fire when I was a girl. Well, I shouldn't have said I was in a fire. Our house burnt to the ground but none of us

47

were in it at the time. It made an impression on me, though. Is your horse afraid of smoke and fires now? I mean, horses are afraid of fire as a rule but is she more leery than the usual?"

"She doesn't like to come too close when people are burning up stumps or if they're burning their garbage. I try to keep her away from that kind of thing out of consideration of her feelings."

Louise didn't say if she was leery of fire herself. She looked at Martha and smiled. Then she patted the girl on the arm. "I'll see what I've got that you might like to read. I always wanted my Miriam to be a reader but she never was, and I've been saving up books for years, waiting for somebody to give them to."

When Martha went up to the house for supper Louise brought out nine or ten books and stood them on the kitchen table next to the girl's plate. Pendleton had had a little public reading room upstairs of the L. B. Hawkins Furniture Store, and later a Carnegie Library on Main Street, and Martha had usually borrowed her books from those places two or three at a time. The only book she owned—she had bought it for a dime from a farm family raising money to move back East—was *Black Beauty*. She was stunned to have so many books loaned to her all at once, which she tried to say, but Louise waved the words off. "I don't suppose any of them is as good as *Black Beauty* but you might like some of them. I liked them, anyway. They're all good books."

Martha said, "I've always just read anything that

came along. I guess I wouldn't know if a book was good to read or bad."

"Oh, I don't either, I just know what I like."

The hired men, waiting for Louise to bring supper to the table, were talking about a cow that had been killed by lightning and they were not taking any interest in the women's talk about books, but George Bliss must have been listening because now he stubbed out his cigarette and said, "I guess you've never met a government handbook then, or you'd know the difference between good and bad reading."

Louise was pulling pans out of the oven and she didn't bother to give her husband a look, she just said, "George, you stay out of this," and George looked over at Martha and winked.

When she carried the books out to the barn she right away opened the one called *Horse Heaven Hills* to look for mention of horses and was pleased to find a girl riding a palomino, though a romance seemed to be the central thing in it. She cleared a shelf in the tack room, crowding the veterinary goods into other boxes and onto other shelves to make room for the books. Their variously colored spines, arranged along the cleared shelf, made a small, distinct change in the room. She unrolled her sleeping bag and sat on it but it wasn't a minute more before she stood again and began neatening and rearranging all the tackle and equipage, clearing a little more space for herself, claiming more of the floor and one wall as hers. With a couple of bent nails, she pinned up a calendar page, a hand-tinted photograph of a chestnut or liver bay Morgan stud in a show pose. *Buck* was written in baroque lettering below the horse's feet. She'd had the picture a long time, and the corners were ratty with tack holes. She once had a horse she'd named Buck after the calendar Morgan, though he was a big-footed old thing with a coarse head in no way resembling a show horse. Her dad had sold him for glue the same winter her mother had miscarried for the third time in eighteen months, which was the same winter her mother had stopped talking to any of them except to complain or command.

Martha got into the sleeping bag and read *Black Beauty* until her hands got too cold and then put out the candle and huddled deeper in the bag. She was only a few pages from the end, but it was her second time through the book so she was untroubled by any suspense and able to put off for another day the short, dreamlike happy ending. She was tired but too stirred up to sleep right away. She didn't know if the two horses she was breaking for George Bliss already had names but she guessed they didn't and, lying there in the dark, she began to make a list of some possibilities. Ollie was one she thought of, and Scout.

◆

4

LOUISE BLISS WAS the eldest of six children. She had worked horseback when she was young—most girls her age living in that part of the world learned to ride almost as soon as they could walk—but when her two brothers, following five and eight years behind, were old enough to take over the range work she had been glad to move inside and learn housework from her mother. Now the garden and the kitchen were her realm and she didn't have a speck of envy for girls like Martha Lessen, girls who worked outside in all kinds of weather and slept in barns and sometimes out in fields under leaking canvas. She had known such girls to marry and become happy wives—Irene Theide was one she could think of—but others who had become eccentric and homely spinsters, like Aileen Woodruff and Emma Adelaide Woodruff. The Woodruffs were old women now, sisters who had spent their whole lives taking rough treatment from the elements and from cantankerous cows and rambunctious horses and were still riding out with the men every spring and fall, declaring they "wouldn't know what to do" if made to stay indoors. Louise liked the Woodruff sisters and admired their fortitude, but considered them misplaced and odd—the unfortunate result when a girl failed to outgrow her tomboy disposition.

"I don't know if that girl owns a dress," she said to

51

George. They were lying in bed in the dark and George was smoking the day's last cigarette. She could see the tip of it brighten and dim every so often. "I haven't seen her in anything but a man's trousers, have you? And those fancy old leather chaps. She dresses like she's headed off to a rodeo." She said this as if they'd been in the middle of a long conversation, which wasn't true, and George was briefly tempted to pretend he didn't know which girl his wife was talking about.

"Well, she's breaking horses, Louise."

"You said yourself she isn't bucking them out. You said the horse just stood there and let her clamber all over him."

"Well, I didn't see what come before. Maybe she give that horse a good whipping first and then bucked the tar out of him."

She didn't let his joking distract her. "I've been thinking I might let her have one of mine. There's that shepherd's check, the blue, but it would have to be let out. She's big-boned."

"You do whatever you think, but don't be too surprised if she don't appreciate it. You ought to know yourself, a raw bronc don't like a woman's skirts flapping around him. The wind picks up a skirt, and even a tame old Shetland pony gets the idea that he ought to go to bucking."

Louise didn't intend to make an issue of it with George. She said, "Well, I won't say anything for now. It's all right with me if she goes on wearing her cowboy getup while she's doing her horse breaking, but if it turns out she's come away from home without even a dress she can wear to dances or to church, that will need to be remedied."

"You do whatever you think," he said again. He patted her hip under the quilts and flopped away from her onto his side.

"Did you put out that cigarette?"

He grunted. "I might switch to those Lucky Strike ready-mades," he said, just to provoke her. "What would you think of that?" She believed there was nothing uglier than an ashtray full of stubbed-out cigarettes and liked to complain that his smoking stank up her curtains and burnt holes in her carpets. She had been trying to get him to quit smoking for thirty years without getting anywhere.

"At this moment I'm just interested in knowing if you've put out the one you were smoking."

"Don't get on me now."

"I'm not on you, I just don't care to die in a burned-up house." Louise in fact was not a woman with a deep dread of fires, but fire was more common in those days than it is now, and people who had been burned out had a healthy wish to keep it from happening again.

George grunted, and in a minute he rocked the bed slightly and she heard the gritty sound of his cigarette rubbing across the bottom of the ashtray. He was asleep almost immediately and snoring like a train. He worked himself so hard he usually would drop right off as soon as he thought Louise was finished talking, or sometimes right in the middle of something she was saying. She was often the one who put out his cigarette. But she always liked to lie awake a little while in the darkness and go over things, anything hanging on from the day's business, before letting sleep claim her.

Tonight what she had been thinking about before bringing up Martha Lessen's dress was something the new young preacher at the Federated Protestant church had said the Sunday before. The Lord, he said, has a way of evening things out in the long run—giving luck and hardship in fairly equal measure over the whole of a person's life—or a nation's life—though you might have to look hard to see it. And he told the congregation, "Now that the war has finally come home to these United States, we must remember that a test can strengthen resolve." Everyone in the church knew what he meant: three American boys had died in the fighting in France just the week before, the first of what would doubtless be many. He had gone on to preach the story of Job's trials, which must have wound its way eventually to a message of hope and solace, although Louise stopped following the sermon after a certain point. She had lost her third-born child, a boy, within a few hours of bearing him, but in other respects had been blessed with luck—had been fortunate in her health and her marriage, had raised three children to be kind and honest adults, was comfortable in her own life and smart enough to know it. Sitting there in the pew beside George, with the Reverend Feldson going on about Job's misfortunes, she felt herself pierced by the knowledge that the first fifty years of her life had been extraordinarily free of travails, and she was due—overdue—for God to even things out.

Her son Jack had gone with the first wave of boys from Elwha County—there had been banquets and public prayer meetings and a parade to see them down the main street of Shelby to the railroad station, Jack with his friends in the back seat of an automobile and all of them grinning as if they were going off like tourists to see the Eiffel Tower. At this point he was still in Kansas learning to be a soldier but she thought he might be shipped out soon—the papers said that by the first of the year troop ships would be carrying fifty thousand young Americans to France every month.

There was never anything in Jack's letters to set her worrying, and in any case Louise was not ordinarily a person who worried. But whenever they had a letter from him—one had come today—her mind would keep going to her son in an agitated sort of way, just as a tongue will keep going to a canker in the mouth, and tonight she had tried to move away from that by turning her attention to the matter of Martha Lessen's dress. Now that George had gone off to sleep and she was left alone, she found she couldn't keep her mind from jumping back to the preacher's sermon, to the part that had stuck with her, the part having to do with the Lord giving and taking away in equal measure. This wasn't something she could talk to George about. She talked to God about it from time to time, her prayers taking somewhat the form of a negotiation.

5

W HEN A COUPLE OF DAYS of corral work and
riding in the stubble field had gotten the worst
roughness off the horses, Martha began riding them up
into the foothills. She rode one and led the other and
after an hour or so she switched off. She always used
the McClelland saddle for this work because, as she
had told George Bliss on that first day, it was almost as
light as a jockey saddle and she liked the horses to be
able to respond to the least pressure from her knees.
She began teaching them words for what she wanted
them to do, "giddup" and "whoa" being the principal
things. She kept a short piece of rope snapped to each
halter so they'd be easy to catch in the corral, and she
always hobbled the horses when she saddled or unsaddled them, a bronc hobble she had made herself out of
straps of rawhide lined with sheep's wool, a hobble
shorter than a camp hobble because she didn't really
want them to take a step while she was getting the
saddle on or off. She always shortened up the near-side
rein when she put her boot in the stirrup, so when the
horse tried to walk out from under her he was forced
into a tight turn that brought the stirrup right to her.
She coaxed them to step over logs, and she got them
used to things they didn't like by hanging tin cans
from the saddle strings, or long silk stockings that
would flutter in any kind of breeze. Those lessons had
started on the second day in the corral and would go

56

on for weeks, presenting them with every kind of thing that might distract or scare them: wiggling ropes, tin cans with rocks rattling inside, rain slickers, ragged pieces of flapping cardboard. She believed a spoiled horse, whether an outlaw or a pampered pet, was a nuisance and a menace, so when one of them bit or kicked she used her elbow or shoulder to cuff him without saying a word or looking him in the eye; she let the horse think it was an accident caused by his own carelessness. She used a low, harsh tone for scolding, which was what Dolly always did, keeping other horses in line, and she kept her voice soft and high for praising.

She made sure they were acquainted with cattle by deliberately riding into bunches of grazing steers and cows, and sometimes she started them loping after solitary cows. Scout, the bay horse, regularly took a cow's frosty breath for dragon fire and would break away with a wild frightened squeal whenever a cow blew air in his direction. Over and over she coaxed him straight up to the cow in question while telling him quietly that this big old mother animal wouldn't set him ablaze.

The chestnut, Ollie, was tractable but he would never make a good cutting horse, being too much on the meditative side; she didn't think he was serious, though, when he kinked up his back once or twice every time she stood on the stirrup. She added "quit" to the words she was teaching him. And as soon as she had both boots settled, she straightened him out and moved him ahead, figuring a horse that's walking forward has a hard time getting his head down to buck.

She liked both horses and liked the work and the clear weather that hung on into the week. She liked Louise Bliss well enough and felt pretty certain Louise returned the feeling, though she continued uncertain whether she had George Bliss's approval.

When she had been there four or five days, Louise asked her to stay on one night after supper so they might "have a visit between women," which was the sort of thing Martha shied away from if she could, but there didn't seem to be any way to say no. She followed Louise into the front room and the two of them sat down in upholstered chairs near the Franklin furnace. Louise brought her knitting into her lap. She was making socks for the army, which was something just about every woman in the country was doing when they weren't rolling surgical dressings or preparing comfort kits for soldiers and sailors. Martha had always worked outside with her dad and her brothers and later for other people, and her mother's attempts to teach her to knit and drive a sewing machine had always come to nothing. Martha knew how to braid horsehair and leather ropes and bosals and she wondered if those might be needed by the army, but it didn't seem the kind of question she could ask Louise Bliss. She kept her hands clasped in her lap.

In the afternoon newspaper the men had been reading about the battle at Cambrai—an attack by British tanks had finally broken through the Hindenburg Line—and they'd been arguing whether it would be better to be in one of those armored cars where you might be trapped and burned alive or to be an infantryman outside on the ground and unprotected when mortar shells fell. Louise never liked their war talk and as soon as she and Martha were sitting down she started out talking about her family, thorough details of some sort of disagreement her daughter had had with her new mother-in-law, and then one story after another about her son Orie in veterinary school, stories to do with people Martha didn't know and problems she expected never to have. She had grown up in a family of taciturn people and had developed a habit of silence—she murmured her slight agreement wherever it seemed agreement was expected, and she watched Louise's hands intently, though they moved too fast to reveal the secret of knitting.

Louise took Martha's quietness as a sign of a good listener and she rattled on for a while without particularly noticing that she was the only one talking. When she did become aware of it she let a small silence fall while she considered what might bring the girl out, and then she asked Martha which book she was reading. It was *Lone Star Ranger*, and Martha couldn't keep from telling a bit of the story as if Louise hadn't already read the book herself—how a fellow named Buck Duane kills a drunkard in a shootout in the street and is forced into being an outlaw. She didn't bring up the way the book had been robbing her of sleep: how there was a good deal in it about the wild blood Duane had inherited from his gunman father, and how Martha had been lying awake searching in herself for bad blood she might have inherited from her dad. Buck Duane had been secretly helping out the Texas Rangers, Martha told Louise, and she hoped that by the end he might get free of his outlaw reputation, that he might even be welcomed into the Rangers himself. Louise smiled at this without telling Martha anything about how the book ended.

They went on talking back and forth about the book and then about Zane Grey, who had written it and a dozen others like it. Louise had heard that Mr. Grey had a house somewhere in Oregon, maybe over on the Rogue River or the Umpqua, which for somewhat parochial reasons made them both think well of him. But when Louise asked if Martha thought Mr. Grey was a real horseman, Martha said, without answering directly, that Buck Duane didn't always treat his horses as well as he should, that he drove them pretty hard on very little feed. And then they talked about the pioneers and whether there were very many towns that had been beset by outlaws, as seemed to happen so often in Western romances. Louise was skeptical. She said in her own lifetime there had been but one bank robbery in the valley, two fellows who were caught by a posse of townsmen and constables and hung the same day. And from her mother she had heard only stories of harsh winters and death by illness or accident and hardly anything about guns and outlaws. Martha didn't say so, but she had the idea Umatilla

County, where she was from, and Elwha County, where Louise lived, weren't part of the West she had heard and read about, the place people meant when they said "the Wild West." She imagined the West Zane Grey wrote about must be somewhere in Montana or Arizona or Texas, and she planned to get there and see those places herself, eventually.

After a while it occurred to Martha that Louise Bliss had deliberately shifted their talk to horses and Western romances, and her warm feeling toward Louise deepened to gratitude. In the middle of something she had been saying about fences—about how there were never any fences and nobody ever had to get down from a horse to open and shut a gate in the Western stories she had read—Martha stopped and said, "I've been wondering if the army might need hair ropes and bosals. That's something I could put my hands to in the evenings when I'm not reading a book."

Louise stilled her needles a moment to look over at Martha approvingly. "Why that's a wonderful idea. I'm sure they do need them."

Martha knew Louise wouldn't want to talk about the war directly but after a moment she said, "I read in the papers about mounted patrols at the munitions plants and other places where there's war work, and that it's girls who are doing it. Girls with their own horses. I don't know how far I'd have to go to find that kind of work—I guess it would be back East? I thought about doing it, but I wouldn't want to live back there."

Louise had resumed knitting but she began to smile, looking down at her hands as they twitched the yarn over and under. "I don't suppose your horses would like it there either."

They went on after that, Louise asking and Martha telling how she'd come by her three horses, and from there they turned to talk of the different kinds of hackamores and bridles preferred for different situations and Martha's opinions of various bits and reins.

George Bliss had been sitting in the kitchen polishing his good Sunday boots. If he'd heard the women talking about Western novels he had kept out of it. But now that the talk had turned to horses and their tack he came into the front room and sat down with his magazine, which was the *Farm Journal.* The war had made farmers out of a lot of ranchers, as thousands of acres of good bunch grass were being turned over in those days to grow wheat for the army—the "Great Plow-Up," people were calling it. The virtue of bunch grass is that it stays green in the fall when other grasses have dried out—horses and cows can winter on it—whereas plowed ground after a string of dry days will lift on the wind and float into space or out to sea in great dust clouds, and that topsoil will never be seen again. That may be why, when the Dust Bowl came along about ten years after the war, some people laid the blame on the Plow-Up. But hindsight is a marvelous thing and if you had asked people then, they would have answered that they were feeding all those hungry soldiers.

George unfolded his magazine and looked at it, then folded it again and said to Martha, "You've got those horses pretty well along, it looks like."

She thought about what she ought to say. "I've got them started, but they're quite a ways from finished. I'll have to keep repeating the lessons to get them solid. And I haven't got very far yet with setting their heads." George went on looking at her and seeming to wait for something more, so she added, "That chestnut has a good nature but he wants to think about everything before he does it, so he's not very quick. I guess I won't be able to make a very good stock horse out of him."

George raised his eyebrows and then winked at her in that solemn way he had. "Well, he must be smarter than you, seeing he's figured out a way to keep from being put to work."

She looked down at her hands. "You can still work him. He just won't ever be too good with cattle."

"Well I guess I could break him to harness but then that smooth trot of his wouldn't do me no good. Maybe I ought to take the son of a gun out and shoot him."

She threw him a flustered look. "He's a good sound horse," she said, and Louise lifted her head and said, "George, stop teasing the girl."

"Oh, she ought to be used to me by now," he said with a laugh.

There had never been any teasing in the house Martha grew up in, just cutting words that meant what they said. Outside the house, on haying crews and ranches where she'd worked and in school, she'd been teased for her size and for loving horses and for dressing outlandishly and for various other things; but it had always come from boys and girls her own age and from the men on the crews, not the boss. She didn't know what to make of George's wisecracks, how to take them. Heat climbed into her face, and she sat staring down into her hands.

"Well, here's an idea I've been thinking up," George said and slapped his magazine into his lap. He was still smiling, so Martha didn't know if she should take his next words seriously. "I was talking to Emil and W.G."—he said this as if he expected Martha to know who belonged to those names—"and they both got some horses need breaking and I told them we had Miss Lessen here, breaking them to beat the band. Which got me to thinking: I just bet there's rough stock all over the county and hardly a man with time to break them out. If you was to line up five or six ranches and start up riding a circle, there might be enough horses for a winter's worth of work just about, and we'd have all our horses broke by spring. What do you think of that idea, Miss Lessen?"

Back then, almost every outfit kept a lot of saddle horses, and the ranches were generally smaller and closer together than they are now. A horse wrangler could line up work with half a dozen places all lying three or four or five miles apart, with maybe ten or fifteen unbroken horses among them, could get the roughness off the horses with a couple of days' work at each place and from then on be riding those ponies one after the other in a loop, beginning in the morning at one spread and heading for the next, running the first horse into the second corral, throwing the saddle on the next bronc and then heading down the line to the next place and the next until winding up back at the first place just about at evening, and repeating the whole thing every day after that. Depending on how many horses were in the circle and how far apart the stops were, each horse would get an hour's riding lesson every day or every other day, which was just about all he needed or could tolerate anyway, and a wrangler could manage to break quite a few horses that way in not very many weeks.

Martha had set out from Pendleton meaning to live a footloose cowboy life and see the places she'd read about in Western romances—she hadn't come down to Elwha County intending to stay. But a winter's worth of work would suit her about right. She had watched a few wranglers riding a circle and she knew the work was hard, riding half a dozen different horses every day, some of them considerably rougher than others and sometimes needing to change saddles or hack-amores to fit their different shapes, and then another half-dozen the next day. You were in the saddle dawn to dark six or seven days a week, pretty much regard-less of the weather. But she wasn't afraid of hard work; she was afraid of having to go back to Pendleton in January or February flat broke and defeated. "I would like to have as much work as I can get," she said to George Bliss, straight and definite, so he would know she was serious.

"Well I thought you might," he said, giving her a look she took to be amused and self-satisfied. "Sunday, you come on out to church with us, why don't you, and we'll introduce you around and see if we can't line you up some horses." He shook his magazine and turned his attention back to it.

Louise Bliss seemed to think more of the idea of taking Martha to church than of lining up horses for her to break. Without looking away from her knitting she said, "There's not a single Lutheran church in the county, I'm afraid, though there used to be one over in Bingham until that minister left for Africa. We've been going to the Federated Protestant church in Shelby, which is a mongrel church in every way, but we have got a new young minister who is smart as a whip. I do love to hear him give a sermon, and the preacher they have at the Methodist church is—" she pulled her mouth into a tight purse—"a bit more on the hellfire side of things than we're used to. There's a Catholic church in Opportunity, because so many of the sheep ranchers at the west end of the valley are Spanish and Bohemian and that sort. You're not Catholic are you, dear?"

She said, "No, I'm not," without offering to say what she was, which was a person entirely without a religious upbringing. Martha's father had come from a long line of nonchurchgoers and had pressed his disre-

66

gard for religion onto his Lutheran wife. Martha and her brothers had grown up knowing next to nothing of the Bible.

"Did you come away from home without a dress for church?" Louise asked her then and looked up from her knitting to collect the reply.

Martha told her, "I did bring one. It's just an old jumper, though, and a middy blouse," which didn't seem to discourage Louise—in fact she perked up a little, just from hearing there was a dress of any kind in Martha Lessen's dunnage.

After a while, she threw the girl a look that was conspiratorial. "Our young minister," she said, "is quite tall," which Martha took to be a comment about the difficulties of a tall woman finding a tall man to marry.

6

THE WEATHER SUDDENLY worsened on Saturday afternoon, a brief cold rain that turned to snow while Martha was still coming down from the eastern edge of the Bliss property, riding Ollie and leading Scout, with long peacock feathers tied into both horses' manes jerking and fluttering in the wind. She had left the ranch in the morning before the cold had moved up over the front of the Whitehorns and into the valley; she hadn't had a warning that the weather might change or she might have thought to put on a sweater under her coat and wear two pair of socks. She might have snugged a silk stocking around her head under the hat, which was how she kept her ears warm in cold weather. As it was, she was caught out in it, and she ducked her cold chin into her coat collar and rode at a swinging trot all the way down to the ranch buildings, stopping to change mounts once but otherwise not working the horses except to encourage their straight-ahead intention.

By Sunday morning there were two or three inches of snow on the ground. When Martha crossed to the house for breakfast George Bliss and El Bayard were out in the field feeding the animals off the back of a wagon. Martha had put on the womanly clothes she had with her, an old-fashioned green corduroy jumper that had had the seams let out a couple of times and a yellow cotton middy blouse with a wide collar. The hat she wore had belonged to her grandmother, a woman's braided hat with the front brim held back by a crushed rosette of worn blue velvet. The men looked over at her, but if the sight of their girl broncobuster in a skirt was a shock to them they didn't give any sign. They went on intently pitching loose hay into a long oval. El Bayard's crippled arm didn't seem to limit him in any way. His sharp-cornered elbow swung out and back in a smooth arc as he worked the pitchfork, and he managed to get every bit as much hay on the ground as George Bliss.

Although it had stopped snowing, the sky was low and slaty and the air was snapping cold. Martha wondered if the weather would keep them from churchgoing, but when she went into the house she found

Will Wright already done up in a wool suit and necktie, and when Mr. Bliss and Ellery Bayard came in from feeding, George changed into a suit too. El, who wasn't a churchgoer, evidently planned to spend the morning mending his socks; Will Wright, who had a regular habit of attending church and sitting down to Sunday dinner with the family of the girl he was courting, said he would head off on horseback as soon as he finished with breakfast. While they were all still sitting around the table, George announced to Louise that he thought they should take the automobile to church, as the mud on the road was good and hard but not icy and there wasn't near enough snow for a sleigh.

Martha at first had imagined the Blisses were either cash-poor or backward-looking, which were the usual reasons for not having a car, but it had turned out they kept a Chalmers in one of their sheds and brought it out only for town trips and certain summer picnics and dances. Usually by this time in November the car would have been jacked up on wooden blocks and set aside for the winter, but the fall had been mild and they'd put off storing their automobile until the weather gave them reason.

George carried water out to the car and filled the radiator and cranked the engine over; then he brought it around, and Mrs. Bliss climbed into the front seat, Martha Lessen into the rear. Martha's family had never owned an automobile but she had ridden in cars more than a few times. She hated their noise and stink but couldn't help liking the feeling of going very fast. The

Blisses shouted back and forth to each other, things to do with people and church business Martha knew nothing about. She leaned out from the car with her hand holding down her grandmother's hat and let the cold, ringing air race into her ears; she watched the white fields going by, the cattle and horses standing in them, and turned her head to keep certain horses in sight a little longer before turning forward again to watch for the next ones. Graves Creek rolled like hammered metal between the road and the rail spur, rummaging and rattling through the bare willow thickets on both its banks. Right after the creek emptied into the Little Bird Woman River the road crossed over the river on a wooden bridge, the car's hard rubber tires riding thunderous and rough across the bare planks, and then up into the streets of Shelby.

The whole of Elwha County, being well off the main wagon routes, had been a left-behind and isolated place during the first big westering push; people hadn't started moving in in any numbers until the late eighties and it was 1905 or 1906 before the OTN&T could be persuaded to run a rail line south from Pendleton through the Ipsoot Pass into the valley. There were three little towns in the valley, strung out along the Little Bird Woman River: Shelby and Bingham and Opportunity, in order from east to west, with Shelby being the largest and the county seat. Early talk about running the line west through the whole valley or south through Lewis Pass to Canyon City had never borne fruit, so Shelby was the end of the spur.

The summer the spur line was put through, Martha's dad had taken work laying ties for the railroad, and the whole family had lived briefly in Shelby. There had been only four or five hundred people living there then, and that was the town Martha remembered—a scant block or two of scattered wooden stores with false fronts. Now she was surprised to find Main Street crowded with two-story brick and stone buildings and the slushy streets around the Federated Protestant church crowded with more automobiles than horses. There were sidewalks and street lights and telephone poles, and the county courthouse was a stone edifice sitting in the middle of its own block of snow-covered lawn.

Martha had left home for reasons having to do with her family and left Pendleton because it had become very settled and overgrown in her view. If Elwha County wasn't much like theWest she had read about in novels it was at least said to be cow and horse country in the old-timey way, which is why she'd headed down here. Seeing the town so changed, she worried that she might have heard wrong and maybe the valley had become peopled and modernized without the word getting out.

The Federated Protestant minister, whose name Louise said was Theodore Feldson, was young and very tall—a couple of inches over six feet—and also very thin, his wrist bones knobby below the cuffs of his shirt. He had a pallid indoors complexion starred with moles and the stooped shoulders of someone who spent a good deal of time slumped in a chair. His voice rang out in the small church, and he spoke in dense sentences of the promise of the Christ Child in wartime, with the season of Advent soon upon them. Martha, trying to follow the line of his discourse, sat forward in the pew, frowning.

When the last of the singing and praying was finished, Louise took Martha by the elbow and brought her along to greet the young reverend, who gave Martha a slightly startled or confused look when they were introduced, which she recognized, and knew had to do with her size—she outweighed him by quite a bit and could have looked him pretty nearly straight in the eye if she'd dared. She had been intimidated by his abstract preaching and his piety, but when he offered her his hand it was a brief soft clasp without squeezing, and when he welcomed her to "our little congregation" she thought his voice away from the lectern sounded reedy and boyish; all of this surprised and consoled her.

Afterward George and Louise introduced her to more people than she'd ever before met at one time, a jumble of faces and names she couldn't keep straight or remember for more than a minute. What she remembered—would remember for the rest of her life, she felt—was George Bliss persuading his neighbors of her good horse work. "I expect she'll just about have them standing on their hind legs and talking American by spring," he told people over and over, every time provoking an appreciative laugh.

Martha held back, blushing furiously, until she was gestured forward for introductions and handshakes. When people asked for the particulars of her methods she mentioned riding a circle, which almost everybody was acquainted with, and otherwise answered in vague terms so they wouldn't have a solid edge to disagree with. A couple of people made remarks that seemed to be about her size—that she sure looked strong enough for a man's work—but most people seemed uninterested in her methods so long as the horses were finished to their needs. It was clear that George's opinion of her was the only thing most people were taking into account.

Martha rode back to the Bliss ranch in the back of the automobile in silence, looking out at the fog-shrouded Clarks Range. The Blisses only occasionally spoke to each other, leaning in close to make themselves heard. When the ranch buildings came in sight Martha leaned forward suddenly and shouted over the rough racket of the motor, "Mr. Bliss, thank you for saying those kind things about me." She had devoted the last many minutes to finding her tongue but the words that came out now were a disappointment to her—too few and too common.

George, without taking his eyes off the rutted road, shouted back mildly, "I guess if you make a mess of things, I'll just have to pack up and move to another part of the country."

When Louise said, "Oh for goodness' sake, George," Martha understood that he was teasing her again.

7

S HE HAD THOUGHT George Bliss might go with her
on Monday morning when she rode out to take a
look at the horses she'd been hired to break, as they
were scattered across six other ranches and farms
around the valley and she didn't know how to get to
any of them. But what happened is that George sat
down at the breakfast table and drew up a little pencil
map and gave it to her.

Any map of Elwha County would have to show the
Whitehorn Mountains and the Clarks Range taking up
the lion's share, with the Little Bird Woman River
carving a valley through the middle roughly twenty
miles long, seven or eight or nine miles wide, where
most of the people had settled and where the towns
had grown up. In those days there were just two roads
through the valley, one that came up through Lewis
Pass, turned to follow the river west through the three
valley towns, and petered out in the steep gorge at the
far west end—the Owl Creek Canyon, which was
home to a few dozen families of sheep growers—and
the one Martha Lessen had come in on, which more or
less followed the rail spur through Ipsoot Pass from
Pendleton and along Graves Creek to intersect the
east-west road at Shelby. But dozens of rutted tracks
forked off from the roads and wandered up to dozens
of ranches and half a hundred little farm claims.

George's map was not much to look at: just a few

squiggles standing in for the bigger creeks and the river, straight thick lines for the two roads that bisected the county, and pointy triangles for the mountain ranges. He had printed the names of the six families who wanted horses broken at roughly the places where their properties lay, with an *x* to mark his guess as to where each farmhouse or ranch house stood, but he had not tried to draw in the ranch lanes or name any of the streams or mark distances.

"You think you can find them places?" George said to her while he was putting on his chaps and hat, and she looked up from studying the map and said, "Yes sir, I'll find them," since there didn't seem to be any other answer she could make.

She rode out on her own horse, the liver chestnut she called T.M., which meant Trouble Maker and which was his name because if Martha let him stand in pasture for very long he forgot every bit of his manners and what he'd learned about being a good horse and he got fractious and full of himself. She set him on the Graves Creek road, which in most places was not much more than a pair of beaten ruts running alongside the creek and the rail spur, veering out here and there around stands of bitterbrush or marshy swales. The little bit of snow that had fallen on Saturday night had melted right off by Sunday afternoon, and the road was muddy enough that there were no automobiles venturing out; Martha kept to the center of the road between the ruts, where the beaten-down weeds made less trouble for the horse to get through.

Romer, George had written on the map at what she judged to be the nearest place to the Blisses, maybe a mile or so south of Dewey Creek and a half mile or so west of the Graves Creek road. These were evidently people Martha had talked to, but she couldn't connect any of the names on the map to the faces of people she had met after church on Sunday.

About the time she started to worry that she'd missed the turn, a faint track bent left off the road and she set the horse on it. She first saw the little brown pond where they'd evidently cleared willow and sage from around a spring and then the house, which was not much more than a milled-lumber cabin with small windows and a sheet-metal roof and a sketchy little front porch. There was a shed and a chicken house but no horses in sight and no proper barn.

In the past fifteen or so years a late homesteading boom had hit everywhere in the West, with more people trying to homestead in the new century than had tried it in the old. And the rush of latecomers grabbing the last pieces of free land happened to coincide, in Elwha County, with the railroad being put through, which meant that for a while just about every section of land in the valley was individually claimed and had a house sitting on it—benighted homesteaders who thought they could make a living from a piece of dry land and a scant twelve or fourteen inches of yearly rain.

The county never suffered the range wars between sheepmen and cattle ranchers written about in the six-shooter Western novels; the steep slopes along Owl Creek naturally lent themselves to sheep, and everybody back then was pretty satisfied with the division. But there was trouble of a sort between the longtime cattlemen and the newcomer farmers. The good farm land had all gone in 160-acre chunks twenty and thirty years before. The homestead acts passed in later days were giveaways of 320- and 640-acre parcels of the dry grassland that Elwha County had a lot of, land without much timber and without the means to irrigate—open range that the old-time ranchers had always been free to run their cattle on. The idea was that the newcomers would take up ranching, but people figured out pretty quickly that you couldn't make a living off the cattle you could grow on 640 acres of dry grass, so of course the newcomers fenced it off and set out to plow and grow crops. In the valley of the Little Bird Woman River, it wasn't quite a war between the old-timers and the newcomers, but a good deal of resentment and squabbling went back and forth. Fences sagged, broke, got leaned on, and range bulls got into fields with dairy cows; every so often a range bull would turn up dead in mysterious circumstances. When a farmer dammed a creek to force the water into his garden and fields, sometimes that dam got knocked out by steers ranging loose and driving through.

This kind of thing didn't last long, because most of the settlers coming late to the game didn't have the cash or other means to get through a dry summer or a deep winter, and most were laying claim to land that couldn't be made to support a crop or pasture dairy cows unless the rain cooperated, which it seldom did. By the war years, a good many of those homesteaders had already given up and moved out, and by the end of the war only ten or fifteen of them would still be farming in the valley out of the nearly two hundred that had been there in 1910 when things were at the peak; the federal land banks and private mortgage companies that had been so free with money for stock, farm equipment, and houses during the boom years would be left holding title to land that was mostly barren through overtilling, land where nothing much would now grow but scrub juniper and weeds. By the 1920s most of the valley would be back to the way it had been before the century's turn: sheep ranging the canyons and lower gorge of Owl Creek at the western end of the county; cattle running over the eastern parts from Graves Creek clear across the valley bottom to Burnt Creek; and a few wheat farms along the well-watered valley bottoms.

But as it happened, the war years were wetter than usual, wheat and cattle prices were high, and any of the dry-land homesteaders who hadn't already given up the fight took this as a sign they could make a living off their little claims, and they settled in for the duration. A couple of the people who hired Martha Lessen to break horses for them in November of 1917 were homesteaders holding tight to their dreams.

The woman who came over from the chicken house

had a face Martha vaguely recalled. "Hello, are you Mrs. Romer?" she said.

The woman visited upon her a stern look of disappointment. "I'm not Dorothy Romer, I'm Jeanne McWilliams."

"I'm sorry, Mrs. McWilliams. I met so many people all at once, I've got everybody's names mixed up."

"Well that's all right. But my husband told you we don't have any horses needing breaking." Mrs. McWilliams's husband blamed George Bliss, whose ranch ran along one side of their property, for letting one of his range bulls break down a fence and claim their milk cow, Jozie, for his harem. If they had had a horse needing breaking, they wouldn't have given it to anybody who worked for Bliss, whom they called Old Mister High and Mighty.

Martha's face began to take up heat as Mrs. McWilliams's face went on being pale and wintry. Martha said, "I'm glad to meet you, anyhow—meet you *again*. I'm sorry I got your name wrong."

Mrs. McWilliams was holding an empty burlap sack in one hand but she put the other hand to her forehead to shade her eyes against the gray winter light. Her fingers were long and reddened. "Well it's all right," she said, without softening the tone of her voice. "I don't remember what your name is, to tell the truth, so I guess I don't have room to complain."

"It's Martha Lessen."

"I'll try to remember it. If you're looking to find the Romer place you can take that little road there, just be sure you shut every gate when you go through." She pointed to a faint trace wandering off across the grass and bitterbrush hills, not a road so much as a path, the kind made by neighbors when they visited each other.

"Well, thanks. I'll just go on and see about that horse they wanted broke."

"You shut every gate."

"I will."

She turned T.M. onto the path the woman had set her on. When she got down at the first gate and undid the wire and walked the horse through, she looked back down the half mile or so of slope to the house and saw Mrs. McWilliams standing on the narrow front porch watching after her, and from this height she could see a man and a pair of horses in a field behind the house, pulling stumps out of the ground. The McWilliams claim had had quite a few good big pine trees on it to start with, but they had cut them all down in the first months of living there.

After Martha wired shut the gate, the woman on the porch turned and went inside.

The sky was gray but didn't look to have any rain in it; it was the kind of high overcast that can make the world resemble a moving picture the way they were in those days, all shades of gray colorlessness. Martha thought it was beautiful country, even grayed out, close to the kind of open, rolling rangeland spoken of in *Lone Star Ranger* and *The Virginian* and other Western romances Martha had read, the country horsemen rode through in novels on their way to trouble with Cayuse Indians or crooked sheriffs. In another twenty years people would wake up to realize that the timber was gone and the native grasses plowed up or eaten right down to the roots, that cheatgrass and rabbit brush and water-hogging scrub juniper had taken over all the disturbed ground. But it was still possible for Martha Lessen to look around and imagine the country as it must have been—the way Nez Perce and Shoshone Indians must have seen it, riding across with their big herds of ponies before white men overran the land, the kind of country where every gully and gorge in the foothills holds a clear, pebble-bottom creek, where the mountain slopes are clothed in timber and the valley floor is a golden grassland with stands of trees in patches, good big timber in the creek bottoms and along the river, the kind of country that leads people to name towns Eden or Paradise or Opportunity.

Martha had read a little book about famous men and their horses: Alexander and Bucephalus, El Cid and Babieca, General Lee and Traveller, the knight Reynard and his charger Bayard, the horse that had outraced Charlemagne's army. She sometimes imagined herself one of them, or a famous woman, famous as Annie Oakley or Joan of Arc, on a famous horse. Riding over the low hills between the McWilliamses' and the Romers' she fell easily into thinking again that she was Mattie (this was how she'd be called, once she was famous), a horsewoman renowned all over the West, on her horse Meriwether Lewis, a tall black with a metal sheen to his coat and a fiery eye behind a long wavy forelock, a horse she had trained, like the Virginian's horse, to come straight to her at a certain four-note whistle and to carry no other rider but her. Always in these imaginings it was forty or fifty or sixty years ago, when she'd have been able to ride all over the valley of the Little Bird Woman River without seeing a fence and without getting down from her horse, not even once, to open and close a gate.

8

DOROTHY ROMER'S HUSBAND, Reuben, had taken up a claim south of Dewey Creek that was unsuited for crops. It was fairly well timbered, so he got most of his income from cutting wood for the Shelby school and for the town electric plant, but he was what these days would be called a binge drinker and he was off somewhere getting drunk and Dorothy Romer was splitting wood for the school so her children would be able to eat that week. Dorothy had set down the maul and the splitting wedge and was stretching her back and catching her breath when Martha Lessen rode into the yard. Martha didn't see Dorothy standing there by the woodshed; she pulled up her horse in the yard and Dorothy's middle child, Helen, who had been kept home from school to stand watch over the baby, cracked open the door and peered out. When Martha said hello to her she shut the door again. Ordinarily Helen wasn't a shy child but Martha

Lessen was a strange and formidable presence sitting up on a big red horse.

Dorothy gathered up some of the disheveled hair that had fallen on her neck and repinned it and then she walked out from the corner of the woodshed. "Hello, Miss Lessen."

Reuben's horses were over in the field of corn stubble rummaging for edibles, and T.M.'s attention was fixed on them. When Martha turned in the saddle to say hello to Dorothy, her horse tried to walk out from under her, evidently to say hello to those other horses in the cornfield. She told him "whoa" in a low voice but he only shook his long head up and down irritably and took another step, so she pulled his head down toward a stirrup and jabbed her blunt spurs into his brisket and whirled him in a tight circle round and round for a whole minute before straightening out his head. After that he stood there well behaved and meek without so much as a glance toward those other horses.

It wasn't a very cold day but Martha's face was pink when she finally turned to say hello to Dorothy. "Are you Mrs. Romer? I've met so many people I can't keep the names straight."

"Yes, I'm Dorothy Romer. Did you come to see the horse we wanted broke? She's there in the cornfield." Dorothy walked over to the fence and Martha got down from her horse, dropped the reins, and followed her. T.M. stood there as if she'd nailed his hooves to the ground.

Reuben kept a gray gelding as a riding horse and he

had four pulling horses he used in pairs so they could trade off the hard work of hauling logs; he had bought the unbroke chestnut mare for no good reason except she was a beautiful horse and he was drunk at the time. "She's that chestnut there, the one standing kind of alone," Dorothy said.

The chestnut shifted her weight just then and moved closer to the rest of the horses, and Martha said, "The one that just moved over? The pretty one?" and Dorothy nodded. Martha watched the mare for a few minutes quietly and then went to the little gate in the cornfield fence and opened it and went through and took off her hat and waved it, which set the horses to moving. She stood and watched the particular movement of the chestnut as the horse bolted away from her, ears flattened, hind legs kicking out. Dorothy couldn't imagine what she was looking for or what she was learning by watching the horse. The mare was an intractable five-year-old that her husband was unfathomably fond of but had never been able to break. She imagined it was the horse's very wildness that her husband admired.

"Was she ever started?" the girl called to her.

"My husband tried to do it. I guess he can get her saddled and get her to take the bit but she always will buck, she won't ever calm down. I think she's just determined not to be rode. My husband off and on has talked about selling her for rodeo stock. If you don't think she can be broke, maybe he'll just go ahead and do that."

The girl walked back toward Dorothy. At church on Sunday Dorothy would have said she looked like anybody's rangy, over-tall farm daughter, dressed in a worn green jumper and worn yard boots, her thick brown hair pulled back behind her ears under an old-fashioned hat that had the velvet worn through. Now she wore a buckaroo getup, fringed buckskin chaps that flared out wide above high-heeled boots and spurs with blunt star rowels, the kind of outfit Dorothy hadn't seen outside of old photographs and rodeo shows. The girl's hair was tied back with a piece of string, and when she resettled her high-crowned hat on her head most of her hair disappeared under it and she looked a good deal like a beardless young cowboy.

"How long ago did your husband give up on her?"

"Oh, I don't know that he's ever given up but if you mean when's the last time he tried to ride her I guess it was a month ago or more." Dorothy remembered this because it was right after Mata Hari, that exotic dancer who had been spying for the Germans, was put to death. Reuben had been calling the horse Mata Hari and joking about her being pure evil, and the day he read about the execution he had gone out to break the horse "for once and all" and he'd been thrown three or four times that day and he hadn't tried to ride her since.

The girl looked down at her boots. "Well I'll see if I can break her for you, but sometimes when they've been tried and bucked like that they just get ruined and they never can be broke. If I can't get her gentled I won't charge you for trying."

"All right. That sounds all right." On Sunday, when Reuben had told the girl broncobuster that she could try breaking his wild horse, he had walked back to Dorothy and laughed and said, "She'll be in for a bad surprise, won't she, when she tries to get up on that mean ol' Mata Hari," but he had looked nervous, and Dorothy knew he was of two minds about whether he wanted the horse tamed at all. And she also knew his pride was in danger if a young girl was able to accomplish what he'd failed at. So there was an odd sort of relief in hearing Martha Lessen speak doubtfully about the outcome.

"I've got about thirteen or fourteen horses, I think, that I'll be breaking on a circle ride. I'm planning to start in the next day or two roughing them out, and I guess I'll start here because you're nearest to the Bliss place and I'm boarding over there. I should know right away whether I can break her or not."

"I'll tell my husband," Dorothy said, though she didn't know where Reuben was and she didn't expect to see him until he had drunk up every penny of last week's wood money. "Would you come in and have some coffee?"

The girl looked off across the countryside for just a moment and when she looked back at Dorothy her face had taken on a shy look. "I've got so many places to visit, I guess I'd better not."

Dorothy had been starving for female company, for

any company really, so long as it wasn't a child, but she didn't say so. She said, "Where are you headed to next? Do you need any help finding it?"

Martha took George Bliss's creased map from her coat pocket and flattened it out and turned it until she could read what it said. "His name is Irwin, I think. Mr. Bliss drew me a map, but I'm still having trouble finding places. Is Irwin's the next one over to the north?"

"The Birtwicks have the place next to ours and then is Irwin's. If you go back to the Graves Creek road and then turn west when you get to the river, you'll see his house setting right on top of a hill; it's painted white. You can't hardly miss it, it's a big house and right out in the open."

"I'll find it. I don't know this country too well yet, but I guess I'll learn it."

"We've been here two years and I still don't know it much. My husband drives me to church in the wagon, and into Shelby for the shopping, but I never learned to drive the horses and I've got to walk everywhere when Mr. Romer is busy. I've got children who get tired if I walk them very far, and that keeps me pretty close to home."

"Was your husband hoping to tame that chestnut enough so you could ride him?"

Dorothy said flatly, "I guess I don't know why Mr. Romer bought that unbroke horse except that he thought it was pretty. But I've never ridden much, and I don't think I'd want to learn on a horse as wild as that, and I don't want her anywhere near my children."

Martha glanced back at the girl, Helen, who had by now come out on the porch and was watching everything from there, and then she said to Dorothy, "Well, no matter how pretty a horse is, if she's not well mannered she's not a horse you'd want to have around. But if I can break her for you, then she won't be wild anymore and you could sure ride her anywhere. You'd just have to keep schooling her, making sure she stayed tame, which are things I could show you how to do."

Dorothy looked over at the chestnut skeptically. "He calls that horse Mata Hari, after the Dutch spy who made so much trouble for them over in France."

Martha smiled suddenly. "After she's broke and not making trouble anymore, maybe you'll have to start calling her Mattie." She was a big girl and had a large mouth, but Dorothy thought she was pleasant enough to look at without quite being pretty. When she smiled it caused her eyes to widen as if she'd been happily surprised. Dorothy guessed Martha Lessen was around nineteen or twenty. Her wide young face, when it was lit up like that, gave Dorothy a terrible feeling of envy. She was only twenty-eight herself, but she felt old, and wise in the sorrows of the world.

"You'll be back tomorrow, then?"

"I think it'll be tomorrow. Anyway I hope I can get around to see everybody today, and if I can then I'll be here in the morning. It'll probably be a good couple of weeks before I start riding the circle, though."

"I didn't say so before, Miss Lessen, but I don't know what you mean by a circle ride."

"Oh, it's just called that because I'll be riding in a big circle every day, one horse after the other from one place to the next, every single day. You'll have somebody else's horse put up at your place most days, or I guess it'll be two horses, because I'll have to get the circle spread out even. I haven't figured out yet what to do about spreading the cost of the feed so you don't wind up feeding more horses than you own, but I'm still thinking about it and I'll get it worked out. Anyway, every morning I'll be riding a new horse in and riding another one out."

Dorothy said, "Oh," as if she understood this, though it was still mostly unclear.

"They need to get used to being ridden," the girl said, "and they need to learn reining and not to be afraid of ropes and all that, so you have to ride them over and over to get the lessons learned. First, though, you've got to get them all used to saddles and so forth, which is likely to take me two or three days at each place." She said this as if she knew Dorothy was having trouble with it, but not like a schoolteacher explaining something to a slow pupil. It seemed to Dorothy she was just quietly pleased to be able to talk about something she knew, something she was good at, and it struck her suddenly that the only things she herself was good at were housekeeping and rearing children, and these were not things other people would be anxious to hear about. Any chance she might have had to be a cowgirl and to go around the countryside breaking horses had passed her by a long time ago.

9

A COUPLE OF THINGS conspired to delay Martha, and it took her the better part of two days to make it around to all six places, talk to folks, and get a look at all the horses.

She found the Irwin place easily enough. Walter Irwin was a bachelor homesteader who had come out from somewhere in New England with money but no knowledge of farming, and he had hired a man named Alfred Logerwell to help him, a man who was lazy and conceited and almost as ignorant as Walter himself. Irwin had an auto-truck and had been slow to discover that he might need mules to get his plowing done and a horse to get down the roads when they were too muddy for his auto. The horse he had bought was not yet broken out, which was an odd choice for some-body with an immediate need of one; but the horse had been bought on Logerwell's advice, it turned out, and from one of Logerwell's relatives. Martha didn't dis-like Walter Irwin—he was mild seeming and decent—but he wasn't interested in coming to any knowledge of horses. He sent her off to talk to his hired man about the roan gelding he wanted her to break, and Martha saw right away that Alfred Logerwell was the sort of person she would never have a use for. He made a false show of knowledge, talking as if the horse was a thousand-dollar prize, though it was a plain cayuse of the worst sort, heavy-jowled and long in the pasterns.

Logerwell would have bucked out the horse himself, could have broken him in half an hour, he told Martha with a crooked smirk, if he hadn't strained his shoulder lifting sacks of cement. This was the kind of thing she was used to hearing from her own dad and hardly ever credited. Moreover, Logerwell liked the sound of his own voice, which was another thing he had in common with Charlie Lessen, and he kept Martha standing there a good hour while he told her every cock-and-bull story under the sun, stories proving how smart he was, and everybody else dumb as cows.

So it was late morning, almost noon, by the time she got away from Irwin's and crossed over the Little Bird Woman River northwest of Shelby and went looking for the Thiede ranch, which was called the T Bar, tucked up against the foothills of the Whitehorn Range. She was pretty sure she had found the right place and was just riding up to the house when a woman on a dun horse popped over the hill and rode down into the ranch yard at a breathless lope. It was a shock to see a little child who couldn't have been more than two years old jouncing on the saddle in front of her, the child's round face wreathed in wool so only the dark eyes showed. The woman's own face was bright pink and her long-nosed horse was damp with sweat along his neck and flank. She rode him right up to T.M., who tossed his head and stepped sideways.

"Miss Lessen," she said, as if they were acquainted with each other, and then at one stroke Martha remembered this was Irene Thiede, whose husband owned the T Bar, and their little boy, who was called Young Karl. "We lost the wagon, it tipped off the road by Little Creek," Irene said in a harried rush. "Emil's trying to get the horses out of harness but he needs somebody stronger than me. I was planning to phone up Gray Maklin, he's the closest, but since you're right here, can you help?"

What Irene didn't say was that her husband, Emil, was German—his father, Old Karl, spoke barely construable English even after twenty-five years of practice—and that Gray Maklin was a Dutchman who appeared to hold the Thiedes to blame for everything the German army had done in the past four years. Irene thought it was very likely that Gray Maklin would turn his back on her and she would have to ride all the way over to Bill Varden's—Bill didn't have a telephone—or phone over to Bud Harper, whose ranch was a good eight miles away. There were homesteaders living closer than that but she hardly knew any of them, and wasn't on good enough terms to ask them for help.

Martha Lessen, who didn't know a thing about any of this, just said, "All right," and they went at a gallop back up the ranch lane and then along a rutted wagon trail that twisted uphill between rising walls that narrowed, following a rock-bedded creek. Mixed stands of yellow pine and spruce stood clumped on shelves and benches along the upper slopes and shadowing the creek. The T Bar Ranch ran cattle clear into the northern slopes of the Whitehorns, and with the open fall some of their wilder cows had decided to stay up in the forest and not come down to be fed at the home-place. Emil had been up to check on the cows and to bring down a load of firewood and maybe shoot at game if he saw any, and Irene had been riding with him to help keep an eye on the bad places in the road and then help him cut and load the wood. It was her fault, she told Martha wildly, all her fault the wagon had tipped over along the rock margins of the creek—she'd been the one riding ahead to scout the potholes, make sure the mud wasn't too deep, see that the wheels had room on that narrow road. Emil's two Belgian horses had been pulled over with the wagon, not badly hurt but terribly frightened, and when they gained their feet they'd made a tangled mess of the harness. They were in a bad place—the wood had spilled out—and Emil was afraid to cut them loose from the lines without somebody to hold their heads and keep them still until he could come around and lead them back up onto the road. "He didn't think I could hold them," Irene said in a tight voice.

As soon as they came in sight of the wagon Martha saw what kind of trouble the horses were in. The wagon had tipped and slid eight or ten feet down the steep, crumbly embankment at the edge of the road and then come to rest on its side against the gnarled boles of trees that clung by stubbornness to the cutaway bank of the creek. The creek made a hard bend just there, running loud and white around the curve, and the roots of the trees sprawled out over a sheer twenty-foot drop to the water. If the Belgians tried to go down instead of up, or if they pitched around and lost footing on that narrow, gravelly shelf, they'd go to ruin.

Emil was on the slope at the front of the rig, standing with the Belgians and leaning into their big bowed necks. His face when he turned it up to the women was scratched and streaked with blood and mud but if he was disappointed to see Martha instead of Gray Maklin it didn't show on him. "Can you climb down here, Miss Lessen? Can you hold them while I get the lines cut loose?" He said it quietly, not to frighten the horses.

She gave T.M.'s reins to Irene. "You'll have to watch him, he's an ornery horse and a troublemaker."

Irene said, "I'll hold him," and smiled whitely. Martha had already seen that Irene Thiede sat a horse as well as anybody she knew. And Young Karl sat in front of her with his mittened hands not gripping the horn but resting on the fenders of the saddle, as if sitting a horse was the most natural thing in the world. His dark eyes looked out at Martha seriously.

She went over the embankment, scrambling down behind the wagon so if she started rocks rolling they wouldn't roll down into the horses. The firewood had spilled in a jumbled jackstraw pile, half in the creek, and some logs had wound up tangled with the whiffletree and the traces. She climbed cautiously onto the spilled wood and squeezed past the upturned wheels and undercarriage of the wagon and spoke softly to the Belgians before coming up on their flank.

"They've calmed down some," Emil told her. "Maybe Irene could have held them but I was a little worried they'd go over into the creek." It was the only thing he had said to Irene—that he didn't want to lose the horses—and not a word about how he would have to get in between the span to get them loose from the whiffletree, and how the big horses, if they reared up or bolted, might crush or trample him or take him over the bank with them.

"Hey, hey," Martha said softly, and breathed against the near horse's muzzle as she took his cheek strap.

Emil stood away and let her take both horses. "You got them? You think you can hold them?"

"I'm pretty sure I can." This wasn't true. Their heads were up, pitching just a little bit, and she could see the white all around their eyes. They had had a bad scare and didn't like where they were standing. She told them what good horses they were, speaking quietly against their warm faces.

Emil sidled around behind them, keeping one hand on the near horse's flank. He was talking to them too, a steady low note, "Whoa, whoa, whoa." Then he said to Martha softly, "Hold them now, can you?" and he stepped around the whiffletree, which stood up on its end in the tumble of firewood logs and half broken through. The wagon tongue had split too, and the shattered ends dangled from the hip straps of the breeching. He crouched down between the big haunches and hocks of his horses. Martha heard the sawing of his limbing knife against the thick tangle of leather as she held the Belgians' heads tightly, bracing her body against their great muscled chests. They leaned into her, wanting consolation, and she told them steadily how brave they were. She could feel her own heart thudding against the hearts of the horses.

"Can you back them up a step, and then ahead?" Emil said. "Just a step, not much."

She clucked to the team and pushed their heads back and they shifted their weight reluctantly. Emil made an inarticulate sound and then he said, "Okay," and she let them step forward. She heard the sound of brush breaking above her, which was T.M. acting up, and Irene speaking evenly to him, something about a bird, hadn't he ever seen a bird before? and it was just then the whiffletree decided to finish breaking all the way through, and part of it slid sideways and struck the ground with a muffled clashing, which Emil would have prevented if he could—it wasn't much racket, but enough to unnerve the Belgians. Martha's heart flew up in her throat and she shifted and clasped an arm around the neck of each horse and let her weight hang from them, which wasn't meant to be force, she couldn't have stopped them with force, but was the kind of reassurance you give a child when you hold him tight, *I've got you, I'll hold you, it's all right,* and they came ahead no more than three or four steps and then stopped, huffing their hot, fragrant breath into the chill air.

"Emil?" Irene called down, and he said, "It's all right, we're all right," and he came around where

Martha was holding the horses and got in front of them and helped her coax them back from the edge of the bank. "Well, that wasn't too bad," he said. Martha was thinking that Mrs. Thiede maybe could have held them. The Belgians hadn't really given that much trouble.

Emil stepped between the horses and took the right-hand one by the headstall. "You take that other one there?" he said to Martha.

They gained the road, one and then the other, scrambling up those few feet of loose dirt and rock without much effort, and then she followed Emil down the road, walking the horses out and back to see if they were bruised or lamed. When they were a hundred feet down the road from Irene, Emil said, glancing at Martha, "Irene maybe could have held them, but she'd have had to leave the baby to come down there and help me."

When she looked at him she saw in his face what he must have meant: that he'd been afraid of what could happen, afraid that if the horses bolted he and Irene might be leaving their son standing orphaned in the road a dozen miles from anyplace.

They turned back toward Irene, who was still sitting on the dun, holding T.M., who had stopped acting up as soon as he discovered Irene wouldn't put up with it. When Young Karl saw his daddy returning he bounced his heels along the dun's shoulders in a restless way, which made the horse think he should move ahead. Irene touched her son on the leg and touched the reins softly and both the boy and the horse settled and became still.

When Emil got to where he could see the tipped-over wagon again he stood with his hand on the Belgian's neck and looked down at it. Irene said in a distraught way, "I thought there was room, Emil," and her husband just said, "There was plenty of room, honey, it was just that the road give way," and he looked over at her and shook his head and that was the last either of them said about it.

They left the wagon where it was—"I'll get Bill or Mike to help me chain it out of there when there's time," Emil said—and he climbed up on one of the Belgians and they all trailed back to the T Bar homeplace. They wouldn't hear of Martha leaving the ranch without sitting down to dinner, and Martha, who would have liked to get a look at the horses they wanted her to break and then be on her way, gradually understood she had to sit and eat to offset their feeling of indebtedness. While Irene went in to heat up the ham roast, Emil took her out to the corrals.

He had a longtime practice of tying his young horses behind the sled when he was feeding out his cattle in winter, or behind the wagon when he was feeding salt in summer, which was a light and easy way to start them; so the two horses he had in mind for her to work with, a black gelding and a bay mare, had already been broken to lead. Up to this point no one had yet told Martha the Thiedes were German, but in any case her judgment of people was always pretty well formed by their treatment of horses. She took warmly to the two T Bar horses right off the bat, could see they were well cared for and that they wouldn't give her a bit of trouble; and this, among other things, caused her to feel well disposed toward Emil and Irene.

While they were sitting at the dinner table they all heard something heavy hit the floor in a room at the back of the house, and the Thiedes exchanged a look. Emil put down his fork and excused himself and went quickly down the hall, and then Irene told Martha that Emil's father, Old Karl, had broken his pelvis falling off a haystack in early October and was laid up in bed. She glanced at Young Karl and then lowered her voice and said they just didn't know if the old man would ever walk again.

By the time Martha got away from the Thiedes it was two o'clock. Then it was a slow five miles or so from the T Bar to the Rocker V, a dozen fences to pass through and a lot of wheat to skirt around. The Rocker V was a big old spread with a gingerbread house, a log barn bigger than a Ringling Brothers tent, and nearly a dozen buildings scattered around the homeplace. Martha imagined Bill Varden must once have run a crew of twenty or thirty cowboys to keep track of his cattle, but he had broken up a lot of his pasture to grow all that wheat, and he wasn't even carrying a foreman that winter. It was Bill himself who took her around to the corrals to see the horses. She had known old-time ranchers like Bill Varden all her life: tough-minded to the point of meanness, unsparing of himself and his cowhands. He was old-fashioned too, in not owning an automobile or a telephone, but he told Martha he had learned the hard way that bucking out a horse was a money-losing proposition—too many horses and men breaking bones or going sour or getting arthritis from a lifetime of bucking the kinks out every damn morning. He hadn't cared about such things when horses were cheap and cowboys a dime a dozen, but now that men and horses were both worth more, he was ready to try a different way, which put him at odds with most of the other old-time ranchers who were his neighbors, men who wished to go on doing things as they always had. He had four horses waiting for her in the corral, although he said the blue roan didn't belong to him but to Tom Kandel, who had the little chicken farm next door. The Kandels didn't have a corral, and the Rocker V had plenty of them, so Tom had brought his horse over to be taken out in turn with the Varden horses.

By the time Martha quit the Rocker V there wasn't much daylight left and she didn't want to get lost trying to find the rest of her customers in the dark. So she rode the eight or nine miles back to the Blisses in a gathering dusk, and the next morning, Tuesday, went out to see the last of the contracted horses. W.G. Boyd lived on a small acreage at the edge of Bingham with his ten-year-old grandson and a black gelding named Skip, which had been given to him because he had a reputation for healing up sick animals. Before coming to the Boyd place, Skip had been tied to a rail on the nailed side of the fence, something most people with good sense will keep from doing, for if the horse is startled and rears back, you run the risk the damn rail will pull loose. Which was exactly what had happened with Skip. He had run about half a mile with a pine pole bounding loosely behind and beneath him, fastened tight to his rein. The pole had beaten his hocks and shanks bloody, and bruised both his cannon bones. W.G. Boyd had gradually brought Skip back from lameness, had done what he could to gentle and reassure him; but although Skip had been tame before he was hurt, he now was wild and frightened of everything under the sun. W.G. was sixty-five years old that year and had arthritis in his hips and hadn't been on a saddle in almost a decade.

Martha listened to this whole story and then told W.G. she would do what she could, but a horse who had been as badly frightened and hurt as Skip might never get over it. She said it wouldn't take much to reaccustom him to being ridden, but his fear might keep him from ever being reliable again. She didn't want W.G. to think he was being cheated if Skip didn't turn out meek as milk.

When she left the Boyd place she crossed the river again at the edge of Bingham and went south along a ranch road that wound and curled through the canyon of Blue Stem Creek for more than three miles before opening up to a pretty little valley where the Woodruff sisters had their Split Rock Ranch. Their land was right up against the mountains without much bottomland for growing wheat, so they were still more or less strictly a cattle outfit. Martha had been told that the Woodruffs' foreman, Henry Frazer, had worked for the Blisses up until June. Then the sisters had lost the last of their hired men to war fever, and Henry had left Louise and George and gone over to the Split Rock Ranch to help out.

The sisters were in the midst of weekly laundry out on the wide front porch when they met Martha; one of them was stirring the boiling pot with a long wooden stick and the other was feeding clothes one at a time through the wringer. They weren't surprised to see her but surprised she hadn't been met by Henry Frazer. "Oh, for goodness' sake, Henry must be taking care of that business with the bull," Emma Adelaide said after a moment, without saying what that business was. Aileen dried her hands on her apron. "Well, you'd better get your barn coat on, Emma Adelaide, and we'll show this girl the horses."

TheWoodruff sisters were two maiden ladies who had grown up on their father's ranch and gone on ranching after his death, unconcerned by convention, riding cross-saddle along with their cowboys even now when they were becoming too old to keep up. They were exactly the sort of women Martha admired and intended to take as a model.

10

B Y THE TIME Martha Lessen got back to the Romers' on Wednesday morning a neighbor had carried Reuben home in a wagon and he was lying liquor-sick and pale in the darkened bedroom. Dorothy had milked the cow before daylight and set the milk in the separator and walked the cow out to their farthest pasture and come back alone just as the sky was lightening. She was splitting wood in a cold gray drizzle when the girl came up the road, riding a different horse from the one she'd been on the other day. Dorothy heard her coming from a long way off, on account of the jangling of a string of little bells she'd tied to the saddle strings. The girl waved a hand and then stood down from the horse in a careful way and stroked his neck and talked quietly into his ear, words Dorothy couldn't make out.

"My husband is sick, Miss Lessen, so he couldn't get that horse into the corral." Martha had told Dorothy on her first visit that the cornfield wasn't a particularly good place to work with an unbroken horse. The girl had asked that Reuben's unbroken chestnut be moved over to their small corral and that they turn the other horses out into the pasture that adjoined the cornfield. Dorothy and her oldest child, Clifford, had tried to do it, but the other horses had refused to leave the corn, and she and Clifford were afraid of the untamed horse; they had given up after she bared her teeth and charged them.

The girl looked over at the chestnut, hiding behind a pair of Reuben's heavy-footed half-Belgians. "That's all right," she said. "I guess if I can get the other horses over into the pasture I can work with her there in the cornfield." But she was thinking she would have brought Dolly along to help her haze the horses if she'd known. She wasn't exactly scared of Mata Hari, but wary. The year before, while she'd been working with a horse that had been bucked out rough like this one, she'd wound up with a dislocated shoulder and unable to remember afterward how it had happened; now she was a little afraid of getting hurt, was cautious around horses likely to give trouble, horses that flattened their ears or lifted a hind leg to kick or swung their head around to try to bite her.

She didn't want Scout standing around tied to a post all morning so she led him inside the pasture fence, got a loose camp hobble from behind the saddle, and buckled it around his front pasterns. Then she loosened the cinch and stripped his bridle, which he was wearing over a soft hackamore. He stood where he was a minute, studying his situation. He knew what a hobble was, but this wasn't the kind he was used to, and he hadn't been turned out in an open field in nearly two weeks. Then he took a couple of pussyfooting steps and lowered his head to lip the cropped-short grass.

Martha took her coiled rope and went over to a wide gate in the pasture fence that let into the back side of the cornfield. She opened it slightly and stood by it and made a kissing noise with her mouth. This was a language some of the horses understood, and two of the draft horses immediately trotted through into the pasture. Then she walked out into the corn stubble and waved the rope, which got the others dodging around, and after some minutes kissing and waving the coiled rope and feinting with her body she got the gray saddle horse to veer out of the cornfield and into the pasture. But the chestnut was leery of her and kept hiding behind the other two draft horses, and those two seemed determined not to be driven out of the corn— they circled and circled, dancing past her. It wasn't a big field but big enough so the horses and Martha gradually got sweaty, even though it was a cold morning.

Dorothy went on splitting wood, looking over at this spectacle every little while. The day before, when she and Clifford had given up trying to separate the horses themselves, she had told her son they would just wait for Miss Lessen to do it, and that Miss Lessen was a cowgirl like the ones she and Reuben, Helen, and Clifford had seen when they went up to the Pendleton Round-Up the summer before the baby was born. Those men and girls roping cows and horses had seemed almost never to miss, and Dorothy didn't know why Martha didn't just shake out a loop in her rope and throw it onto Mata Hari's neck. Maybe this was what you had to expect from a girl who was not a rodeo cowboy, just somebody doing an ordinary job of work on foot in an open field, but it was a disappointment.

Just about the time Helen and Clifford were going out the door to school, Martha finally persuaded the Belgians to move over into the pasture. Then she shut the gate and stood in the middle of the cornfield stubble with a little whip and began snapping it around Mata Hari's hind feet, which made the mare dodge back and forth or circle, looking for a way out or a corner to hide in. The girl began singing quietly, a song Dorothy didn't recognize, something dirgeful about a cowboy who had died. Dorothy's children walked slowly backward down the road, swinging their lunch buckets, watching Martha Lessen and the horse every last moment until they went over the low rise at the edge of the pasture fence and lost their view.

Dorothy was as curious as Helen or Clifford. She went on with her housework but every little while she looked up to watch the girl in the field. She expected bucking and noise but none of that seemed to be happening. Early on, she saw that the horse had stopped racing around and was standing quietly letting the girl's hands rove up and down her neck and withers. Dorothy could hear Miss Lessen still singing—when she came to the end of her cowboy song, she just started at the beginning again—and from this distance it looked for all the world as if the chestnut horse was in thrall to the girl's low voice. When Dorothy looked out a few minutes later, Martha had a halter on the chestnut and a long lead rope and was following the horse around the field, letting her go wherever she wanted and keeping slack in the rope. It was a mystery to Dorothy what this had to do with teaching a horse to behave. Without dust or noise to keep her interested, she sometimes forgot there was anything going on out in the cornfield. Once, when she looked up from what she was doing, she saw the girl walking around the field and the horse seeming to follow her like a pet. But things progressed so quietly, it wasn't long before Dorothy was hardly watching at all.

She had been simmering a pot of beans and a ham hock on the stove ever since the breakfast dishes were washed, and she had been looking forward to having Miss Lessen to visit with at lunch. But late in the morning the girl came up to the house and said she was finished with the chestnut for now and was going on to the Irwin farm to start his gelding. Dorothy said, "Oh," in surprise and believed she'd hidden her disappointment, though she hadn't come anywhere near it.

Martha shifted her weight, which caused her spurs to jingle lightly. She had not given much thought to it, but imagined that a woman like Mrs. Romer, a woman with a husband and three children, wouldn't have any cause to feel lonely; now she remembered suddenly, seeing the look that came into Dorothy's face, there might be all kinds of reasons for a person to need the company of strangers. She herself had suffered from loneliness, living in a house crowded with five brothers and her parents and sometimes grandparents and a sickly aunt. She said shyly, looking away, "I might come back here this afternoon, if that's all right. It wouldn't hurt to spend some more time with your horse," and Dorothy's face lit up with something like relief.

All the rest of that morning Dorothy fitted in the wood-splitting when she could, between caring for the baby and her sick husband and washing clothes and sometimes sitting down to sew for a few minutes on outfits she intended for the children's Christmas. Reuben was able to keep down some soup, which Dorothy brought to him in the bedroom. His hands were shaking, so she spooned it into his mouth, and after a minute or so he began to weep quietly and she wept too and kissed his sweating forehead. He dropped his head down on her bosom. "Don't give up on me, Dorothy," he murmured, "just don't give up on me. I won't drink no more, I promise you." She had heard this promise three or four times a year for all the ten years of their marriage. She cried and said, "All right, Reuben, all right," and stroked his greasy hair. He was a good husband and father when he was sober, but he had lost jobs one after the other on account of his drinking, and they would lose this farm if the wood wasn't delivered to the school and the electric plant in a timely manner.

Martha Lessen rode back into the yard in midafternoon. Dorothy's children, who had just come walking up the farm lane from school, stayed out by the cornfield to watch her work with the chestnut horse even though the day had gone on cold and damp and they stood there shivering, their shoes muddy and their cold hands fisted around the handles of their lunch buckets. Dorothy didn't call them in until she had supper nearly on the table, and then she walked out in the drizzling rain to get the children and tell Miss Lessen that she hoped she would come in and eat too. She was startled to find Martha riding the saddled horse at a walk round and round in the stubble field.

Dorothy stood a moment at the railing with her silent, enraptured children, and then she called out quietly, "I hardly can believe it."

Miss Lessen kept her attention somewhere along the bobbing neck of the horse, as if something was written there and she was trying to make it out. "Well, she's not finished," she said, "but she will be, by spring."

"My husband will be so surprised." Dorothy looked over toward the house, the drawn curtain at the window of their bedroom. Then she swatted Helen lightly on her little behind. "Go on and feed the chickens and then you wash up for supper. Clifford, the cow is out in that pasture that has the hollow tree, you'd better run all the way if you want to make it back in time to eat." Her children scattered. She said to Martha Lessen, "Come in and have supper with us, will you? I made a big pot of beans and hocks."

It might have been a quiet meal if the children had gone on tongue-tied and if Reuben had stayed in bed; Dorothy had imagined the two women might have a chance to visit like adults. But the children suddenly discovered their voices and peppered the heroic Miss

Lessen with every possible question about horses and cowboying and her life in the Wild West, and in the midst of it Reuben came out from the bedroom dressed but unshaven and smelling ripe.

"I've been getting over being sick," he said shakily to Martha Lessen, a kind of apology. In fact he looked thin and sallow, the tender skin around his eyes standing out bruise-dark. He sat at the table and took a little food onto his plate and cleared his throat and said, "I bet that horse is giving you lots of trouble."

The children's faces flashed bright with their news. "She's already broke," Clifford said, and Helen, tumbling her own words over her brother's, said, "She never even bucked one time."

Reuben drew back his head in surprise. Slowly, while his children went on chattering to him about the wonderful Miss Lessen, his face reddened and he lowered his eyes to his plate and began quietly to pick at his food with a fork. The children might ordinarily have gone on talking—they were irrepressible children, really—but they felt something come into the room, a strain or rigidity they recognized, and gradually they fell quiet and sat looking from one to another of the adults. Dorothy threw Martha Lessen a distressed glance, which the girl gathered the meaning of. Like the two Romer children, Martha was pretty well acquainted with men who drank themselves sick. In her experience they often spent their shame in the coin of anger and swagger. She said, intending to soft-soap him if she could, "Well, she's not broke yet, she's just somewhat started, and she took to the saddle so easy, I guess you must have been working with her and done most of it already."

Reuben looked at her and after a moment carried a forkful of beans up to his mouth and held it there while he pretended to consider the matter. He cleared his throat again. "I did think about going on breaking her myself, I had her that close. Only I don't have the time. I've got plenty to do without bothering over a stubborn horse." He chewed the beans deliberately and chased them down with milk. His hand holding the milk glass trembled slightly.

In a while Martha said, without looking up from her plate, "Mrs. Romer told me she's called Mata Hari, and I guess she must be named right, she tried to take a bite out of me when I had my back turned."

This finally seemed to please and mollify him. "You be careful, now. That horse would as soon kick you as look at you." He went on after that, talking about the execution of Mata Hari and the progress of the war, particularly this recent business of Lenin and his crowd overthrowing the czar and making peace with Germany. Reuben had signed up for the draft, he told Martha, and "wished to get a chance to kill Heinies." But he didn't expect to be called, given that he was a farmer and father to three children. It was true they were still calling up the unmarried men and the men without children ahead of the family men, but Dorothy doubted the draft board, if it came to it, would ever grant her husband a farmer's exemption. He had hardly managed to make anything grow on his claim, and after the last poor pea crop he had turned almost entirely to woodcutting for his income. From time to time she found herself daydreaming, in very nearly a hopeful way, about Reuben being shipped off to France while she packed up her children and returned to Wisconsin to live with her parents.

Her notion of a pleasant female conversation over the supper table had already been surrendered, so when the baby started to fuss, Dorothy left Reuben sitting at the table gravely delivering to Martha Lessen his opinions on the conduct of the war, and she put Clifford and Helen to clearing plates while she settled in a chair to nurse little Alice. Miss Lessen's eyes followed her with a shy-seeming glance and after a minute or two she stood and carried her own empty plate to the sink, murmuring a word of excuse to Reuben, who was still talking knowingly about the mistakes the British had made in their conduct of the war. Martha had taken off her big cowboy hat and canvas coat on coming into the house, but not the heavy leather chaps and spurs. When she crossed the room to retrieve her coat and hat, the scuff of her boots across the board floor and the jingling of her spurs made Dorothy's children stop and gaze after her in rapt worship, and even Reuben fell silent and stared.

"Are you going back to the Blisses' now?" Dorothy asked her.

"I've got a couple more things I want to do with your horse before I leave—I want to get her moved over into the corral, for one thing. But I'll be finishing pretty soon. I'll come back here tomorrow to rub a little more of the rough off her, but if you can make sure she's left alone until then"—she glanced pointedly at the children—"that'd be the best thing. She's awful tired from so much schooling. She's not used to it, and needs to be left to rest up overnight." She stood at the door a moment, settling her hat on her head and gazing out the front window at the dark afternoon. It had begun to rain harder, and Dorothy wondered if the girl was dreading going back out in it, the Bliss ranch a good three or four miles down a muddy road in the coming night.

She said to Martha, "You could stay over if you want. You'd have to sleep on the floor here in the front room but it's warm by the stove and we don't have a dog that would step on you."

Martha showed the quick white edge of a smile. "I wouldn't know what to do without a dog stepping on me." But she wouldn't stay: the Blisses were expecting her, she had horses of her own to see to, she didn't mind the rain so long as she was dressed for it, and so forth.

Then she turned and said to Reuben, "I hope you're feeling better, Mr. Romer," and Reuben, who by then was leaning forward with his elbows on the table and scrubbing his face with his palms, replied glumly that he had too much work to do to lie around in bed for long.

It occurred to Dorothy that Martha Lessen's words

about letting the horse rest might have been meant for Reuben as much as the children. If he wasn't the worse for liquor, it would be like him to try to show his children and his wife and the half-tamed horse just who had the upper hand and how little need he had of a girl broncobuster.

But later, when Dorothy had helped him take a bath and shave his whiskers and they were lying in bed together, he murmured again how sorry he was and how he would try to do better, and then he told her piteously that he was a damn worthless hand with horses and he never should have bought that unbroke chestnut and if Miss Lessen could finish the horse, by damn, he would turn around and sell it just like that, to make up the money he'd lost while he'd been off on his drunk. He began to cry as he told her these things, which drove Dorothy to feel she had to argue with him, she had to tell him it wasn't true that he was worthless around horses, and she tried to think of times when he had acquitted himself well around a horse or a team, bringing up, for instance, the time he had stopped his brother's horse from bucking just by grabbing hold of its bridle—just by hanging on and talking firmly to it. She murmured these things with her lips touching his temple and her hands stroking his hair. Slowly he quieted in her arms. He was so childlike at times, she despaired of seeing him a man, and childlike too in his temper and his need to strut and boast. She was shot through suddenly with an understanding: if he ever was drafted and sent to France, he would not survive it. He'd be killed in the first minutes after stepping into the trenches, and he would die weeping for her like a child.

11

SOME OF THE PEOPLE Martha had contracted with gave her just one horse to break, and others three or four, which meant she had to go to some trouble to get the horses spread out evenly, two in each corral. It was something she did little by little, moving a horse late in the afternoon after working all day at saddle-breaking. The first week in December she went over to the Woodruff ranch intending to pick up one of their three uneducated horses and take it to the corral at W.G. Boyd's place. She'd been working at the Rocker V all day in a steady rain, and one of Bill Varden's horses had given her a rough time—he was a big gelding pretty well blinded by his own glory. She hadn't any expectation of getting back to the Bliss homeplace until well after dark, well after the others had eaten their supper, and her back hurt, her feet were cold and wet inside wet boots. She rode the six or seven miles from the Rocker V to the Split Rock in a discouraged temper, with her chin down and her shoulders hunched under a rubber poncho.

Somebody—one of the Woodruff sisters or their foreman—had corralled the three horses for her, which was a relief. When she climbed the rails the horses crowded together in a far corner of the fence and watched her warily, ears pricked. Two were seal brown—they were out of the same mare, not twins but born two years apart—and one a flashy palomino. Martha had known palominos to make a show, to strut around as if they knew they were beautiful; but this one had a somewhat shamefaced way of holding her head low to the ground as if she thought herself plain. There was just no rhyme or reason to such things; the Rocker V horse, the one so proud of himself, had a long, rangy body, a Roman nose, a ratty tail.

A man came out of the little house Martha thought must be the foreman's place and crossed the muddy yard to her, shrugging into his coat as he came. She had been told his name but couldn't remember it. He climbed up next to her and looked at the horses a minute in silence. It was still raining lightly; she could hear it ticking on her rubber slicker and the crown of her hat.

"None of them is broke to lead," the man said, as if he and Martha had already been introduced and were in the middle of a conversation.

Her mood being what it was, Martha took this for some kind of criticism. "I know it," she said.

She felt him glance in her direction, but then he turned back and watched the horses another minute. Finally he said, "You care which one gets moved?"

Most of the horses she was moving were entirely unbroken, they were horses she hadn't gotten around to yet, horses who didn't know a thing about being led. She'd been roping their necks up close to Dolly and

116

bringing them along that way, so if the young horse gave trouble, pulling or trying to rear up, it was trouble only in the first minute or two. Dolly wouldn't stand for any nonsense and educated them with stern school-marmish discipline. Martha had been studying these three, looking for the one easiest for Dolly to handle, one small enough it wouldn't pull Dolly off her feet. "I thought I'd take the one with the white snip on his nose," she told the foreman, and waited for him to find some objection to it.

After looking them over a bit longer, he said, "I'll get a rope and wrangle him out for you," which brought him into her better graces. She had been worrying somewhat that she might have to try to rope the horse with the foreman standing there watching her. He looked over at Dolly. "Were you thinking you'd pony him up to your horse there?" This was said matter-of-factly as if it was just exactly what he would do if it was up to him. Martha gave him a look. He had by now put himself in a good way with her.

"Yes sir. They usually follow her pretty good and if they don't she takes a bite out of them."

He made a low sound of amusement. "I'll bet. She doesn't look like she'd take any monkey business off a youngster." He was studying Dolly. "I heard you had a horse that was all scarred up from being burnt."

"Yes sir."

He turned and gave Martha a slight smile. "I wish you wouldn't go on calling me sir. I'm just the hired help."

She glanced at him. "I don't know your name."

"It's Henry Frazer. And I've been presuming you're Martha Lessen, but if you're not then I guess I'm helping a horse thief get off with one of our horses." His smile widened good-humoredly. He had a round, clean-shaven face that was a long way from handsome: a large fleshy nose running up to a heavy brow bone almost bare of eyebrows. His nose had been broken once, and a front tooth chipped off at a slant, which Martha thought must have come from adventures with bulls or mother cows or horses, though what had happened was more complicated than that, and involved an automobile on an icy road.

"If I was to steal one of them, I'd steal that one there, the palomino," she said.

"Is that right? You like her color, do you?"

"I like thinking about ways to coax her out of her shyness. She's a pretty horse, pretty as anything, but she doesn't know it yet. I like thinking about ways I could get her to hold up her head."

This evidently surprised him. He studied the horses a minute and then said seriously, "I hope you don't have a favorite aunt named Maude because I want to say that's just about the homeliest name in the book, and that's what the sisters have been calling that horse, and maybe she's just ashamed of her name. I bet you could get her to bring her head up if you just started calling her Ginger. Or Babe. Or Dolly."

Martha hid a smile. "I've already got a horse named Dolly," she said.

"Is that right? Is she that one there, the one you rode in on? Well, she's holding her head right up, so I guess that proves my case." He didn't try to hide his own smile, in fact he seemed pretty pleased with himself for his little joke.

He stood down from the fence and went into the barn and came out with a coiled catch rope. While he stood building his loop he asked her, "You want to get a hackamore on him before you neck him up close to Dolly?"

"If he's got a hackamore on him he'll be easier to handle, but I don't always do it. It's a lot of trouble when it's just me."

"Well, there's two of us," he said, glancing up at her.

Martha went over to Dolly and opened up the corral gate just wide enough to lead her inside and then Henry stepped in too and Martha shut the gate. She had spent maybe a hundred hours of practice over the years trying to get better at roping without making much improvement. Henry Frazer shook out a loop and neatly forefooted the horse Martha had said she wanted. The horse hit the ground with a heavy thump, mud splashing everywhere, the other horses leaping wide, squealing, and Henry in nothing flat had his knee on the horse's neck and the head twisted up against his chest like a rodeo bulldogger before that horse had any idea what had happened. It wasn't how Martha would have gone about it—she never liked to throw a horse, which maybe was part of the reason she had never been able to get very good at roping—but she knew she'd have been half or three-quarters of an hour getting the damn horse ready to leave the corral if she'd been left to manage it alone. In the rain, at the tail end of a long day, she hadn't energy left to concern herself very much with the horse's fear, and she wasn't sorry at all to have him in a hackamore and snubbed up to Dolly in five minutes flat.

When Martha climbed onto Dolly again it caused a brief flurry—the brown horse squealing, trying to buck and shy away, Dolly baring her teeth, Henry Frazer jumping back to keep from getting kicked or stepped on—but Martha didn't have any trouble keeping her seat and in a moment, after everybody settled down, Henry came up again to Dolly's shoulder and rested a gloved hand on her and peered up at Martha. He had odd, downturned eyes that gave people the idea he was always squinting. Boys in those days always tagged each other according to some part of how they looked—every gang of kids had one called Slim and another called Red—and when he'd been a boy Henry Frazer had been called, even by his friends, Chink, or Chow Mein, for those screwed-down eyes of his. He said, "You all set?" and Martha answered, "I guess we are. Thanks." He nodded and peered across Dolly's withers to the brown colt. "That one's not very happy."

She could feel the horse where he touched against her lower leg, his wet heat, his pulse racing almost as quick as a rabbit's, and she could smell the fear rising off him. He was licking his muzzle over and over and eyeing Dolly sideways, the whites of his eyes showing. "He's wondering how this happened and what's going to happen next."

Henry looked up at her briefly. "Well, he doesn't have much cause to worry, I imagine." He patted Dolly once and stepped back. "You take it easy." His overalls and coat were badly muddied, and there was a clump of mud on his chin and mud in a long streak across the crown of his hat.

When she was out of earshot of the ranch Martha began to talk to the brown horse in a low steady voice, telling him everything they would be doing together in the next days and weeks, and she told him she was sorry he'd been thrown and bulldogged but he shouldn't take it as a sign of what to expect, and she told him she thought Henry Frazer was someone who wouldn't hurt a horse unnecessarily. The rain had pretty much come to an end by then, and they rode in a cold gray dusk, the horse's ears flicking sideward to catch every word she said.

12

THERE WAS AN OFFICIAL call in those first months of the war for folks to "pray hard, work hard, sleep hard, play hard, and do it all courageously and cheerfully." Of course not many people in Elwha County needed this direction from the War Office, for they had always been hard-worked without ever complaining much, and most of them lived in isolated circumstances without feeling particularly put-upon. They would travel ten miles for a pie social or a basket supper or an evening of cards or dominoes and not think a thing of it, even in the winter months when the roads might be troublesome and the ten miles to be covered on horseback. Such pastimes went on only slightly abated after war was declared, and in fact Liberty Bond drives and gatherings of women knitting socks for the army had to be squeezed onto the calendar.

Martha Lessen was drawn into this intense sociability almost as soon as she came into the county, though at first she had to be persuaded. Late in the first week of December, in the middle of saddle-breaking the fourteen horses in her circle, Louise Bliss pressed her to go to a Christmas dance at the Bingham Odd Fellows Hall. Will Wright, the young hired hand, told her he was riding over there himself on Saturday night and she might follow him up. Even in Pendleton, where she had lived most of her life, a town already pretty settled and gentrified, all the girls from the farms and ranches would ride to a dance with their dresses and shoes and stockings tied behind their saddles and would change when they got there; so she wouldn't feel odd in that respect. But she had come down to Elwha County intending to spend the winter breaking horses and sleeping in barns. She'd packed only the one dress in case someone pressed the point about the impropriety of a woman wearing trousers, and she had not brought any but barn shoes and boots with her. She tried to say this without saying it, but Louise Bliss would have none of it. She brought out a pair of shoes, patent leather with an opera toe, which she said had become too narrow for her feet now that she had bunions. The Cuban heels were worn down at the corners, and the patent was creased across the instep, but someone had polished the leather recently and they were better shoes than Martha had ever owned. Louise urged on her also a large silk scarf figured with red and pink and cream peonies and fringed in red, which she said could be worn tied at the waist or around the shoulders and would make any dress in the world presentable for a dance.

So Martha wrapped up her corduroy jumper and the loaned things in a bundle tied behind the saddle and rode over to Bingham with Will Wright. She took one of her own horses, the brown gelding named Rory, and Will Wright rode one of the Bliss horses, a pretty little blond sorrel with a flaxen mane and tail, whose name was Duchess. Rory was plain colored next to the sorrel, and as she was saddling him she whispered in his ear that he shouldn't have any reason to feel bad about himself; that even though Duchess was a beauty and also well mannered, with a sweet look and lots of width between the eyes, Rory was every bit as good a horse. He had been given to her in payment for last summer's work on the L Bar L, and he had nicely sprung ribs and plenty of depth through the heart, good shoulders, a reasonably long neck well cut up under the throat. He was heavy-barreled but easygoing, imperturbable, a horse she could trust without loving very much; the truth was, Martha would have traded him for Duchess without a minute's thought.

The day before, the papers had been full of news about a munitions ship and a troop ship colliding in Halifax Harbor, thousands of people killed, square miles of the city flattened, and there had been a lot of talk at the supper table about whether it was an act of Hun sabotage. While they rode over to the Odd Fellows Hall, Will Wright launched right in, repeating to Martha his opinions about Halifax; but then, without stumbling over the switch, going on to tell her he was in love with Elizabeth—Lizzie—the daughter of the county road supervisor, and when he was eighteen—in a little less than two months—they would marry, and after that he expected to enlist. Of course by then they might have extended the draft to men younger than twenty-one and it wouldn't be necessary to enlist, but in any case he expected, by late winter or early spring, to be shipped off to France to kill Huns. Like Rory, Will Wright was easygoing and imperturbable, and the idea of going off to war as a new bridegroom seemed not to perturb him anymore than anything else.

He asked Martha about the horses she was breaking, and she told him about the three that belonged to Bill Varden's Rocker V Ranch, one of them a narrow-headed Roman-nosed horse with a little pig eye, a horse that was always on the lookout for a chance to act up or get away or give her trouble of some kind. Will laughed and passed her an admiring look. "I never seen a horse get the better of you yet," he said, which wasn't completely true but near enough that it made her blush. Will had good balance in the saddle but he was sometimes a little heavy on the horse's mouth. Tonight, though, he had loosened his hands and Duchess was stepping along lightly.

He told her, "It's not the Round-Up, but we got a rodeo going on somewhere in the valley just about every Saturday in the summer, and if you're still here you ought to get into one. The one in Shelby has got two chutes and a bronc stall for saddling, but the one at Opportunity hasn't got no fences, they just snub the bronc and ear him down in the open while they get the saddle on." He looked over at her and grinned. "Some of those broncs are pretty mean, but I bet if you walked up to one of them and give him the eye and climbed on, he wouldn't buck at all, and wouldn't that be something for people to see."

By summer she planned to have moved on to some other part of the country, and anyway she knew it wouldn't be that easy to just walk up to a bronc and climb on, but she laughed and said she'd like to try it. She had been to the Pendleton Round-Up plenty of times, had even worked the chutes when they'd let her. There had been times she'd thought about becoming a rodeo broncobuster herself—those girls got to wear outfits that nobody teased them about. She had some-times thought the saddle broncs mostly didn't mind the life: they liked bucking people off and got to do it pretty regularly. But the bronc riders raked the horses bloody with sharp-rowel spurs, and every so often a horse would go down in the chute or out in the arena and have to be shot; plus, bucking out a horse wasn't horsemanship, and she didn't think she'd like doing it every day even with crowds of people admiring how she did it.

Bingham lay about five or six miles west of Shelby along the Little Bird Woman River. They crossed the river on the plank bridge at the edge of Shelby but then skirted the town and followed the River Road west. The weather was cold and dry. Under a fair moon and a sky dense with stars, they met several other young people riding over to the dance. Will introduced Martha as "our bronco-girl," and they laughed and seemed to understand who she was. Word of her had spread to most of the ranches by then, which she had no objection to; when the circle ride was finished she thought she might head down to Canyon City, and she hoped her reputation for good horse work would make it down there ahead of her. But the ease of Will's friends with each other, and their laughter, gave her a quick, helpless feeling of being a misfit and an out-sider, a feeling she was familiar with. She let Rory fall behind the other horses.

The street in front of the Bingham Odd Fellows Hall was crowded with horses and automobiles, and the long porch crowded with people. Martha followed the other girls into a small meeting room off the main hall and stood alone with her back to the others as they chattered in their underwear. She was the last to change her clothes and go out, having stood for minutes alone in the room fussing over the best way to tie Louise Bliss's scarf around her jumper.

The hall was beautifully dressed, the doorways and windows wound round with garlands of pine boughs, mistletoe, and strings of cranberries, and charmingly lit by dozens and dozens of bayberry candles on the tables and hanging in wire chandeliers from the center roof beam, their flames jumping and fluttering when the doors opened or shut. A three-piece band—autoharp, fiddle, and accordion—had begun warming up in one corner, but so many people were crowded inside the room that the air shuddered with their voices and the only instrument anyone could hear was the accordion.

Martha's furious hope was to go unnoticed and be left alone, but as soon as Will Wright spotted her he brought her straight over to a group of his friends, some of them the ones she had met on the ride in. The boys were all as young as Will or younger. Oliver was a ranch hand, Roger worked in his father's sawmill, and Herman drove an auto stage on the Lewis Pass road between Canyon City and Shelby. If the girls came from ranch families, they didn't say so: Mary Lee was a teacher, Jane was a normal-school girl who had come home for the Christmas holiday, and Will's girl, Elizabeth, who wished to be called Lizzie, was working at a candy store in Shelby until she and Will could marry. Their talk was all of friends who had gone off to join the army, and girls they knew who had taken up nursing in hopes of being allowed to drive an ambulance in France. Martha stood at the edge of their crowd in an agony of loneliness.

There were half again as many women as men in the hall, and the men were mostly very young, like Will and his friends, or they wore the burnt and leathery look of farmers and ranchers who must stay at home and raise wheat and cattle to feed all those soldiers—half the barns in the county had been painted with the slogan FOOD WILL WIN THE WAR. Martha knew some of the people from her horse-breaking circuit and others she had met through the Blisses or at church. The young minister, Theo Feldson, stood in a group of admiring girls, his stooped shoulders and bowed head rising above the girls' tortoiseshell combs and feathers. She recognized Henry Frazer, the Woodruff sisters' foreman, who was standing with some of the other ranch men, holding his cup of punch and idly watching the musicians get themselves organized. He looked over at her, smiled, and nodded.

Once the musicians began to play in earnest, people crowded to the sides of the hall and left the center of the floor for dancing. Martha was called on to dance with Will Wright and each of his friends and then with other men and boys in the room, although more often she danced with one of the girls—the few boys at the dance were obliged to have a turn with as many girls as possible. Mary Lee was as pretty as Duchess and barely five feet tall in her shoes, her arms and cheeks plump and soft, which made Martha, dancing with her, conscious of herself as a dangerously mannish giant. She was taller than any of the girls, taller than many of the men and boys in the room, which she was used to but still never happy about.

She had been to a fair number of dances in her life, from a wish not to be thought entirely eccentric. She knew the two-step and the polka, the march and the waltz, but when Theo Feldson, the tall young minister, tried to teach her a dance called the bunny hug, she had trouble keeping the steps straight, and shortly he switched back to the two-step. He held her with moist hands and after a long stiff silence began to talk to her about prospects for Prohibition.

Later Henry Frazer, as he was moving her around the dance floor, suddenly said, "You're good and tall," as if he hadn't noticed it before. She was about an inch taller than him. She didn't know what sort of answer that needed, or if it needed any at all. "How tall would you be without those shoes?" he said to her, looking down at her feet.

She realized he might be teasing her, and she thought to say, "I'd still be tall. When I'm not wearing these shoes I'm wearing my boots."

He smiled slowly, which crinkled his slanty eyes more than usual; the edge of his broken tooth showed below his lip. "I've seen you in your boots. You seem taller in party shoes. But I guess we weren't dancing whenever you've been over to the Split Rock."

It was hot in the hall—the press of so many bodies, and the stove stoked with pine logs—and Martha's face was flushed and shining. She said, looking past his shoulder, "I can't help if I'm tall."

He said nothing for a few turns and then he said, "I don't mind it."

They said nothing more to each other until the dance was finished and then Henry Frazer said, "I guess next time we see each other we'll both be in boots," and he smiled briefly. Martha watched him walk off. He had an odd, rocking stride, seeming to kick his feet out to the side with each step. His boots were worn down at the heel but the creased leather was shiny with saddle soap or boot wax.

She didn't dance with Walter Irwin. He was tall and was known to be a bachelor of means, so he was a popular partner; but when he finally worked his way around the room to Martha she told him she had promised to meet Irene and Emil Thiede out on the porch, which wasn't true—she had only just that minute seen the Thiedes cross the dance floor and go out to the porch. In point of fact, it wasn't Irwin she disliked but his hired man, Alfred Logerwell. The week before, watching her work, Logerwell had called out to her, "I can tell you right now, if you mollycoddle a horse he'll turn out spoilt, and I've had to unspoil plenty of horses that've been girl-broke. You ought to take a stick and beat some sense into that one." He wasn't the first man to ridicule her for the way she broke horses, the first man she'd met who believed in brute force, but he was the only one she knew of here in the Odd Fellows Hall. She had made a private promise not to dance with him; but by now Logerwell had danced with every woman and girl in the room and was starting around a second time without asking Martha, and she had begun to suffer from the unexpected feeling that she was being shown up or snubbed. Which was a roundabout and irrational reason for refusing to dance with Mr. Irwin, but there it was.

Irwin went away with a surprised look, but unperturbed. "Well, all right," he said, and strolled off to select another girl.

When she went out on the porch she found Emil Thiede smoking a cigarette and leaning on the porch rail, talking quietly to Irene, whose eyes were fixed past him on the low moon above the roof of the hardware store across the street. What they were talking about was Old Karl's broken pelvis, a subject that ran through their minds and through their conversation daily, but Emil stopped and raised his chin when he saw Martha Lessen, and Irene turned to see who he was looking at and they both smiled and came to her as if the story she'd given Walter Irwin had been true and the Thiedes had just been waiting for her to come onto the porch.

In those first months of the war there was a lot of foolish flag-waving. Orchestras banned the playing of Mendelssohn and Beethoven, people insisted sauerkraut was "liberty cabbage," vigilante committees in some places back East tarred and feathered people who spoke the German language. The Thiedes might have been entirely shut out by their neighbors, except the old ranch families in the valley had known Emil all his life—Old Karl and Hilda had come over right after the Franco-Prussian war, Emil had been born in the valley—and in any event Irene was English through and through, her family among the first to settle along the Little Bird Woman River. And with Old Karl laid up in bed, the worst of people's patriotism may have been forestalled. But Irene and Emil had been frozen out by quite a few of the townsfolk and homesteaders in the crowded hall—"Heinies" and "Krauts" had followed them in low whispers—and they were both glad to see Martha Lessen, who had evidently made up her mind that people who treated horses decently must be decent people.

Martha hadn't yet started riding the circle, so Irene said, meaning to tease her, "We've got a couple of horses just dying for Miss Lessen to come and give them a ride."

Martha didn't quite take this for criticism but she said in exasperation, "I'll be riding in and out every day once I get them all started, but I've still got two more to get to." She had just finished the rough work on W.G. Boyd's black gelding and still had two of the Woodruff sisters' horses to saddle-break before starting the circle ride. She worried about how long it was taking her to get around to them all.

Emil smiled. "Well, I guess pretty soon we'll be seeing too much of you then."

Irene, who had picked up on Martha's tender feelings, pushed him lightly. "Quit it, Emil." She fingered Martha's scarf. "This is so pretty."

Martha had tied the borrowed scarf at the waist of the jumper and then had stood in the changing room, turning the scarf one way and another trying to find the right place for the fringed points to hang down. Louise had told her the scarf would spruce up any dress, which Martha had understood to mean it might partly hide the shabby condition of her jumper. "Louise Bliss lent it to me," she said, not to mince matters.

This didn't lessen Irene's admiration of it. "It looks so nice. And the color is right for you. If I had your hair I'd wear red all the time. There's nothing prettier than a red ribbon in chestnut hair." Martha never had thought of her brown hair as chestnut, and she realized with something like dissatisfaction that she didn't own a single piece of red clothing, not even a ribbon.

She looked down at her feet, wriggling the toes. "These are borrowed, too. I've got sore feet from wearing them."

"They're pretty, though. Every woman should own a pair of patent shoes."

Martha kept looking down at her feet. "I never have."

Irene laughed. "I never have either." When she put one arm around Martha's waist, the last of the girl's unhappiness went out of her, and the two of them leaned together.

Irene had taken warmly to Martha from that first day in Little Creek Canyon when Emil's wagon had gone off the road. She had grown up in a family where horse sense was considered a heroic point of character, had heard repeated all her life the particulars of her grandfather's story—how he'd come West alone and penniless and worked as a cowboy and horse wrangler before managing to build up a decent ranch of his own from a small donation land claim and half a dozen cow and calf pairs. Irene had always been a good hand with horses, better than her brothers, every bit as good as her granddad, but she'd been a schoolteacher before marrying Emil. Martha represented to her some part of her old childhood notion of becoming a cowgirl.

After a moment, Martha thought to ask Irene, "Where is Young Karl?" Old Karl, even with his broken pelvis, stubbornly took care of his own needs so long as Irene left a sandwich and a pot beside his bed, but the two-year-old couldn't be left with his invalided grandfather.

"He's in that little room we all changed clothes in. Some of the younger girls are watching the babies and small children so we mothers can dance." She met Emil's look and flushed.

Emil said to her, "You're not dancing, though, are you?" He winked at Martha. "She'd rather stand here and fret. Her and the baby don't like to be in separate rooms, ever."

Irene looked away from her husband, frowning around the crowded porch without seeming to see anyone. "He's attached to me is all. He doesn't like to be held by strangers."

Emil took her hand and played with the short, blunt fingers without saying anything else about Young Karl. He said to Martha, "So I guess you'll be starting around the circle pretty soon. When? In a week or so?"

"It might be sooner than that. It might be Wednesday. Those horses have been standing around quite a while, some of them. I want to start as soon as I can."

Irene, who was remembering the start of school every autumn and how the children always had to relearn their lessons, smiled and said, "If those horses are anything like children, they'll have forgotten every bit of what you taught them by the time you get them back in the schoolroom."

This was fairly close to the case. Martha had tried to get back to the first of the horses every couple of days while also going on with the rough work on those remaining, and she'd ridden some of them a short way, getting them spread out evenly around the circle, two horses at each stop. But by now they were restive and tending toward wild again. She knew she'd have to remind some of them who she was and what a saddle was for and what was expected of them.

Emil grinned and said, following a trail Irene had opened up, "I always had to relearn my times tables over again every year. Did you?"

Irene looked over at him, laughing, and then said to Martha, "He still doesn't know them. He leaves all the book work for me to do."

It was cold on the porch, and in a few minutes they

would be driven inside again, but for a while the three of them stood along the railing looking out at the horses and autos in the street. Martha looked for Rory among the many brown horses and found him standing close to Duchess with his cheek resting affectionately against her golden red neck.

"I guess I'd rather teach horses than girls and boys," Martha said, and Irene answered briefly, dreamily, "Oh, I would too."

The T Bar comprised almost a thousand acres, a hundred cows, and they'd been short-handed even before October, when Emil's dad was hurt. Irene wouldn't have felt right saying it, but she'd been happier since then—since Old Karl was laid up and Emil needed his wife to ride out with him on horseback every day, just to keep up with all the work.

◆ 13 ◆

THERE WAS A LOT of rain early in December, followed by a hard freeze and then a thaw and another freeze. Sometime during the thaw a bunch of Split Rock mother cows discovered a desire to swim or wade over to Baby Island, a long narrow acre of land lying just beyond a U-turn in Blue Stem Creek. This would not have been trouble except they had pushed down a farmer's fence to get there, and the grass on the island was a little field of his winter rye just coming green after the rain, and they were still there when the temperature dropped and put a ledge of ice all around the island. After the cows finished up the rye and came to an understanding of their predicament, they began bawling to be rescued, which could be heard from half a mile off. The farmer rode over to see what the noise was and then rode over to the Split Rock Ranch and told the Woodruff sisters he was planning to shoot every damn one of those cows if they weren't off the island and off his property by the time he got back from seeing a lawyer about a lawsuit. He and the Woodruffs had enjoyed a long-standing dispute having to do with their range bulls covering his dairy cows.

Henry Frazer saddled a big dun horse called Pardner and went to take a look at the problem. The ledge of ice around the island was four or five feet wide, thick and white at the brushy margins, thinning out to a brittle skin shuddering and transparent at the edge of the current. Henry called over to the cows, his lowing, wordless mother cow call, hoping they might be inspired to jump out on the ice and break it with the weight of their bodies and then swim across to him. They went on milling along the bank and bawling fretfully. It was late in the day and a little wet sleet was drizzling out of a low sky, and Henry, studying the trouble these cows had got themselves into, considered whether he ought to just let the farmer shoot them. Then he hunted up a short thick pole for breaking up the ice and put his horse into the water.

The Blue Stem came straight off the Nelson Glacier far back in the Clarks Range and was numbing cold even in August; and in December, after a week or so of rain, it was deep enough to require a horse to swim. The whole adventure went against Pardner's better judgment. When the water climbed over his big haunches he decided to turn right around and climb back out, and Henry had to convince him pretty firmly to get back in and swim for the island. Henry wasn't happy about any of it either. He tucked his coat up to keep it out of the water but his boots flooded icy cold and then his overalls and long johns up to the hips.

When the horse bumped up against the ice and found his feet on the gravel bar under the water, Henry shoved the pole out and beat at the ledge of ice and broke away enough so the horse could climb up, and it must have been the shattering of the ice and Pardner scrambling and splashing up from the water that spooked the cows. They had been asking him to come rescue them but now they went hightailing away from him to the upstream tip of the island. The lead cows walked or got pushed out onto the ice until it broke under them, and as soon as they went down in the water the other cows jumped in after them, bawling and rolling their eyes, and the whole bunch started swimming hard upstream, which made no sense, except a cow will get herself into trouble and take you with her if she can.

Henry yelled and swore, which didn't help matters, and spurred the horse back into the water. The cows were swimming toward the hairpin curve on the Blue Stem where the bank had been sheared away in a high bluff, and afterward he would tell the sisters and any-body else who asked him about it that he'd been thinking they would pile up there at the oxbow and drown and that he meant to turn them back down-stream. But the truth was, he wasn't thinking at all, he just went in after them. And he never did know what caused Pardner to go under, if it was a rock or a stump under the dark water, or the shock of the cold, or a seizure of some kind, but the horse lurched suddenly and then sank, and Henry kicked his boots loose of the stirrups and swam away from him. The horse didn't come up, and then he did, floating on his back. Henry was at the bank by then, climbing out on the slick frozen mud, and he stood there with his teeth chat-tering and the stream running off him, stood there looking at his horse floating down the high creek with his legs sticking out of the water.

The cows upstream were already turning for the bank, finding their feet, beginning to lumber up into the farmer's frost-killed field of peas. If Henry had left the damn animals to their own devices he wouldn't have killed his horse was what he was thinking as he watched them. He started walking downstream after the horse and then he broke into a trot to keep his blood from freezing up on him. The saddle wasn't more than a year old and had cost him a pretty penny, and if the horse was dead he at least hoped to save the tack that was on him. He got ahead of the horse, and where the creek widened and creamed across a gravel bed he waded into the water and caught the reins.

When the dun's back scraped on the pebbly shallows the horse suddenly righted himself, snorting and blowing, and stood up wild-eyed and wobbly and streaming water.

Pardner was a big dark dun with zebra stripes down the spine and the shoulders—Henry never had thought he was much of a looker. But of course, when it comes to color a plain horse has his virtues. The fact is, a white-faced horse's eyes will weep. A horse with white feet is prone to split hooves. Palominos, claybanks, skewbalds, piebalds, some strawberry roans, have amber hooves that are brittle and prone to cracks. White hides will scald, chafe from sweat and heat. Some paint horses, the ones with mostly white on them, and blue eyes, are not right in the head. A pure black horse will sunburn in hot weather, fade out under the saddle and the harness. Left to go their own way, horses will pretty much always revert to bay, with black legs and hooves; or they'll fall back to grulla, with black feet, black zebra slashes above the knees and hocks and down the spine and shoulders of a dun-colored hide. They seem to know, most horses, the plain colors that will save them.

"Hey, Pardner," Henry said in surprise, and put his wet glove on the horse's neck affectionately. He and the dun were both soaked through and shivering and he didn't have a damn thing to dry off with, so he set out leading the horse at a trot to get some heat going in both of them. It was near to a mile back to the Split

Rock. He got into the yard just about the time the sleet quit, and went into the barn and took off the wet saddle and rubbed down the horse as well as he could with gunnysacks and then went over to the house and stuck his head into the kitchen.

"Miss Woodruff, I've got to get back to those cows and bring them in, but there's a horse in the barn needs to be warmed up and looked after, he near drowned in the creek."

Emma Adelaide took in Henry's sopping clothes and said, "Oh for goodness' sake," and she stood up and reached for her barn coat on the rack by the kitchen door. "You put on some dry clothes," she yelled after Henry as he went back out, and then he heard her calling Aileen's name.

His wet boots were a slow chore to get out of, and the wet long johns, the goose flesh bright pink when he peeled them back. He stood by the box stove in the foreman's house for the little bit of leftover heat coming off it and dried himself with a towel and rummaged around until he found dry clothes that weren't too muddy—he hadn't got around to doing laundry that week. He didn't have another winter coat to put on, so he put on his summer coat over a flannel shirt, and a raincoat over the top of that, and his barn boots caked with mud and manure.

It was just about dusk by then. He took a coffee can of corn out to the pasture and shook it, and his red horse, Dick, came up. He was saddling him when Aileen brought over a steaming cup that turned out to be tomato soup, and he drank it down before he went ahead with tightening up the cinch. While he was standing there next to the horse, Aileen let herself through the pasture gate and chirped to the horses, and her paint horse called Paint came up to her and she led him over to the fence and went ahead with saddling him, even though Henry called to her, "Miss Woodruff, I don't need help bringing those cows home." The sisters were both stubborn that way. When he and Aileen rode out of the yard, there was a light on in the barn and through the half-open door he could see Emma Adelaide walking Pardner up and down the runway with a blanket over his back.

The pea field the cows had climbed into was fenced on three sides with wire strung between posts and rockjacks, and on the fourth side by Blue Stem Creek. The cows were too spent to go to the trouble of pushing the wire over and they had had enough of the flooded creek, so they were standing in the near-darkness, bunched up together for comfort and heat, waiting for what would happen next. Henry got down and opened the gate in the fence and Aileen went through and began driving the cows toward the opening, clucking and chirping to them quietly. Her white hair and the white on the paint horse seemed lit-up and luminous against the darkening sky, the dark field, the dim glooming shapes of the cows.

When Pardner sank under him in Blue Stem Creek, Henry had reached down for the horse, had tried to hold on to him, hold him up, a thousand pounds, which he had not remembered doing and now suddenly remembered.

In April the year before, Henry's older brother, Jim, had been driving him and El Bayard back to the Bliss ranch from Bingham after seeing a moving picture. El's sister Pearl was in the car too, as she and Jim were engaged to marry. Jim had moved to Elwha County in 1914, persuaded by Henry's letters about the mountain air, the scenery, the prospects for growth in the valley, and now Jim had a law practice in Shelby and a brand-new Model T Ford car. At the curve where Cow Creek comes down and joins the Little Bird Woman River the car slid off the road and overturned. It had been a deep winter, but a Chinook wind had blown up warm the previous week and the roads had opened up, though most people hadn't taken their cars off the blocks yet. The four of them had been talking about Wilson's declaration of war, which had happened just the week before; they had been arguing about the need for it—Jim was adamantly against the war—and about the moving picture, which was *Kaiser, the Beast of Berlin.* Henry never did know what caused the car to swerve, if it was ice or if a tire blew or if they hit a pot-hole and Jim lost his grip on the wheel, and he didn't know if their arguing had taken Jim's attention away from the road. The car went over on the driver's side and pinned Jim's head to the ground and he drowned in four inches of cold snowmelt at the flooded verge of Cow Creek.

While he watched Aileen bring the cows through the

gate he was thinking about that night on the Bingham-Shelby Road, the luminous whiteness of Julius Audet's bald-faced half-Shire horses coming toward them out of the darkness, and how Julius had unhooked his horses from his hay wagon and run a chain from the horses to the Ford and righted the car just that easy, releasing Pearl Bayard's pinned legs forty minutes after Jim was dead.

14

SOME OF THE FELLOWS homesteading up and down the valley in those years were such poor farmers they could hardly raise Cain. They would break up the fields of bunch grass to grow pinto beans or turnips and nothing would thrive but star thistle. If there was timber on the land—and it grew thickly in those years, yellow pine and spruce and fir up to four feet through—they'd log it off and pull out the stumps and be surprised to find scrub juniper and rabbit brush growing back instead of the grass they'd expected to pasture their dairy cows on. When they cleared the sage and willow from around a spring, sometimes the spring would silt up, and when they opened up a spring to make a farm pond, as often as not the water dried right up or got salty. Quite a few people who might have given a good account of themselves under other conditions were just taken in by rosy visions of "rain following the plow," which was the widespread, spurious claim of not a few commercial and government interests. In those years it seemed as if all you might need to grow wheat or alfalfa or field peas on the dry slopes of Elwha County was a stack of pamphlets and bulletins from the Department of Agriculture or a handbook put out by one or another of the companies making farm equipment.

Tom Kandel had come into the county to homestead about 1910, with his wife, Ruth, and their young son, Fred. He was a college man, which made him different from most of the rest of his neighbors but not always in the ways you would expect. He was a thinking man with a curious mind, who if he happened upon a petrified bone or a fossil in weathered rock was not content until he found the book that could tell him what animal it had come from, and he took subscriptions to magazines and journals of a kind not seen in other houses and always had a book he was reading or quoting from—he had read every word of Ridpath's *History of the World* for instance—all of which might be exactly what you'd expect of him. But Tom had a healthy mistrust of anything a government bureaucrat might say about the scientific methods of dry-land farming and he had more common sense than most.

The Kandels had filed their homestead claim on land that had once been winter range for a sheep outfit, and Tom was smart enough to plant his garden vegetables in the old sheep corrals on his claim. While his neighbors were breaking up grass to plant wheat and draining shallow lakes to grow corn or timothy hay, he set about growing chickens as a full-fledged enterprise.

Every farm family raised chickens in those days as food for the table and sold a few eggs if there was a market for them, but Tom put into practice the most modern methods of incubation and scratch feed and found a thriving home market among the big crew at the McGee Creek Lumber Mill over on the slopes of the Whitehorn Mountains. "My blooded stock is in egg yolks," he would say, and laugh outright as if he found everything about it deeply amusing. It was never an easy thing in that part of the country to keep chickens alive—hawks, especially, would plan their visits according to the time of day you regularly went to the privy. But until he got sick Tom did as well as anybody could hope, and better than many of his friends and neighbors.

He took cancer sometime in the fall of 1917. In November, when Martha Lessen came into the county offering to break horses, he bought a coming four-year-old blue roan gelding and left it at the Rocker V corral to be taken out in its turn with the horses Martha was breaking for Bill Varden. This struck some of his friends as a foolish distraction from the business of dying, and other friends as the necessary business of going on with your life. Tom didn't know which of those it was, really. He had wanted to buy the horse and have it broken, so he had seen to it. It was something he and Ruth had talked about before he'd become ill—they wanted to give their son a horse when he turned thirteen—and now he had become anxious to see it through. He wanted other things done as well, things they had talked about for months or years while lying in bed at night, things they had always said they would do when they had the money for it next year or the year after—a new rug for the front room, a new mohair cover for the old chair that had been Ruth's grandmother's.

The Rocker V was one of the big old spreads, a cattle outfit, although Bill had sold off about half of his cows and broken up a lot of his grass to plant wheat in 1915 when he could see the way the war winds were blowing. He'd always had trouble keeping cowboys and foremen—Bill was a harsh old man and he worked people hard—so when he found himself with less need for skilled cowboys, he took to hiring local men, homesteaders for the most part, to dehorn his cattle in the fall and feed them out in the winter and haul ice from Lewis Lake to be laid up in sawdust in his root cellars and icehouses for the coming summer when, for a few weeks, he'd be feeding a big harvest crew.

Tom Kandel had taken winter work with Bill just once, for a few months in 1915 when extraordinarily cold weather had frozen half his flock of White Leghorns. But in 1917, that last winter of his life, he went over to the Rocker V and signed on again to feed cows. On Sunday, late in the afternoon, he was working with a team and wagon laying out a racetrack of hay in one of the Rocker V fields. A cold fog had settled over the valley, and the trees on the surrounding slopes were soft gray shapes against a white remoteness; so when a horse and rider came off the hill, they seemed to take their form out of the ground, and only slowly became something he recognized. They were almost upon him before he realized it was Martha Lessen riding his son's blue roan horse.

"Hello, Mr. Kandel."

"Miss Lessen, you ought to be sitting down to Sunday dinner about now."

She smiled, which had a way of transforming her face. She was a big, serious girl, but when she smiled her eyes widened and you saw how young she was, as green and unhandled as one of her horses. "We had fried oysters for breakfast, and Mrs. Bliss's sweet rolls, but I wouldn't know what to do if I sat inside all day, and anyway the horses need to be taken out every day so I went ahead and started the circle." She looked over at the cows coming up to the long oval of hay behind his wagon. "I guess cows have to be fed even on Sunday."

Ruth was holding off roasting their usual Sunday hen until Tom finished with his work, but she hadn't been happy about it. They had quarreled over it the night before, and then she had cried and told him she didn't care about getting a new carpet. "I wish you would quit working for Bill Varden and stay home with me and with Fred every day," she had said to him, and he had finished the sentence in his head, *until you die.*

He nodded and looked back at the cows and then over at the girl. "That's my horse you're riding."

"I know it is. I don't know if he has a name but I've

148

been calling him Dandy because he's coming along so good." She put her gloved hand along the horse's neck affectionately and he bent his ears back to her. Miss Lessen was devoted to the trappings of old-time cowboys, and Tom looked at her buckskin chaps and loose starred spurs with an odd pang of yearning.

"Dandy," he said, as if he was trying it out. "He'll be my son's horse so I imagine we'll let Fred name him. I'll tell Fred you've been calling him that." He smiled.

No one had told Martha that Tom Kandel was sick. He had lost a good deal of weight over the past few months but she hadn't known him long enough to notice it. He had a thick shock of brown hair that hung down over his forehead, and in the cold whitish daylight he was slightly flushed with one of the fevers he'd been running off and on for days. If you didn't know, you'd have thought he was bright with health. He was forty years old and in a little over two months he would be dead.

"I guess we'd better both go on if we want to be in time for dinner," she said to him, and began to move the horse along.

He found that he didn't want the girl to leave, that the idea of being alone again in the center of a shapeless, shadowless vagueness was suddenly terrible to him. He said, "Ruth's roasting a hen. I imagine it will be stuffed full of onions." He didn't know how he expected this news to keep the girl from riding off, and already she was half gone, the fog eddying around her. She called back to him, "I saw a horned owl this morning, I hope he didn't get any of your chickens," and she threw him a last look, one of her childlike smiles. He stood at the back of the wagon with his hands on the handle of the pitchfork, and watched the shape of the girl on the horse soften and whiten and sink down again into the formless ground and leave no trace. He sat on the tailgate of the wagon and took out a handkerchief and wiped his forehead and drew cold air into his chest and let it out again and after a minute he was all right, able to go on as he had been, feeding cows in the late December afternoon without noticing the fog too much and without thinking too much about anything except the work.

He always made sure the weaker cows got their share. They would come late to the first dump of hay, after it was already trampled on by the fat, healthy cows, and while the fat ones would follow the wagon around the oval, those weak cows would stand where they were and make do with muddied feed. So he always went all the way around again and dumped fresh hay for them at the beginning place. Today when he had finished his work he sat a while on the tailgate of the wagon and watched them feeding, their dark shapes softened by the fog, before he drove the team back to the Rocker V. The windows in the ranch house were mostly unlit, although he could see Bill's housekeeper, a tobacco-voiced woman named Ella, moving through the dimness attending to her weekly chore of cleaning the lamp chimneys and trimming the wicks. Bill Varden was a divorced man and he drove himself as hard as his hired help. Tom thought he was probably not in the house at all on a Sunday afternoon but was somewhere out on the ranch, maybe hauling wood off the mountain for fence poles or going up into the canyons to set traps for coyotes and mountain lions.

Martha Lessen had already changed horses and ridden off toward the next place on her circle ride. The blue roan and another horse, a chestnut, were standing in the corral, both of them looking morose and slighted, staring yearningly toward the other horses in the fenced pasture on the east side of the barn. Tom unhitched his team and turned the big Percherons out and stood along the rails of the fence watching them drift off into the whiteness, their breath gusting out and stirring the frosty air. The cancer was in his liver. His side ached with it and with the effort of getting the horses out of their harness. He leaned on the fence and when he was feeling better he walked home slowly along the hard ruts of the ranch lane.

The windows of his own house were brightly lit in the darkening fog, and he could see Ruth moving about in the single room that was both their kitchen and their parlor. He had built a wooden sink for her with a pitcher pump that drew from a well drilled under the house. That well had never yet dried up on them, though most of his neighbors were hauling water in barrels from the Little Bird Woman River in the dry months of the year, their hand-dug wells sucking mud by then. He stood outside in the cold, watching his wife work the pump and carry a pan of water to the stove. His flock of chickens had already gone in to roost, and the yard was quiet—chickens will begin to announce themselves hours before sunrise as if they can't wait for the day to get started but they are equally interested in an early bedtime. Tom had grown used to sleeping through their early-morning summons, all his family had, but in the last few weeks he'd been waking as soon as he heard the first hens peep, before even the roosters took up their reveille. The sounds they made in those first dark moments of the day had begun to seem to him as soft and devotional as an Angelus bell. And he had begun to dread the evenings—to wish, like the chickens, to climb into bed and close his eyes as soon as shadows lengthened and light began to seep out of the sky.

He let himself into the woodshed and sat down on a pile of stacked wood and rested his elbows on his knees and rocked himself back and forth. His body felt swollen with something inexpressible, and he thought if he could just weep he'd begin to feel better. He sat and rocked and eventually began to cry, which relieved nothing, but then he began to be racked with great coughing sobs that went on until whatever it was that had built up inside him had been slightly released. When his breathing eased, he went on sitting there rocking back and forth quite a while, looking at his boots, which were caked with manure and bits of hay. Then he wiped his eyes with his handkerchief and went into the house and sat down to dinner with his wife and son.

15

ON THE SATURDAY before Christmas the Woodruff sisters invited their friends and neighbors—not the newcomer farm families, but all the old-time ranch families and their hired hands—to the house for a holiday dinner. Emma Adelaide took on responsibility for roasting the pig, and Aileen for baking the cakes, and they asked Henry Frazer to see to the eggnog. Elwha was a dry county, but several moonshiners living down in Owl Creek Canyon regularly brought whiskey up to the valley, packed under loads of tomatoes or inside bales of sheep's wool, and the Woodruffs expected Henry to see that the punch was sufficiently stiff.

It was not a lack of liquor that kept most people from making eggnog that winter, it was the sugar. But for years the Woodruff sisters had been experimenting in their garden with various plants their neighbors said wouldn't grow in the valley, and they had grown a crop of sugar beets in the summer of 1917. Now that the country was on a wartime footing the Woodruffs had sugar while others were going without. There was no easy way to separate the molasses from the sugar crystals though, so the Woodruffs' sugar was black. Aileen's chocolate cakes took to it easily, but Henry Frazer's eggnog, floating in a silver punch bowl with a grating of orange nutmeg, was the color of snuff, and people had to be persuaded to drink it. Henry, ladling cups of dark froth, took the chiding and ridicule with a smile. He had ridden over to Tom Kandel's and bought up several dozen eggs, pretty much all Tom had now that the days were short and his hens reluctant to lay; and cream from the Bowman Dairy, all the cream Timmy Bowman could give him now that his cows were reluctant to lactate; had whipped up the egg yolks and the cream with the dark sugar and then folded in the beaten egg whites and the whiskey bought from a sheepherder who kept a still down in the canyon. It was as stiff and rich an eggnog as he could make, and after the first round people stopped teasing him and began wandering back to the silver bowl on their own.

Martha Lessen let Henry fill her cup twice before the liquor took effect, and he was watching her when she looked around the room in dismay and then found a chair and sat in it. Other women must have had an eye on the girl too; Henry saw Irene Thiede and Louise Bliss exchange a telling look and then Louise came straight over to Martha and sat down in the next chair and leaned toward the girl and said something Henry couldn't make out. Martha looked down at her stockinged ankles or her patent shoes and made some sort of reply and then the two of them went on talking over there in the corner while Henry stood with his cup in his hand, listening only now and again to the men standing around the punch bowl going over the past season, grass and cattle and horses and wheat, and the war news, which had to do with electric signs in the towns and cities staying dark twice a week, and how that didn't have a thing to do with any of them or anybody they knew, since electricity hadn't yet made it out of the towns into the countryside. Of course nobody in those days would have guessed: it would be 1946—on the other side of another great war—before electric wires were strung to all the farms and ranches in Elwha County.

When finally Mrs. Bliss stood and went off toward the kitchen, Henry left the men and sat down in the chair Louise had surrendered. The flush of liquor had almost gone out of Martha Lessen's face by then but Henry went ahead with what he had planned to say. "The sisters wouldn't stand for eggnog without liquor in it," he told her, which he meant her to know was an apology.

When Henry had seen the girl the first time, riding up to him on a scarred and earless mare, she had looked gravely sure of herself, even vain, outfitted in showy fringed chaps and a big vaquero hat as if she was headed for a rodeo and her mare was the famous Justin Morgan. But it hadn't taken him long to realize she knew her horses and was bashful and skittish away from them. She gave him a wild sort of look that he took for embarrassment. "I told Mrs. Bliss I have a terrible sweet tooth."

He turned her words over until he got her meaning: the eggnog was sweet, and she'd gulped it down for the sugar. He grinned and said, "Aileen made three cakes and I never saw her put any liquor in them, but

I imagine she won't bring those out until we've ate up the pig."

She silently twisted her fingers in the scarf tied at her waist—her hands were pink from hard scrubbing, and still there was a thin rime of black around each nail—and looked out at the two dozen or so people standing around the room. After the girl's silence had gone on a while, Henry looked up into the dusty realms of the roof beams and said, "Old man Woodruff built this house himself."

People in Elwha County considered the house an unfashionable museum piece—it had been a throwback to an earlier time even when new—but Henry guessed Martha Lessen, with her old-fashioned cowboy trappings, might think well of it. The roof of the main room was supported by hand-peeled pine logs, and the walls and ceilings were faced with rough-cut lumber. Bear rugs were scattered on a floor of pine boards twelve inches wide, planed and fitted together as tight as a ship's deck. The fireplace would take four-foot logs. "Every bit of the wood came off this ranch," he told her. "The old man cut the logs and snaked them down off the mountain and then he built a sawmill and planed the boards himself. Those fireplace stones came from Short Creek and Blue Stem Creek and the Little Bird Woman. The windows and the nails, I guess those came from outside, but just about everything else he made with his own hands."

Martha had desperately loved the house from first seeing it. She turned her face up to the great wrought-iron chandelier suspended on a chain above the center of the room, its heavy wheel supporting six kerosene lamps, and adorned with horseshoes and small iron replicas of the Split Rock brand. "Do you think he made the hanger for the lamps?" She glanced hesitantly at Henry. "He might have made the nails for the house, too, if he was used to making his own horseshoes."

"He might have. I guess if you can make horseshoes you can make nails, and he sure did his own shoeing. Those old-timers knew a little bit of everything. I can shoe a horse if I have to but I try to keep from doing it if I can."

She warmed to this. "I never took it up either. Roy Barrow taught me to break horses and showed me how to shoe but I never really wanted to do much of it. I can trim hooves all right if the nippers are sharp, but I don't even like doing that if I don't have to."

He didn't know who Roy Barrow was but he said, "Every farrier I know of has got a hunched-over back and bad knees."

She gave him a quick look, smiling. "Roy couldn't stand up straight, and his legs were all bent out like broken fence rails. I guess that's why I never wanted to shoe."

"Well there you go." He thought of something else she might be interested in. "You ought to ask the sisters to tell you some of their stories, those pioneer days when old man Woodruff first came up here. I guess wild horses used to herd onto those alkali flats over by

Teepee Hot Springs to lick the salt and take a bath and roll around in the grass and just have a time. I guess it was quite a sight, hundreds of them."

"I wish I had seen it." She had seen, plenty of times, big herds of horses gathered in one place. Combine crews making the rounds of wheat ranches in the summer would come through Pendleton with as many as a hundred and fifty horses, but those were coarse and heavy-footed pulling horses, kept bunched up together in corrals or herded close between wire fences. And at the railroad corrals in Pendleton horses were brought in by the carload; on weekends it was popular sport for folks to go down there and watch cowboys bucking out dozens of horses in a melee of dust and noise. But she hadn't ever seen more than four or five wild horses at one time—not range horses, but wild horses—and then just a glimpse before they spooked away. They'd been pretty well hunted down, shot, or rounded up, until the ones that were left were skittery and canny and quick as cats. When she was younger she had daydreamed about going up into the high parks of the Blue Mountains or the Wallowas or the Clarks and camping there quietly until the wild horses got over being afraid of her and came out of their hiding places, and in her daydream she rode them bareback without a bridle, guiding just with her knees and heels and her voice, and she never came down from the mountains.

After a brief silence he said carefully, "I guess you don't get thrown too much, breaking horses." She raised her chin and gave him a quick look, her face as pink and shining as it had been at the Odd Fellows dance when he had said that stupid thing about her tallness. He spread his hands. "I was just thinking about the horseshoers, and how bronc stompers can get pretty broken down too."

She looked away from him. She had been bucked off in the corral that morning by one of his horses, or anyway a Split Rock horse, one of the brown ones she had been calling Big Brownie, but she didn't tell him so. "Well the horses don't hardly ever buck when I bring them along the way I do," she said, which was mostly true.

In the silence afterward, they became aware of the room clamorous with voices. The men standing around the punch bowl were arguing, and Emil Thiede made a loud, high declaration—"No, no, that sure ain't what I meant!" Irene was standing by the fireplace with several other women, holding Young Karl against her bosom. Henry and Martha both saw her look over at Emil with a worried frown. The old-time ranch families hadn't been shutting out the Thiedes, but everybody in the room knew: sometimes words were traded that didn't seem to be about the war or patriotism but had that meaning anyway.

Henry said to Martha quietly, looking down at his hands, "I guess you know the Thiedes are German."

She did know. Louise Bliss had told her, and in the same breath had vouched for them as one hundred percent Americans. But Alfred Logerwell had come up to her one day while she was changing saddles and said he had heard she was breaking horses for that damned Kraut spy Thiede. When she hadn't given him any answer, he had puffed himself up and said she must be a sauerkraut sympathizer herself. She and Logerwell had been on poor terms from the first time they met, but she didn't know where his hatred of the Thiedes came from—she didn't think he had ever spoken to Emil and Irene. Later on the thought occurred to her that she'd better keep Logerwell from knowing which of her horses belonged to the Thiedes—that if he knew, he might take out his hatred on the horses.

She said to Henry, "They're Americans," just so he'd know where she stood on the question. She had heard he was friends with Emil.

He looked over at the men gathered around the punch bowl. "I guess Emil would have to join up and get killed over there, and I guess Irene would have to leave Young Karl in an orphanage and start driving a Red Cross ambulance for some folks to believe that family's on the right side in the war." His smile was grim.

After a moment they went back to talking about horse breaking. Martha told Henry that one year at the Round-Up she'd seen a showman named John Rarey offer to tame any horse in about an hour without a bit of bucking and that she had picked up some of her methods from watching how he did it. Henry had read in a magazine about how the queen of England's horses were trained without bucking them, and he told

Martha what he could remember. Martha said she'd heard from Roy Barrow how some Indians liked to put their horses into deep water or a muddy marsh where they'd get tired of fighting in a hurry. Roy would have used this method himself if he'd been able to find any water deep enough; he was from Minnesota, which had its fair share of muddy marshes and deep-water lakes, and he liked to complain about the lack of them in Umatilla County.

When they began talking about the bells and so forth that Martha hung off the saddle to get the horses used to all kinds of noise and distraction, Henry said, "I guess there's nothing they'll be afraid of, once you get done with them."

Martha hesitated, but then she said, "Roy liked to bring out his accordion and play it close to the horses until they quit being scared of the music. I guess my horses will have to go on being afraid of accordions, because I can't play a note." Henry laughed, and Martha gave him a pleased, sidelong look.

Just about the time the roasted pig was brought out, Henry looked into his hands and said to her, "I ought to have warned you about the liquor in the eggnog."

She frowned. "I don't usually drink. I wouldn't want you to think I did."

"I know that. You were lit up too quick for somebody that was used to it." She glanced at him, seeming to look into his face for whether this was true. She had a good, open face, and with her hair pulled back and tied with a red ribbon she looked to him painfully

161

innocent and unguarded, a child. He was thirty himself, and his coffee-brown hair was already shot through with gray; nobody had ever mistaken him for handsome, and he knew he had more than the usual wear of weather around his mouth and eyes. He imagined Martha Lessen must think him old or a bachelor too set in his ways to ever be housebroken.

16

THE WEATHER TURNED COLDER, the ground frozen so hard it rang under the horses' feet. The sky on Christmas Day was Chinese blue, brindled with long streaks of dry cloud. Martha pulled a silk stocking close over her head under her hat and rode the circle from the Bliss ranch to the Romers' farm, then Irwin's, the Thiedes', the Rocker V, old Mr. Boyd's, the Woodruff sisters', and back to the Blisses'. It was roughly fifteen miles around the circle—would have been only eight or ten as the crow flies, but she sometimes had to let the crow find its own way while she took a roundabout path skirting fences and getting through gates and going up- or downstream to cross the Little Bird Woman River on a bridge or find a place to ford where it was shallow. At each corral she stripped off saddle and bridle and turned the horse she had ridden up on into the corral, caught and tacked up the horse that was waiting there for her, and climbed once more onto the cold saddle. Certain of the horses had to be hobbled while she saddled and unsaddled them, and some others had to be hobbled whenever she got down to open a gate and then unhobbled after she mince-walked them through.

Before finally starting to ride the circle, she had been thinking she knew the peculiarities of each of the horses and what to expect from them—which ones were tractable and which ones mean-spirited or cold-jawed—but she became better acquainted in the first couple of rounds. By Christmas Day her back and neck and legs and arms were aching from the long jarring ride over frozen ground, the jerk and pull whenever a horse took sudden fear of a shivering blade of grass or made up its mind to try again to throw her off and reclaim its old unfettered life.

She carried lunch with her and ate it as she rode. People on the circle were astonished to see her riding through on Christmas Day, and some of them—the Thiedes, the Woodruffs—tried to get her to come inside the house and get warm, eat something hot from the stove. She stood by the corral and drank down hot coffee if they brought it out to her, but otherwise told them she was determined to get around the circle as quick as she could so as not to hold up the Blisses' Christmas dinner—Louise had announced that they wouldn't eat their beef Wellington until Martha was able to take her seat at the table.

It was well after dark when she rode into the Blisses' yard around five o'clock. There were two unknown cars, a black Ford and a dark green Willys Knight, standing alongside the Chalmers, and the house was lit up behind its draperies, people's voices sounding dimly through the walls.

Martha made a poor toilet for herself by carrying water from the pump to the tack room, stripping down to her underwear and running a cold wet rag over every bit of bare skin. The water in the pail turned murky—she'd been shouldered and knocked to the ground by Irwin's horse that day. She put on the corduroy jumper and the peony scarf, combed her hair, and retied it with a ribbon. Christmas had never been much celebrated in her family, which had given her the notion she might like to celebrate it, but the corduroy dress went on cold and stiff over her shoulders, and her boot-sore feet didn't like the patent shoes, and her unwashed hair smelled of horse sweat; she was bone- and muscle-weary and she dreaded meeting the people who had driven over in the cars. If she could have gotten out of going to the house, she would have. What she wanted now was to eat a quiet supper and crawl into bed with a book.

The Ford car belonged to the Blisses' daughter, Miriam Bliss Hubertine, and her husband, who had driven down from Pilot Rock; and the Willys Knight to a friend of Orie Bliss, who had taken two days to drive Orie down from the university at Pullman, Washington, where they were both studying animal medicine; the Bliss car was in the yard because Ellery Bayard had borrowed it to bring his sister Pearl out from Shelby. All these people were gathered in the house when Martha let herself in through the back porch door, although the men were in the front room and the women in the kitchen, which at least relieved her from meeting everyone at once. Louise, who had been in the kitchen since before the break of day and was bent over the roast with her head half inside the open oven, merely said, "Well, there you are," when Martha came in, and left it to her daughter and Pearl Bayard to introduce themselves.

The young woman who had been employing a potato masher set it down and reached out with both damp hands. "I'm Miriam," she said with a light laugh. She was the very image of her mother, which should have put Martha at ease, but mother and daughter behind their aprons were both daintily dressed in dark red Christmas frocks, which made her heart fail her. Pearl Bayard too was finely dressed in a gown of blue watered silk still elegant despite being bleached out a bit and worn around the seams. Pearl sat in a kitchen chair, her hands idle in her lap, and though she smiled slightly and said to Martha, "Hello, I am Pearl Bayard," she didn't stand up from the chair.

Louise, as she began to lift the roaster pan out of the oven, said, "Maisie, you had better—" and Miriam made a clucking sound of amused exasperation. "Mother, you haven't called me Maisie since the boys were little."

Louise straightened with a startled look and stood a moment holding up the heavy roaster in her towel-wrapped hands. "Oh my goodness, why did I do that."

Miriam said to Pearl and Martha, "Jack couldn't say

'Miriam' when he was a boy, so that was what they all called me when we were children. I had just about forgotten that."

Louise set the roast down on the kitchen table. "I wish they would have let Jack come home for Christmas, but there it is," she said, and smiled stiffly. She made quite a business of folding the towels.

Miriam Hubertine had by now gone back to mashing potatoes, leaning over the handle of the masher and turning the bowl rhythmically with her left hand. She said matter-of-factly, "He might telephone. But even if he doesn't, you know he's sitting down to roast goose or something. We read about it in the papers, how they're feasting all the soldiers." Of course she knew this wasn't what was on her mother's mind. Jack had written just this week that he expected to ship out right after the first of the year.

Louise puckered her mouth once and said again, as if making a particular point, "Well, there it is." She frowned and bent over the roast, which was entirely wrapped in a golden blanket of pastry decorated with bits of dough in the shapes of flowers and leaves. Martha had never seen such a fancy thing in her life.

Shortly afterward, Louise put Martha to work ferrying things to the dining room, which was a room she had not seen in six weeks of coming and going in that house. It was larger even than the front room and more formal, its corners occupied by tall parlor palms and the walls dressed with oak paneling, graceful kerosene fixtures with figured shades, and large photographs in gilt oval frames of people Martha had never met, posed stiffly in full dress suits. The table had been laid with an ivory lace tablecloth, and lamplight gleamed upon fine china and silverware. The pickles and the salt were in cut-glass bowls, the cream in a delicate pitcher embossed with ceramic roses. Martha had known the Blisses to be well-off compared to her own family—most every rancher she had worked for in Pendleton had been better off than the Lessens; this was something she was used to—but the sight of a table set with so much finery gave her a shock of dismay.

When she went back through the door into the kitchen, she had another shock: Pearl Bayard coming toward her supported on a pair of canes. Her locomotion, swinging her slippered feet through, then stabbing one cane and the other, was the action of a child staggering along on stilts. Martha, who had been feeling snubbed by Pearl, flushed and dropped her eyes to the floor and tried to move aside.

Pearl's face was pink, her eyes fixed on Martha. "I wonder if you'd hold the door for me," she said with a faint smile. Martha afterward could not remember if she replied at all or just fumbled backward with one hand to catch the swinging door and hold it; she worried that she may have stared down in silence while Pearl passed through to the dining room.

The men had been called to the table, and in a flurry of formality Mr. Bliss and the others began pulling out chairs for the women. Martha guessed it was Orie

Bliss who seated her—he resembled his father, and he had George's dry, joking manner. "I bet Ray two bits that you're Martha," he said to her as he took hold of the back of her chair. She flushed, which had nothing to do with Orie's mild joke but with not knowing whether to let her weight rest on the seat as he pushed the chair in or to lift up her behind and let him slide the seat under her. Clumsily, she tried to do a little of both.

She was introduced around the table to the men she had not met. Howard Hubertine, Miriam's husband, was older than his wife by quite a bit, his sandy hair already balding at the forehead, his red whiskers streaked with gray. He talked in a slow drawl and didn't say too much. His silence was made up for by Orie Bliss and his friend Ray Buford, who talked and laughed easily and had to be stopped from describing, at the Christmas dinner table, the intimate details of surgeries on horses struck by automobiles. Ray Buford was small and sinewy-looking and wore glasses in wire frames. His large family was all in Pittsburgh, where his father managed a steel mill.

Martha's hands trembled as she took the dishes passed to her. In her world, the world of horses and working out of doors, everything was natural to her and came easy; but in this world she was, as old Roy Barrow used to say, *a fish wearing clothes*. The others at the table, even El Bayard, seemed at ease with the elegant food, the dainty dishware, seemed familiar with the rules of good manners. Martha was in an agony that she might spill gravy on the lace tablecloth or break a plate by pressing down too hard with her knife. She was acutely conscious of being the only left-handed person at the table and was embarrassed by the horsy smell of her hair and the way it had become stubbornly bent around her ears from being confined under a silk stocking all day. George and Louise made a point of talking her up, of saying to the others how glad they were to have her teaching manners to their horses, and how clever she was in the way she went about it, but this only made her hot with self-consciousness.

There was a good deal of war talk around the table, especially the question whether the draft would be extended: it had been rumored in the papers that men as young as eighteen and as old as forty or forty-five might soon be on the call-up list. It came out that George had been asked to serve on the Elwha County draft board and that he'd turned it down. When Ray Buford mildly chided him for it, he said stubbornly that he didn't want to be hated by his neighbors— they'd all been hearing about charges of favoritism and unequal treatment flung at draft boards elsewhere in the country. He didn't say his deeper fear, which was that he might, in fact, be tempted to favor young men he had known all their lives and the children of his friends over the sons of homesteaders and Basques and Mexicans, and he didn't want to have any sort of hand in choosing which men were sent off to their deaths.

He had said yes to being a Four Minute Man,

though, and expected to start in soon delivering Liberty Bond speeches during reel changes at the moving picture shows in Shelby. George had a streak of the evangelist in him, which wouldn't have surprised anyone at the table except perhaps George himself, and after the dinner plates were removed and the desserts brought in he didn't need more than a wisp of persuasion to stand over the pies and cakes and the frosted yule log and deliver, with broad gestures of a cake knife, his practiced four-minute sales pitch for Liberty Bonds in a voice Martha thought must carry clear out to the pastures and the barn.

The evening went on quite long. When the women had washed and put away every last plate and spoon from dinner, they joined the men in the front room, and the lamps were turned down so the candles on the tree could be lit in a great show of romance. Martha, who had spent the late hours of Christmas Eve helping Louise string cranberries and popcorn, was by that point almost too worn out to take pleasure in the sight, and when they began to sing carols she was agonizingly conscious of being the only person in the room who knew none of the words to the songs. She had thought that if gifts were traded they would be traded only among the Bliss family members, but of course was surprised in that as well and made to accept popcorn balls and then open a little package from Louise and George, which turned out to be a pencil box and six pencils. Pearl and El Bayard and Ray Buford, she was relieved to see, were given the same things; but

Ray afterward brought out what he said were "little tokens"—hair combs decorated with feathers for Louise and a nickel-plated watch fob engraved with a stag's head for George. Even Pearl and El had come with an offering of fudge candy and taffy that Pearl had cooked and pulled herself, which left Martha the only one who had not brought a gift for anyone.

All the guests were staying over. At the end of the night Miriam and Howard went up the stairs to Miriam's old bedroom, and Pearl, who couldn't climb the stairs with her canes, was settled on a fold-out cot in the front room. Orie, who might have slept in the unoccupied bedroom he and Jack had grown up in, trooped out to the bunkhouse with Ray and El. It was a long time, though, before the place settled into quiet, as one by one people stepped out in the moonlit darkness to call upon the privy.

Martha was entirely used up from the long day of work and the long night of nervous strain, but nevertheless she waited until all the others were finished before taking her own turn. Standing in her coat and her underwear just inside the cold barn, she could hear people murmuring to one another as they passed in the yard, and she expected eventually to hear Pearl Bayard struggling across that great distance on her canes; what she heard, finally, was Pearl saying softly, "I'm all finished, El," and through a gap in the barn wall watched El Bayard carry his sister from the privy back across the yard to the house. Martha had been thinking Pearl was crippled from polio—a plague of it had gone around the country the summer before—but now, seeing El's shadow in the darkness, his elbow jutting out stiffly, it occurred to her that the Bayards might both have been crippled in the same mishap.

Very much later—it was after midnight—Will Wright, who had spent the evening with Lizzie's family, got back to the homeplace and blindly crawled on top of Ray Buford, who was asleep on Will's bed. Martha didn't hear about that until morning. The shouting and the laughter weren't enough to wake her.

17

DOROTHY ROMER HAD HEARD from Jeanne McWilliams shortly before Christmas that Tom Kandel had a cancer and that Dr. McDonough had told Tom there wasn't a thing that could be done about his tumor. She had been trying to get over to Tom and Ruth's since first hearing Tom was sick, but the days had gone by. Finally in the first week of the new year she gave up trying; she walked out to the corral where Martha Lessen was changing horses and asked if Martha would mind dropping something off at the Kandels' on her way around the circle. Dorothy had put several jars of homemade jelly and applesauce and a small jar of orange marmalade in a splint basket with a note tucked under the jars: *I am so sorry to hear you're sick, Tom. I'm praying for you every day. If there's anything I can do for you or Ruth or Fred I hope you'll let me know.* She knew they wouldn't think of asking her for help. They would know she had three young children and that she didn't have any way to get around on the roads except walking; and they would have heard the gossip about Reuben's drinking—like news of Tom's illness, it would surely have gone around to all the homesteaders in the county by now—and they would know that Dorothy was sometimes called on to split and haul wood while still keeping up with her housework. They would know she hadn't any time left at the end of the day to help Tom with his dying, and they would excuse her. She was distressed by her willingness to be excused, but she'd finally grown tired of arguing with herself about it. She liked Tom, and she felt deeply sorry for him and for Ruth and for their boy, but she was afraid of being around anybody who had cancer—she had heard it might be a disease you could catch, like influenza or a chest cold. In any case, she couldn't imagine what she would find to say to them—a man who was dying and his wife, who might be expected to burst into tears at any moment in the conversation. Without being able to put words to the feeling, she was also afraid being around Tom would remind her, in the most potent and stark way, of the inevitability of every person's—of her own—death.

Martha rode away from the Romers' with the splint basket carried across her lap. The Kandels' farm wasn't on Martha's circle—their blue roan horse had been corralled at the Rocker V next door—and since Dorothy hadn't said anything to her about Tom

Kandel's illness, Martha was slightly put out about making the extra stop. The Woodruff horse she was riding was entirely placid but she changed horses again at the Thiedes' and then she was riding a bright bay gelding that had given her a fair amount of trouble in the past. She had tied a string of tin cans to the back of her saddle that morning, and riding over to Tom and Ruth Kandel's place she had to worry about the basket of jellies in case she suddenly needed both hands to control the bay. As it happened, the horse tolerated the rattle of the cans well enough and the basket didn't suffer any mishaps. She didn't trust the horse with the chickens, though, and sat outside the gate to the Kandels' yard thinking about the best way to get to the porch through that white sea of hens. She was about to climb down and hobble the horse when Ruth Kandel must have seen her there. She came out of the house and waded toward Martha, knee-deep in chickens. Their flurry and scattering made the bay nervous and he tried to rear off his front end and scoot back from the fence, and Mrs. Kandel, startled by the commotion, stopped where she was, which allowed the chickens to gradually smooth their feathers and wander off on their own affairs, which was more help to Martha than anything else, though the whole thing never came near the point of disaster. She spoke firmly to the horse and settled him, and then she said, "Dorothy Romer asked me to bring this by," and she coaxed the horse up to the fence and handed down the basket.

Ruth took it by the handles and said with a very brief smile, "Thank you. How is Dorothy? How is their baby? Well, she must not be a baby anymore, I guess she's got to be more than a year old by now. It's awful, the way time gets away from me." A moment later she heard her own words, which suddenly had a different meaning than they might have had a few weeks before. She looked past Martha without expression.

Martha said, because it was the only thing she could think to say, "Your horse is coming along well. He's a good horse."

"He's not my horse. I guess he'll be Fred's, but it was my husband's idea." She had been against Tom spending their money on an unbroken colt. If she and Fred had to give up the farm and move back East after Tom died, the horse would just have to be sold again: that was what had occurred to her. But there never had been a way to say it to Tom.

Martha looked down, having heard something she thought was aggravation or resentment and knowing only that it had to do with the horse and therefore with her. She had met Ruth Kandel just one other time, coming by their farm to talk to Tom about the blue roan.

Tom had been amazingly forthcoming to all his friends about the cancer that would kill him, and in the past month, as word had gone around, people had been coming by to say hello to Tom and to offer their sympathy without mentioning his illness. Ruth hadn't ever needed to speak the words, even once, that she now said to Martha Lessen. "My husband has a cancer and is dying."

"Oh!" the girl said, and looked at Ruth in shock. "I'm sorry."

Ruth immediately regretted she had said it so bluntly. She didn't know why she had. The girl was very young and there was something in her manner, a kind of tenderness. She wouldn't know what it meant to lose a husband; she would imagine it was like losing a favorite horse or a dog.

"It's all right. But my husband shouldn't have bought the horse, I don't know why he did." She was strangled by sorrow suddenly, and couldn't go on with what she had meant to say, or even remember what it was.

Ruth Kandel had seemed to Martha to be an unhappy and unfriendly woman, distracted, restless, which Martha now thought was due to Tom's illness. And she hardly knew Tom Kandel—she knew his blue roan horse, the one she had been calling Dandy, better than she knew Tom. Now that Mrs. Kandel had told her Tom was dying, she thought of those few minutes when she had met up with him on the Sunday before Christmas, and how he had spoken of his son, Fred, with a look of soft affection in his face.

Martha said again, "I am just so sorry."

Ruth looked toward her briefly and nodded without answering. The sympathy of her friends and neighbors felt like nothing to her, was just a weightlessness in her arms. She accepted it because it wasn't their fault they had nothing else for her, nothing she could hold on to, nothing that was any help at all.

Martha, whose mother had suffered a string of miscarriages, had often watched neighbors come through the door with casseroles, and with their arms full of the Lessens' clean, pressed laundry; she had learned early the kinds of things that were useful when people were sick. Now that she'd heard about Tom's cancer, she had already given up thinking about the Kandel farm as an extra stop. She said, "I'm going around the circle every day and coming right by here. If there's anything I can bring for you, or take out, it wouldn't be any trouble at all. I could bring your mail or the groceries. I'm already carrying mail around to some of the other people on the circle and I could just bring yours too." Thinking of Tom feeding cows over at the Rocker V, she said, "If you want to send him a lunch over there where he's working—if he's not walking home every day for it—I could pick it up and take it to him." She said all of this matter-of-factly, as if there was no reason at all for Ruth Kandel to refuse.

Ruth looked up at her and then said in quite a different voice, "Thank you. I do want him to have a hot lunch but it's too far to expect him to walk back and forth." She smiled slightly. "His appetite is gone but I keep trying to feed him." She had to hold back an impulse to tell the girl every damn thing that had been running through her mind these past few weeks. This had more to do with Martha's open face and the patience with which she sat and waited on that horse than with anything she had said.

They went on talking together for a few minutes more, working out the business of taking lunch to Mr. Kandel and getting mail from the Bingham post office, and then Martha rode off toward the Rocker V while Ruth stood at the fence a little longer. She was bundled in a thick coat and a worn felt hat—they had had a string of cold days—but her hands were bare, the knuckles red and chapped where they gripped the basket. She didn't watch the girl ride away but stood holding the heavy splint basket and looking north toward the Clarks Range, or where the Clarks Range would be if you could see the mountains. Fog had been coming down to the valley floor in the mornings and then sometimes clearing out in the afternoons but today had only just lifted above the tops of the trees.

Ruth Kandel was not one of those women for whom husbands or fathers made all the decisions. She had been as eager as Tom to come West and try herself against the land and raise their son on a farm. The world out here was large and beautiful as nowhere else, and she loved it, every part of it, and their life in it. She was never tired of the view from her porch, the ground sloping off north across their neighbor's wheat fields to the river and the white mountains braced against the sky, had never felt as she did here, every day, a sense of herself alive in the world.

She had barely begun to think of all she would lose when Tom died.

18

W.G. BOYD'S WIFE had died in 1910 after an illness. Then in 1913, as if a terrible family inheritance had been passed down, his son, Clyde, lost his wife in a train derailment as she was returning home from a visit to her parents in Chicago. For the next few years, Clyde and his young son, Joe, went on living in a rented house in Pendleton, where Clyde worked as a telephone lineman, but when he was called to Kansas in the summer of 1917 to teach soldiers how to string telephone line, the boy came to live with his grandfather.

W.G. owned about ten acres of land at the edge of Bingham and got his living primarily from a small planer mill in the summer and from making butcher knives and pocket knives from old saw blades in the winter. He had another line of work as well, although it gave him little in the way of income. People up and down the valley of the Little Bird Woman River brought him sick or mistreated animals for rehabilitation—horses, milk cows, goats, dogs, rabbits, pigs, as well as wounded owls and orphaned fawns and once a coyote pup whose foot had been mauled in a leg-hold trap. Sometimes he was paid for his veterinary work in cash or barter but more often people simply dropped off sick or dying animals, conferring not only ownership but the trouble of disposing of the carcass if the animal failed to thrive. W.G. never turned away an animal, and although he was unschooled he had a natural gift for seeing what was troubling these creatures; fairly often he was able to help them to a recovery. Two or three times a year he took to auction a few head of livestock he had seen through to health and in that way managed to recoup his costs for feed and assorted healing agents. Several dogs, including one with three legs, lived at the Boyd place, as well as numerous cats and an assortment of scarred and aged or otherwise unwanted livestock. It was a paradise, more or less, for a ten-year-old boy.

Among the animals W.G. was feeding that winter was the young black gelding, Skip, who had been left with him after being badly scared and hurt by dragging a loose pole behind him. W.G. was working in his shop on a cold day in the middle of January, showing his grandson how to whet the burr off a finished knife, when Martha rode Skip into the yard. They had shut the dogs into the cowshed to keep them from causing a ruckus if Martha rode in while they were working, and when they heard the dogs barking and scratching at the door Joe looked out and said, "Grandpa, she's got Skip."

There were fourteen horses on the circle, and seven stops, which meant the horses got ridden every other day, and it took a horse a couple of weeks to make it clear around to his home corral; the Boyds had seen Skip only one other time since Martha had started the horses. "Now don't run up at him," W.G. called after the boy, who had already wormed past the workbench and was out in the yard. But the boy knew how skittish the horse was—he hadn't needed W.G.'s warning—and when W.G. came out of the shop, Joe was walking up to Skip slowly from the side so the horse could see him coming and he was crooning soft words of praise he'd picked up from listening to Martha Lessen, "Well my goodness, aren't you a good old horse, I sure think you are," and so forth. W.G. stopped where he was and watched them come together, the boy and the horse and the girl. Joe thought the world of Martha—there were children all over the valley who worshipped her—and it amused and charmed W.G. to see the shining look that came into the boy's face whenever he got near her.

Martha gave Joe a brief, approving look and stepped off the horse and held the headstall up close under the throat while Joe touched the horse along the shoulder and the neck. Skip stood patiently. W.G. could see that he'd come a long way in the last two weeks. Horses evidently thought the world of Martha Lessen too.

"Hello, child," W.G. said.

"Hello, Mr. Boyd. Skip is coming along pretty well."

"I can see he is. You'll have him steady as the Rock of Gibraltar before long."

She flashed a brief smile of satisfaction. "I don't know about that."

"Do you have time to come inside? I've got some coffee on the back of the stove that'll wake you right up. You can stand a fork up in it."

She laughed. "I'd better not. I'm starting to think we

might get some snow tonight." She had gone on working as she talked to him, had already loose-hobbled Skip and was pulling off the saddle.

It had been a cold dry day—this winter seemed to have an excess of such days, parading methodically down the valley one after the other like solemn children going Indian file—but W.G. had been smelling something damp in the air all afternoon, a certain quality to the cold. "We might," he said, and looked toward the northwest, where the gray overcast had grown dark along the crown of the Clarks Range. "All those farmers with winter wheat must be hoping for a real snowfall. We've had an awfully dry winter. But I guess that's not what you're hoping for."

"No. But it's all right. I won't mind as long as it doesn't get too drifted." She led Skip to the corral. Joe went ahead of her and swung open the gate and then shut it behind her. She said, "Thanks, Joey." He wouldn't stand for his grandfather to call him Joey anymore, but he let Martha Lessen get away with it. When she had stripped the horse of his bridle and hobble she stood a moment in front of him, scratching his neck. W.G. had noticed she never liked to let a horse walk away from her until she had walked away from him. Skip reached his head forward and rubbed her shoulder lightly with the side of his muzzle, as if they were two horses standing head to tail grooming each other. "Goodness, you're such a pretty old thing," she murmured to him, which made W.G. smile.

After a bit, she turned to the two other horses in the

corral, one sandy brown and one chestnut. The big chestnut belonged to Bill Varden's Rocker V Ranch; he'd been in the Boyd corral a couple of days and was due to go out. She clucked to him and held the bridle out to the horse like a gift. He turned his head to look, and after thinking about it he walked right up to her. Even the sandy horse looked as if he might have liked to be invited.

Joe, who had climbed up on the corral rails to watch her, said, "He wants to go out for a ride."

"Yes he does. He doesn't much care for standing around in a small corral all day." W.G. had seen early on that this was a good part of Martha's plan. The horses were bored and quickly learned to welcome being ridden out; they were usually happy to see her.

"Is he called Nickel because he's not worth a plugged nickel?" Joe knew the name of every horse Martha was riding around the circle.

"I don't know. He's sure worth more than a nickel, though, if you ask me."

Joe said with a huge grin, "I'd take all the nickel horses I could get," and Martha laughed. "I would too."

It was part of her ritual to always brush the dirt and mud off a horse before she saddled him, and to run her hands all over his body, especially his legs. While she was wiping down the chestnut horse with a burlap sack, Martha said quietly to W.G., "Mr. Boyd, did you hear about Tom Kandel having cancer?"

W.G.'s wife, Anne, had died of a cancer that had

started in one of her breasts and then flared up in her spine. In the nearly eight years since Anne's death, he hadn't personally known anybody else taken by the disease. There was a way in which the very word *cancer* had seemed to belong to him and to Anne. He didn't think Martha Lessen knew any of this—folks might have told her he had lost his wife, but probably not anything about how she'd died.

He looked down at his hands and then over at his grandson, who was straddling the top rail of the corral looking down at Skip or watching Martha rub down the nickel horse, pretending not to overhear Martha and W.G. talk about a dying neighbor. "I did hear about it," W.G. told Martha. "How is Tom doing, do you know?"

Martha crouched down, and W.G. heard her say something quietly to the horse as she ran her hand down his hind leg. To W.G. she said, "Mrs. Kandel told me today that he might have to give up his job on the Rocker V. I didn't see him, she said he was inside the house resting, but I guess he was too sick today to go over there and feed cows." She met W.G.'s eyes briefly. "I've been taking him a lunch the past two or three weeks but I don't know if he's been eating it. He's awful thin."

They didn't say anything else about the Kandels but talked a little more about the weather as she saddled the chestnut and then put her boot in the stirrup and climbed up on the horse. She liked all the horses to know they weren't to move ahead until she gave them the say-so, and the chestnut stood quietly under her. She asked him to bring his head toward one of her knees and then the other, which she had told Joe was to keep him soft in the mouth, and then asked the horse to take a few steps back, his neck soft, before she let him know it was all right to move ahead.

Joe jumped down and swung the gate open to let them through, and then W.G. and Joe stood out of the way and watched her put Nickel through the quick turns and spins and *whoa*s she always started with, there in the yard. The Boyd yard had been hard-packed earth but by now was pretty well broken up and cratered from horses' hooves digging in to turn and stop. When she had the horse good and warmed up— it always looked to W.G. like a sort of dance—she lifted her voice to carry over to where W.G. and Joe were watching. "I'd better go along before the snow gets here."

"Bye, Martha," Joe called to her.

"See you tomorrow, Joey," she called back to him, and rode off at a trot.

W.G. and his grandson went back into the shop to finish work on the knife. While he was guiding Joe's hands to hold the knife and the whetstone at proper angles to each other, W.G. said, "I guess you don't remember your grandmother."

Joe had been barely three years old when his grandmother died. His father and his grandfather spoke of her from time to time in some story they were telling about the past, but Joe didn't remember her. Sometimes a particular smell—the starched, boiled-water smell of freshly ironed clothes—put him in mind of her, and he had a brief recollection of floured hands on a rolling pin, which he thought were his grandmother's hands. He had been six when his mother was killed, and his secret fear was that his mother was becoming as vague to him as his grandmother, no more than two hands and the smell of clean clothes. He charmed himself to sleep sometimes by going over and over certain memories of his mother in order to keep them fixed in his mind, like the lines of a poem he might be expected to recite at any time. He didn't say any of this to his grandfather. He said, "No sir," and kept his eyes on the whetstone and the blade of the knife.

"Your grandmother had cancer, like Tom Kandel," W.G. said to him. "I wondered if you knew that."

He did know, although no one had ever told him directly. It wasn't entirely clear to him what kind of sickness cancer was, but the word spoken by his father or his grandfather had a certain terrible meaning associated with his dead grandmother, and he understood implicitly that if Mr. Kandel had cancer then he must be dying. None of this did he say to W.G. He said, "How did Mr. Kandel get it?"

"His cancer? I don't know. It just happens, I guess. But you know your mother never was sick. She wasn't sick at all. I didn't know if you were worried about that." This was what W.G. had been heading toward all along. He had seen something in the boy's face when he and Martha Lessen were talking about Tom Kandel, and he had guessed that it might have something to do with how the boy's mother had come to die.

"The train tipped over," Joe said. "That's what my dad said."

"Yes. It wasn't sickness." Then, as if they hadn't been talking about death at all, W.G. said, "Now you don't want to sharpen a knife any more than this. When it gets that little feathery edge, that burr, you know you've got it thin to the point of perfect." He held the knife up to the light and squinted along it as he gently rocked it back and forth. "What do you think?"

Joe squinted and looked. His grandfather had shown him how a dull edge reflected light and would show up as a shiny narrow surface, while a sharp edge would appear just about invisible. "It looks pretty good," he said. "I think this one is about done."

W.G. said, "I think you're right." They gathered up the hand and bench stones and the whetstone and washed them in a pan of water and then rubbed them with gasoline and put them away under cloth covers. The knife was one of a matched pair he was making for the Woodruff sisters. He folded it in a piece of oiled leather and left it on the workbench beside the second knife, which was barely started.

Later on, after they'd eaten supper and were sitting at the table playing dominoes, Joe said to his grandfather, "I was thinking, if cancer just happens, it could happen to anybody." He looked down at his unplayed tiles, touching and rearranging them.

W.G. frowned and played a tile and said, "Eighteen," and wrote his score down while he turned things over in his mind, puzzling out Joe's question and what it might mean. He had a pet cat he allowed to live in the house, a part-Angora who was crippled from being caught in a coyote trap. The cat was on his lap, and he put his hand down and stroked the thick ruff while Joe was looking over the pattern of the dominoes spread out on the table.

"Well, it doesn't happen very often, Joe," he said slowly.

The boy had learned about death at an early point in his life. He frequently worried about his father dying, or his grandfather, and sometimes late at night was visited by the knowledge that he, too, would someday die. He particularly worried about certain illnesses and accidents, the kind that occurred frequently among their neighbors—tuberculosis, food poisoning, typhus, runaway horses—and he wondered if cancer, which he had imagined to be exclusive to his grandmother, was something he should now add to his list of things to worry about.

None of this had he said to his grandfather, but he might as well have, because W.G. understood suddenly that it was this, and not confusion about the particular way his mother had died, that must have come into the boy's mind when he heard his grandfather and Martha Lessen talking about Tom Kandel.

By the last weeks of Anne Boyd's life a profusion of suppurating lesions had spread across her chest and back, and she was paralyzed by a tumor on her spine. Her left breast had grown nearly to the size of a woman's head, and as hard. In Chicago or New York she might have been sent to a surgeon, but in Bingham that sort of radical treatment was not practiced. When W.G. could no longer lift and turn her on the bed without help, she was taken by wagon up to Pendleton, which at that time had the nearest hospital to Bingham. He thought afterward he should have fought against removing his wife from their home, but he had felt overridden, defeated by his own ignorance and tiredness.

It was the opinion of the hospital staff that W.G., who followed Anne to Pendleton, would be better served not to witness the agonies and indignities of her last days, and they strictly limited his visits to half an hour in the mornings and half an hour in the afternoons. In the hospital, they dressed her ulcerating skin and her bleeding nipples, applied caustic poultices and pastes that gave her excruciating pain, lifted her sobbing into a chair once a day while her bed was neatened and rearranged. When the morphine stopped her bowels, they began giving her daily enemas, and W.G. spent his visits, morning and afternoon, sponging his wife's limbs, her lean buttocks, the soiled valley of her privy parts. She was in a moaning, agitated semicoma for the last eight days before she died.

Since Anne's death, W.G. himself had had an irrational fear that he might someday have to watch someone else, someone he loved, die in that terrible way. Or that his son and grandson might have to watch him. He knew he should say to Joe—he wanted to say—*You don't have to worry about cancer. It won't happen to you or to your dad or to anybody you love,* but the words wouldn't come out of his mouth.

19

SNOW BEGAN TO FALL out of the darkness that night and fell straight down all the early hours of the morning, and by daybreak it stood about half a foot deep everywhere in the lower valley, though the sky then cleared off and a pale sun lit up the newborn world. The horses were excited by the snow, and just about every one of them wanted to frisk and jump, which wasn't quite the same thing as giving trouble but was trouble anyway, and slowed things down. It was already late afternoon, almost dark, when Martha left the Rocker V, and then she had to take the long way around to get to the Woodruff ranch because a flock of sheep had bedded down in the road between Bingham and Opportunity. Some Owl Creek sheepmen had taken delivery of over a thousand ewes and yearlings at the railhead in Shelby late in the day, and they had stopped for the night at the first place they came to with a stretch of wire fence along both sides of the road. Martha knew the trick: you used the fences on two sides to hold the flock, and that way you only had to post one nighthawk and a dog in the narrow lane at each end to keep them from drifting.

There were so many sheep they were packed into that stretch of road for almost a mile, and it took her a good long while to get around them and back onto the ranch road that went up to the Woodruffs.

So she was a couple of hours past her usual time getting to the Split Rock Ranch, and she found Henry Frazer in the yard saddling a piebald horse. He didn't say he was about to come looking for her, but when she rode up he gave her a look that could have been relief; then he quit buckling the cinch and pulled the saddle off the horse again. Martha guessed that the sisters had been about to send him out in the cold dark to look for her. When she stood down from the Thiedes' sorrel mare, Henry said, "You'd better go in and say hello to the sisters, so they don't go on worrying and fretting about you like they have been. I'll change your saddle. Is it the bay horse you're taking out now?"

"There was a bunch of sheep in the road and I had to go way around," she told him in defense, so he wouldn't think she'd been bucked off somewhere along the line. She was tired and cold and just wanted to get back to the Bliss place and eat some warm soup if there was any waiting for her on the back of the stove, and go to bed. But she let Henry Frazer take the sorrel's reins and she said, "Yes, the bay, his name is Boots," and she went off to see the Woodruff sisters.

Emma Adelaide came to the kitchen door in a long beltless dress that was in great disrepair and at least fifteen years out of style, and when she called out, "Aileen, here she is," her sister came in from the front room in an identical dress. The Woodruffs weren't twins but looked much alike, large in the nose, built thin and straight, with skin the color and grain of a wooden ax handle from all those years working out of doors. Aileen's hair had gone entirely white while Emma Adelaide's had grayed in streaks, and this was the most significant difference between them in the way they looked. They never had gone so far against convention as to wear trousers or overalls—riding cross-saddle, they hitched their skirts over, and expected boots to do the work of concealing ankles—but it had been many years since either one of them had bothered to wear a corset.

They forced on Martha a hot supper: Emma Adelaide had already phoned the Bliss ranch and told Louise they would feed their broncobuster before sending her on. But it seemed clear to Martha that she had misread the extent of the sisters' worry. In fact, the Woodruffs had spent their lives on horseback and seemed to take for granted the idea of a girl riding alone through darkness and snow on an uneducated colt. They appeared entirely unperturbed by her late arrival.

The kitchen was so warm it made Martha's skin itch. She ate quickly, afraid of stiffening up or falling asleep if she sat too long. Emma Adelaide sat across the table from her, doing book work with a pencil and a mechanical adding machine, while Aileen stood at the sink washing up dishes from their own supper.

"How are the horses coming?" Emma Adelaide asked her.

"Good." She was shoveling in mounds of rice that had been fried up with bacon and onion. She swallowed what was in her mouth and gulped coffee, and said, "I like your palomino horse, and that other one, the one called Big Brownie."

Aileen laughed. "I bet you never met a horse you didn't like."

This was close to the truth, so Martha didn't bother to disagree. She said, "I guess there's a couple that are giving me trouble, one of those Rocker V horses is full of himself, and that one ofMr. Irwin's is pretty mad at the world."

"Irwin. Is that one of the homestead farmers?"

"Yes ma'am. He has that white house that sits up high on Lodge Butte, right before the road goes down into Lewis Pass. He has a hired man named Logerwell."

Emma Adelaide lifted her head. "Oh, I know which one Logerwell is. His wife raises pigs and sells them."

Martha kept from saying what she thought of Alfred Logerwell's wife. Every horse she rode out of the Irwin corral was ravenous—she'd begun to believe that Logerwell's wife was stealing oats and corn from the horses to fatten up her pigs.

Aileen clattered dishes in the sink. "That one? Then he's the one I saw that time beating his horse with a piece of pipe for refusing to go over the Graves Creek bridge. If he works for Irwin, I expect Irwin's horses are getting that same treatment." She was silent a moment. "Mad at the world, I should think so."

Martha grew flush and still. She was remembering the time she had lifted her arms above her head to stretch a kink out of her sore back before putting a boot in the stirrup, and how Irwin's roan gelding had screamed and reared away from her. She felt stupid, now, not to have guessed what that was all about. She had been all these weeks imagining Logerwell's temper had only to do with her.

The sisters were overly conscious of their responsibility to set an example for Martha Lessen: without ever speaking of it, they had both become aware that she took them as paragons. Aileen turned from the sink and gave Martha a look. "Now don't imagine that I just stood there and watched. I took that piece of pipe right out of his hand. I cussed him, too, and I believe I might have hit him with his own pipe if I hadn't been with Mrs. Stuart, who turned about the color of buttermilk when she heard what I said."

Emma Adelaide had been entering figures in her ledger but this made her stop and laugh, a mulish bray, which was another thing the sisters had in common. After a moment she became gravely serious. "Well, and don't think for a minute he's the only one who would beat a horse, Aileen. There's plenty of them would."

"Oh, I know that. Of course I know that, Emma Adelaide. But they'd just better not do it in front of me, that's all I'm saying."

"Or not in front of Martha, I should imagine."

"Yes, I should imagine not."

Henry Frazer came in the back door with a burst of noise and cold and stood there shedding snow, peering into the kitchen. He was thick-set and looked more so in a sheep-lined jacket and a sweater. He had wound a wool scarf around his neck and it bulged out the collar of the coat. The whole of his broad face was lit up with color just now. "All saddled and ready to go," he said unnecessarily.

When Martha went out to the yard, Henry followed her, and she found that he had saddled his own horse again. "I might as well go along with you," he said when she gave him a look. "I'm headed over there to play cards with El."

She thought she saw in his face, in his unwillingness to meet her eyes, that this was a lie, and she was suddenly struck by the thought that it was Henry Frazer, and not the Woodruff sisters, who had been fretting over her late arrival, that his look of relief when he saw her had nothing to do with being saved from going out in bad weather. She said without looking at him, "I don't need any help, if you were thinking I did."

He didn't act surprised by what she said; he smiled and answered placidly, "I was just thinking we might keep each other company, riding over there."

She had risen into the saddle by that time, and the bay horse kinked up his back a couple of times just for the fun of it, which aggravated and embarrassed her. By the time she had him settled down into a trot she had forgotten what Henry Frazer had said to her that had made her go warm in the face; the keyed-up feeling, though, stayed with her.

The moon had risen and was three-quarters full, which was enough light to find the way. Martha was forced to keep a tight hold of the bay, who had a wish to run, while Henry Frazer ambling along on his piebald could be light on the horse's mouth, and this was a further embarrassment to her. Not a single thing came into her head to say to Henry, but she leaned into Boots's neck and murmured quietly, "I wish you'd give up your idea of running, because this is not the night for it."

They went along in silence for more than half the way. At one point a coyote ran across the snow ahead of them and both Henry and Martha pulled up their horses at the same time and sat watching until it trotted off into the deep shadow under a copse of trees, and they resumed riding after a minute, without either of them saying a word about it.

It wasn't long after that Henry said, as if the words were ones he'd been turning over in his head for quite a while, "It can weigh on your mind, if you think very hard about a horse's life."

He might have meant anything, but what came into her own head was Alfred Logerwell beating his horse with a pipe, and her dad's horses, and other horses she had known, horses who were gaunt, thirsty, lame, wounded, broken-winded, frightened, discouraged.

"There's a look I've seen in some horses," Henry Frazer said, still going along as if this was part of a long conversation he'd been having with himself, "like they're just reconciled to taking whatever comes. Like they've given up, and they don't have much expectation of anything good ever happening to them. You see it in their eye." He didn't look at Martha. "But some others never do get reconciled. I had a horse once so determined not to be broke that he bucked under me until his heart busted and he died." His face in the night was without expression.

She was startled beyond words, not by the story of a horse breaking its own heart—she had seen that sort of thing herself—but by Henry Frazer telling it to her that way, quietly and at the end of a few words about pondering a horse's life. They rode on silently. It was cold, and the air held a bluish light. The horses' unshod feet moving through the snow made a dry, quiet, steady squeaking.

Finally she said, "I know a wrangler who joined up with the Canadian army, and he was telling me about the horses over there."

He didn't ask her where she meant; in those days people understood that "over there" meant the trenches of France and Belgium. He said, "They don't say much about it in the newspapers," and Martha said, frowning, "No they don't."

Martha had known Bud Small from working with him up in Umatilla County, where he was known to be a good hand with horses—better than most, in Martha's opinion. Bud had spent a year working at a Canadian remount depot in France and then had shipped home when a horse fell on him and broke both his legs. He had told her everything that she now began telling Henry—everything about the terrible plight of the horses over there—how they died on the transport ships from fear and trampling; how they pined with homesickness and consequently took cold or pneumonia and died at the remount depots before they ever got to the front; how they were often starved and thirsty to the point of eating harness or chewing their stablemate's blankets; how as many horses were invalided by war nerves as were killed in battle—their hearts and minds not able, any more than the men's, to bear the airplane bombs and grenades, falling fuses, the shrieks of wounded men and animals.

These were things that had been on Martha's mind for months, ever since she had gone to visit Bud at his sister's house, where he was laid up in heavy plaster. But she had not talked about them to anyone before now, and saying them to Henry—in snatches, with silences between—her voice rose and rose until she became aware of it and fell silent in the middle of what she was saying, which was something terrible and distressing about horses being whipped and beaten for rearing back from the smell of blood.

Henry Frazer had listened to her without interrupting, and he glanced at her when she stopped talking, then waited to hear what else she might say; he let the silence spin out so long that finally Martha felt she couldn't keep from telling him one more thing. "I think if they would let horses stick together, the ones who come from the same farms and ranches, the ones who are acquainted with each other, if they let them stick together maybe they wouldn't get so homesick and they might hold up better." She said this to Henry as if he was the one able to do something about it. "Isn't that how it is with the men? They do better when they go over there with a pal or a brother."

Buyers had been coming through some parts of the country almost from the beginning of the European war, gathering up American horses and mules to ship to the British army. But Pendleton was in a far corner and there hadn't been much of a push to send local horses to the war effort until lately. Some horses well known to Martha had been among the first batch of two thousand shipped out in the autumn just past, and it was those horses she was thinking about now. Some of them had been raised together on the L Bar L since they were foals, and she knew they'd bear up better if they were kept together.

Henry said, after another short silence, "I guess you know Will Wright is planning to join up."

She looked over at him. She thought he might be making a point about the men, whose suffering ought to be more important to her than the horses. She wondered if Henry even believed her, that horses had their horse friends and that they might become homesick and lonesome among strangers.

Then he said, "I heard the other day Roger Newbry's planning to join up too. They've been friends since they were born, just about. So I guess they'll try to keep each other company and out of trouble." He didn't say this lightly, as if he was making a joke about boys going off to the fairgrounds in Pendleton; his look was solemn, humorless. Martha saw that the only point he had wanted to make was about friendship— friendship between men, just as between horses.

After several moments had passed, she said, "Two of my brothers went in together."

Henry looked over at her. He and his brother wouldn't have joined up together, he knew this—Jim had been hard set against the war. Although he hadn't thought it through exactly, he knew his brother's death was in some way the reason he planned to claim his farm worker's exemption and stay out of it if he ever was called up. But a brief, ridiculous pain sometimes still rose up in him, as if Jim's death had cheated them both out of the chance to go off to France and die together as heroes. Whenever he heard about brothers joining up he felt a momentary, inexplicable pining.

"Where are they now? Are they over there yet?"

"I guess they're still in Georgia, one of those forts where they're training soldiers." She hadn't thought she would tell him any more of it, but then found she was going ahead. "They got into some trouble, a fight I guess, and both of them are in the stockade. I heard Davey broke somebody's nose, a sergeant or a captain. So I don't know if they'll even get shipped out." She said this without looking at Henry and without seeming to offer an opinion about it.

They stopped at the fence line above the Bliss homeplace and Henry held on to Boots while Martha got down to work the wire on the gate. Below them the lights in the house and the bunkhouse made a pale geometry behind drawn curtains. Someone had hung a lamp from the eave of the barn, and its light fell out on the trampled snow.

When they started down the hill, Henry Frazer said quietly, going on with something they'd left in the air, "I suppose whenever a horse gets traded to somebody new he must wonder. Will he get beaten? Will he get enough to eat? I hate to think what goes through a horse's mind when he's hauled off and set down in the middle of a war."

Martha looked toward Henry. He was riding with his shoulders hunched, his elbows held in close. The planes of his cheeks were rounded and soft, his once-broken nose wide and fleshy below that heavy brow bone. His eyes had a certain aspect, as if they were always peering into something interesting. He was looking out across the snowfield where the dark shapes of cows and horses stood against the blue-white snow, clumps of two or three of them standing together, as still as anchored boats on a millpond.

20

IF DR. MCDONOUGH had had his way, he wouldn't have told Tom Kandel the nature of his illness at all—he felt people shouldn't have to suffer that kind of knowledge—but Tom and Ruth had been stubbornly of a different mind, insistent and unrelenting in their demand to know, and finally he had been forced to tell them the mass in Tom's belly was a cancer.

In those days, a lot of what people thought they knew about cancer was wrong. Some people, even some doctors, hadn't let go of the idea it could be spread from one person to the next or that it might start from eating tomatoes or drinking water out of a trout stream. And of course for the most part the only treatment was surgery, which in just about every case wasn't resorted to until the cancer had manifested itself in some visible way on the body. Dr. McDonough didn't know the cause of Tom's cancer so he didn't offer the Kandels any opinion about it, and because the tumor was in Tom's liver he was careful not to mention surgery. The Kandels were both educated people; Tom was the son of a doctor. When Dr. McDonough told them where the cancer was located neither of them asked him about a cure or regimen of treatment, nothing of that kind at all, which was a relief to him.

After Tom learned what he had—that his body was incubating cancer cells—he carried on the ordinary affairs of his life for a month or so out of the same sheer stubbornness that had made the doctor give way. But by the middle of January he had become too weak and tired to keep up his job feeding cows for Bill Varden, and Dr. McDonough began coming by the house every morning to give him a hypodermic of morphine. Tom and Ruth then passed through a brief, almost pleasant interlude in the course of his dying. Fred took over the job of feeding and caring for the chickens now that his father was too sick to do it, but otherwise carried on behaving as if Tom wasn't dying, and saved his parents from having to think very much about him. Friends came in and out of the house with gifts of food and sat down to talk with Tom for what they expected would be the last time, and then went home and left the two of them alone. A good part of every day Tom would sleep, leaving Ruth to do only the quiet things that would not disturb him: she spent the bulk of those hours reading, writing letters, embroidering, knitting, free of guilt for not keeping up with the hard housework. When Tom was awake she wanted to spend every moment with him. They clung to each other, held hands as they had not done since the early days of their marriage, and Tom sometimes teased her or joked with her—he came out into the front room one night wearing nothing but his winter underwear hooked up to striped suspenders. He talked a blue streak, as if by keeping silence at bay he could reassure himself that he was still alive. He even talked to her interestedly about his own funeral, smothering her refusals with his mild persistence and offering firm opinions about what hymns should be played and who the pallbearers ought to be, and making a list of poems he wanted read in addition to the Gospels the minister would insist upon. He made a dark joke about the failure of his appetite—how it would lighten the load for his friends carrying the coffin—and when Ruth burst into tears he laughed, but then cried too, and held out his arms to her in a tender way.

At one time in his life Tom must have been a church-goer, because it was well known he could sing any hymn you might name, and quote long verses from the New Testament. But during the years he lived in the Elwha Valley he was a famously shameless agnostic. Before he became ill, it had been his habit to walk with his wife and son to the Presbyterian church in Bingham every Sunday, then stroll on down to the riverbank and fish for an hour before going back to retrieve his family; cancer did not cause him to embrace God as some people had expected. When the Presbyterian minister visited him Tom listened, and then mildly and without pleasure pointed out the inconsistencies and defects in the man's reasoned arguments for heaven and a life after death.

Sometime during the middle part of January, Marcella Blantyre, who hardly knew Tom at all except to nod and smile, went over to the Kandel house to see him. She was a devout member of the Bingham Presbyterian church but she was not on a church mission to kneel down and pray with Tom and Ruth. Marcella imagined Tom was the sort of person who wouldn't ordinarily have given a woman like her any credit, but Ruth Kandel had asked her to come to the house, and Marcella didn't have to think twice before saying yes. She told Ruth truthfully that she didn't know if she could do Tom any good, but she would come by and see.

Marcella had a reputation in the Elwha Valley for healing people's illnesses merely by the laying on of hands. This wasn't something she advertised or made a boast of; in fact, Marcella was a garden-variety farm wife who lived with her husband on 160 acres of river-bottom land and devoted herself to raising five children while her husband raised onions. But she'd been struck by lightning when she was about nineteen years old, a new bride expecting her first child; and after she recovered her senses, and after the baby was born perfectly formed and perfectly healthy, Marcella had begun quietly to work cures. The people in her church all knew at least one person who knew a person who had been healed of some ailment or affliction by her hands. After the Presbyterian minister's son was cured of stammering, the minister had preached in his Sunday sermon that miracles were still taking place in the world, two thousand years after God's son walked the earth. Marcella, sitting in a pew toward the rear of the church, had bent her head and looked at her shoes. She was entirely a sensible woman and she knew she might not have had anything to do with curing his son of stammering; she knew many of the sick people she'd laid hands on would doubtless have gotten better without her help. But some of them, yes, she felt sure she'd made them well simply by passing her hands over their bodies. She could sense when this happened: a shivering electrical vibration as if a spark had jumped the space between the tips of her fingers and the skin of the person she was treating. She didn't know what it was that had entered her body when she was struck by lightning, but she knew it to be a gift of some kind, a gift from God.

Tom had been dozing in a chair—he was sitting with a quilt spread over his lap, his legs stretched out so his slippered feet could rest on a leather stool—but as soon as Ruth opened the door to Marcella he stood up from the chair and began folding up the quilt and said cheerfully, "I imagine I've given you a real job of work today, Mrs. Blantyre," as if he had hired her to chop several cords of wood or paint the entire house from top to bottom. She understood from this that Ruth had told him she was coming and why, and this relieved her of her mild anxiety about the visit. She smiled and said, "Well, I can only do my best, Mr. Kandel," which he seemed to find unexpected. He smiled slowly. "We can't ask for more than that," he said, and looked at Ruth, whose eyes immediately filled with tears. Ruth didn't believe in Marcella's gift—neither did Tom—but it was impossible for them both not to hope they were wrong.

It turned out to be a strange contradiction in Tom, that he was more willing to entertain the idea of a magical healer than of a Benevolent Creator and a life after death. They sat down, the three of them, and while Marcella quietly told him the story of what had happened to her and what she had seen during the moments she'd lain dead in her garden—*a bright white light and then colors I've never seen in life, and a figure in white coming toward me through the rainbow, and his hand when it touched my shoulder just going right down into my heart to shake it awake*—Tom leaned forward in his chair and listened with terrible attention and yearning. He asked her interestedly about the time when she first became aware of her gift, and asked her to tell him about some of the people she had cured. When Marcella said to him that she hadn't ever healed anyone of cancer—hadn't ever been asked to—Tom said quietly, "I guess you're not expecting this to be one of your cures," but lifting the last words so he appeared to be asking her something.

"I don't know, Tom. Only God knows," she said, which made him smile slightly.

"Well, God holds his cards pretty close to the vest, which is one of the things I intend to complain about if it turns out there's anyone to complain to." He looked at Ruth, but she had become very still and shuttered and was looking out the window at the cold afternoon dusk.

They carried on talking a little while longer. Marcella told him she would, in a moment, ask him to lie down quietly on the sofa with his eyes closed while she touched him, but that in fact she wouldn't actually be touching him, just passing her hands close to his body, and that he might feel the force of her hands as an electrical spark, a warmth on his skin; then after a short silence she told him she was ready to start. He looked quickly at Ruth, a naked look of need and fear, and Ruth turned her face to him and pursed her mouth to stop something equally desperate from showing there. Then she crossed the room and bent down to pull off her husband's slippers as if he were a child. He touched her hair, and she reached tremblingly for his hand, a moment so intimate Marcella felt she should look away. He stretched out on the sofa and Ruth stood over him a moment, straightening his clothes, not meeting his eyes, then she kissed him lightly and smiled and went back to her chair. Tom's eyes followed her. He took a breath that could be clearly heard in the room, and then another quieter one and closed his eyes. Marcella went to the sofa and let herself down on her knees beside it. She prayed silently a few moments to clear her mind of all the scraps and candle-ends of the day, and then she began passing the flat palms of both her hands over his body slowly, long sweeping strokes downward from the top of his head as if brushing the cancer out through the soles of his feet.

He was pale and thin, but so absolutely endowed with the force of life, even lying flat and still on the sofa with his eyes drawn closed, that it was almost impossible to believe his death might be only days or weeks away. Marcella had watched over the deaths of, now, seven people, people who had been beyond her help for reasons known only to God, and she knew the suddenness with which the animating soul of a person could fly out of the body and leave behind a meaningless clay corpse. If she hadn't believed so strongly in God the Comforter, death would have seemed to her almost a parlor trick, an unfathomable disappearing act.

She closed her eyes and emptied her mind as well as she was able, of this and other distractions. She let her cold hands rove above Tom in slow, rhythmic strokes. There was no sound in the room except a ticking clock and the breaths of three people. Tom, through his closed eyes, felt a slight sense of the shadow of Marcella's hands when they passed over his face, a slight sense of her body leaning above him as she plied her mysterious art. His skin, seeking some feeling of heat, of electricity, yearned toward her helplessly.

21

IN THOSE DAYS, plenty of men thought nothing of being rough with horses. A horse had to have his spirit entirely broken was what a lot of men thought, had to be beaten into abject submission. Martha didn't know Walter Irwin very well, didn't know his feeling about horses, but she knew if he held the usual opinions it wouldn't do a bit of good to tell him his hired man was beating horses and shortchanging their feed. And she knew there wasn't a damn thing she could say to Logerwell himself that would change his mind or improve the situation for the horses. In her experience, anything she said to him would be sure to make things worse.

At Irwin's corral she began to grain the horses herself while she was changing saddles and mounts, which was time she could hardly spare, but it took care of the problem of Logerwell's wife shortchanging the horses on their feed. Through the next few days she went on undecided whether to speak to Irwin about the other part of it. She seldom saw Logerwell but kept an eye out for him warily and watched all the horses for any sign they were being casually mistreated. And she thought back to every mark of injury a horse had suffered, trying to remember if it had happened while the horse was standing in Irwin's corral. On a Sunday morning, after a week of watching, a black gelding named York, which belonged to the Thiedes and had spent the past couple of nights at Irwin's, showed up with a long red weal across his cheek. It could have come from scraping himself nervously against a fence rail or from another horse—stablemates didn't always get along and would sometimes chew on each other— or it might have come from somebody slashing him with a whip or a stick. Martha felt pretty sure she knew which one of those it was. She stood there holding the McClelland saddle against her chest, looking at that stripe across the long plane of York's face, those beads of scabbing blood, and then slung the saddle over a corral rail and started on foot up the muddy track to the farmhouse.

Irwin's family money set him apart from most of his homesteader neighbors. His house was a white clapboard two-story built high up on a logged-off rise above the north bank of the Little Bird Woman River. He had built his barn and corrals a fair hike down the hill from his house, which was meant to keep the smell of the animals out of his kitchen but also meant he couldn't keep much of an eye on what was going on down there. In addition, the house was poorly situated in terms of the practicalities of snowdrift and wind, and he'd had to drill his well a long way down to reach water; but sitting up high like that, the house could be seen by pretty nearly everybody living at the eastern end of the valley, which his neighbors thought was his reason for putting it there, and which he would have been surprised to hear. He had built on that rise almost entirely for its aerie view across the river to the White-horns.

The property was a relinquishment he had bought from the railroad when another homesteader gave up on it, and the Logerwells now occupied a small house the first nester had built in the lee of the hill, about halfway up from the barn. When Martha went past that house the windows were dark and there wasn't any sign of Logerwell or his wife. Several hogs were sprawled in a deeply muddy pen across the runway from the house. One of them, a black and white sow, lifted her head and blinked her small pink eyes at Martha before lowering her cheek into the mud. A black dog, underfed and every bit as muddy as the pigs, lay in the yard tied to a post by a short piece of rope. He watched Martha without moving.

She went on up to Irwin's porch and knocked at the door and tightened the throat-catch of her hat against the wind and when he came to the door she said quickly and forcefully, "Mr. Irwin, your hired man has been whipping some of the horses I'm working with and not feeding them the grain they need."

He looked at her in bewilderment. "Logerwell?" he said, as if he had more than one hired hand and was sorting out which one she meant to indict.

Walking up the hill, she had become just about as sore as a boil—at the edge of blazing up if Irwin gave her the least reason for it. She said more loudly than was needed, "If you're planning to keep on letting him work for you, I'll have to take your horse out of the circle."

His brain gradually took in what she had said. "He's been beating on your horses," he said, without questioning it.

"Yes sir, and yours too, and their feed's been going to his wife's pigs, I'm pretty sure."

He stood stiffly in the entry of his house with a book held down in one hand and the other hand resting on the doorknob. He was dressed in his Sunday suit with a plan to attend church, but the book he was holding, marking the page with his thumb, was not the Bible but a history of the French monarchy. "Is he down there right now?" he said, and stepped out on the porch to look down the slope toward the barn and the hired man's small house. The wind caught the front of his hair and lifted it in a cockscomb, caught the pages of his book and flapped them against the back of his hand.

"No sir, I don't think he is."

With the recent change of weather, the mountains across the way were dressed in snow clear down to the valley floor. Irwin turned his head toward them and studied the view for a long minute and then tightened up his mouth and said, with a glance toward Martha, "All right, then. I'll take care of it." He started back into the house.

She couldn't let it stand that way. She said again, "If you're planning to keep him on, I've got to take your horse off the circle." She would hate to leave Irwin's roan horse behind, hate leaving him in Logerwell's custody, but she would do it to protect the rest of them.

Walter said to Martha in a slight tone of umbrage, "I'll make it clear to him, he's to quit mistreating the animals." He had had trouble from the first day getting his hired man to do much of anything he asked, but he believed his own words: he would make his point with Logerwell this time and get control of the situation. He had seen the man cruel to his own wife's pigs and to his dog for no good cause; he wasn't much surprised by what the girl had told him.

"He'll go on doing it," she said fiercely. "He'll find ways to do it without you knowing." It was her belief—her experience—that when Logerwell heard it was Martha who'd brought the complaint he would start looking for ways to take out his grievance on her horses.

In truth, Walter Irwin wouldn't have been sorry to see the man go. But he had no experience with firing anyone and little hope of finding somebody else to work for him now that the war had taken so many men off to the army. He said to Martha in exasperation, "If I turn him out, I don't know where I'll get another hand."

Martha flared up. "I don't know either, but if you let him go on working here he'll go on hurting the horses until he kills one, which I won't let happen." Her voice shook from deep feeling, and she cleared her throat a couple of times to try to hide it. She put her hands inside her coat pockets and fisted them.

Walter stared at her, taken aback, startled to see tears standing briefly in her eyes. He hardly knew the girl, but on the evidence of her dress and the masculine work she'd chosen for herself he had formed an opinion of her as hard and leathery, not very much different from the ranch men who were his neighbors, men he believed to be without an ounce of soft feeling or the capacity for sentiment. Martha went on looking at him heatedly, with her chin squared and her fists working inside her coat. Her silence and her stubborn stare made him feel put upon, provoked into taking some kind of action. He turned from her again and looked out at the mountain range without seeing it, and in a moment found the gumption to put himself on the right side of the question.

On Monday morning when she rode up the lane to Irwin's corral, Martha passed Mrs. Logerwell headed downhill toward the River Road pushing a handcart loaded with their household goods, and Mr. Logerwell behind her driving their half-dozen pigs and leading the ribby black dog on a short length of rope. Mrs. Logerwell's face turned pink when she saw Martha, and as they passed each other she said, "If you's the one got him booted out—" in a hoarse, threatful wheeze that was more self-righteous injury than promise of harm. When Martha came even with the first of the pigs, Logerwell began jabbing the hindmost ones viciously with the homemade prod he was carrying—a stick of wood fitted with a metal hook—and the pigs squealed and broke into a frantic trot, which evidently was meant to unseat Martha from her horse. She was riding the Woodruffs' palomino mare, the one named Maude, and when Martha said "Whoa," Maude planted her feet and held still until the stampede of pigs had gone by; the horse hadn't liked any of it, but she'd long since come to trust Martha Lessen in these matters.

Logerwell's look was white-lipped with venom, and as he came on down the middle of the lane he slung the stick back and forth alongside his leg, the metal hook making a thin whistle through the air. Martha shifted her weight onto her toes resting in the stirrups in case she needed to ask Maude to move quickly, and she brought the horse over close to the fence at the side of the lane: she had seen that look on her dad, and even once or twice on her oldest brother, Davey. But when the man came alongside her he only let out a wordless sound of loathing and yanked on the dog's rope hard enough to make him yelp. He didn't look at Martha or say anything to her, just went on whipping his stick back and forth as he followed the pigs and his wife down the hill.

22

S TANLEY CAMBRIDGE HAD A 320-acre timber claim along the north side of Lewis Lake bordering the outlet of the Little Bird Woman River, and sometime around 1910 he cut a road through from the lower valley to the lake, a narrow double-track negotiable by wagon or sleigh. He built four little lodging cabins and a livery barn on his property and advertised the place as a mountain encampment. Elwha County families would come up by wagon or car in the summer, rent a cabin or put up a tent for a week or two at a stretch, take Stanley's little excursion boat up the lake for picnicking and sightseeing, or spread nets for the spawning sockeye salmon and salt away fish in ten-gallon kegs for winter use or sale to the mines down in Canyon City. And in the winter Stanley would flood a low pasture to make a skating rink and rent out toboggans and sleds, which brought people up to the lake by horseback or sleigh to spend the day skating and sledding.

On the third Sunday of January in that first winter of the Great War, Martha Lessen went up there with a big group of Will Wright's friends, including Henry Frazer and El Bayard. She had been riding the circle seven days a week for nearly two months, and Louise Bliss wouldn't hear of her spending another Sunday on horseback. Martha thought this would lead to a morning at church with the Blisses and an afternoon playing pinochle with George, or sitting by the stove in the bunkhouse reading *The Last of the Mohicans* while El mended harness or knitted socks; but it turned out Will Wright's friends had planned a skating party at Stanley's Camp, a last revel before his upcoming wedding. Louise paid no attention at all when Martha tried to beg off. She had already telephoned the Woodruff sisters, she said, and borrowed a pair of skates for Martha. Henry Frazer would be around in the Woodruff sleigh at the earliest hour of Sunday morning to collect El and Martha, the Bliss sleigh having already been loaned to Will and Lizzie, who were going up on Saturday with several of their friends, the girls to stay in the cabins and the boys to camp on the snow in tents.

The Blisses kept a great oak-trimmed steel and enamel tub in its own small room off the kitchen, and at Louise's instigation the ranch hands had the regular use of it. Although the hot water had to be carried from the kitchen stove, the tub was a grand luxury for all concerned—it was the only fixed bathtub in the rural parts of Elwha County in those days—and especially well regarded by Martha, who was completely unaccustomed to the privacy of a separate bath room and had never before had the use of a tub deep and long enough for soaking and stretching out her legs. Ordinarily she had her bath every Thursday night, but with the skating party in the offing Louise shifted her to Saturday night, clear evidence of female favoritism but not remarked upon by any of the men nor objected to by Martha herself. On Saturday night she slid down in the water until it lapped the underside of her chin and soaked for a quarter of an hour.

She had been careful in the past to bring her own bar of lye soap and not make use of any of the Blisses' collection of ointments and toilet preparations, but this night after thinking twice about it she cautiously helped herself to a lavender-scented hair soap, worked it into her hair, and rinsed it out with particular care; and she took a hard little brush from the washstand and used it to scrub around her fingernails and toenails and then behind her ears until she wore the skin thin and bright pink; after brushing her teeth with baking soda, she made a paste of the Blisses' gritty tooth powder and scrupulously cleaned them again. By then the bath water was cool. The tub had a waste plug and drain that emptied into a barrel behind the house, which Louise used to irrigate her kitchen garden. While the water slowly emptied around her, Martha went on sitting in the tub grimly examining her body, which was a map of bruises and half-healed scrapes. Finally she stood on the rag rug and dried herself with a towel and applied Louise's almond lotion to her cracked heels and hands and worked her oily fingers through her hair in hope the lotion might act like a hair tonic and keep her hair from flying away once it dried. She couldn't have said why the skating party had become a matter of such concern and importance to her.

In the morning, Martha and El waited on the porch with the provisions and furnishings for the day's expedition piled around them in boxes, waiting in silence after eating in silence in the shadowy kitchen, a cold breakfast Louise had set out for them the night before. They'd been afraid even to boil a pot of coffee, since it would have meant rattling wood in the stove while George and Louise were still asleep upstairs. But if there was ever in the world a better sound than sleigh bells in the early morning Martha didn't know what it was, and her throat just about closed up when Henry Frazer drove over the hill in the Woodruffs' sleigh, bright red and yellow with new paint, the pretty chestnut Belgians in their silver-chased harness, a high arch of Swedish bells over the hames.

Before the sleigh had come to a good stop Henry called out, "There's about half a foot of snow on the ground and not much wind," in a voice too loud for the time of morning, loud enough to rouse the Blisses out of sleep, which made Martha wonder why she had bothered to give up her morning coffee.

The floorboards at the back of the sleigh were already crowded with foodstuffs brought from the Woodruffs, and Henry was amused when he saw they were carrying more groceries. "I guess we won't starve," he said. His round face, caught between a scarf and a pulled-down hat, was pink with cold, and he looked even more barrel-chested than usual in layers of coats and sweaters.

They sat three in a row on the leather cushions, and Henry brought forward a wool army blanket and two quilts, which he spread across their knees. Then he spoke to the horses and they stepped out with their necks bowed, their breath smoking the air. Martha had earlier pulled her hair back in a damp knot—it had not quite dried overnight—and pinned it under a wool cap Louise had loaned her, which was not as warm as the silk stocking she wore when she was riding the circle but considerably prettier; she wore her warmest wool trousers and sheep-lined gloves and had twisted a scarf around her throat under the collar of her coat. Even so, waiting on the porch in the pale dawn she had been cold and shivery, and now the race of sharp air made her eyes water, her nose run. But she found, squeezed between the shoulders of the two men, that she wasn't cold at all and was suddenly wide awake—too nervous to feel dull from need of coffee.

Henry offered an opinion about the recent weather, how this snow was a good thing for the wheat but they would still have to hope for more of it, or a wet spring, to make any kind of wheat crop. He asked after George and Louise's health, and he said to Martha that he had been painting York's cheek with carbolic as she had asked him to and that the mark on the horse's face looked to be healing up all right. At one point when they were passing close by the rail yard in Shelby, Henry said, "I guess it was last year when we had all that snow pile up, there was a hobo jumped off the train when he saw the lights of town, and then he must've got cold and wet. Anyway, they found him dead the next day, just in that field between the rail yard and the river." Since this didn't seem to be in reference to anything, neither Martha nor El gave him much in the way of response.

Martha, for her part, had made up her mind not to always rattle on about horses, which meant that every minute she became more self-conscious and tongue-tied. And El was never a talker in any circumstance. Henry spent a few minutes working uphill against the untalkativeness of the other two and then gradually fell silent himself, which was not an uncomfortable state of affairs as far as Martha was concerned. The jangling of the bells and the rhythmic stride of the horses and the slight squeaking of the sleigh runners over the snow made her entirely happy. Her dad had never seen the need of a sleigh, so in snowy weather they kept close to home or drove a heavy democrat wagon behind laboring horses, which may have been why she was uncommonly fond of sleigh rides and glad for half a foot of snow, which was barely enough to warrant one.

They were the better part of two hours getting across the twelve or fifteen miles to the lake. Henry let the horses follow the roads quite a while, but once they were west of Bingham they left the road and headed southwest across the countryside. El got down and opened gates a time or two, but the foothills came down close to the river at the west end of the county and the timbered slopes hadn't been taken over by wheat fields or little homestead farms; when they finally crossed the boundary into the Whitehorn Forest Reserve they left all the fences behind and began climbing through an open country of pine and spruce and white fir and crossing shallow creeks one after the other, the sleigh runners cutting neatly through ice that ledged the stream banks. It had been foggy along the valley bottom but now the sun broke white and glittery in a dark blue sky. The snow here was deeper, and the limbs of the trees sagged under heavy cloaks. They rode in and out of tree shadow and bright sun.

Right after they struck the road going up to Stanley's Camp they overtook a man riding a well-built stock horse and towing behind him a burdened pack horse and three worn-out-looking horses who were making a slow job of it, going uphill in the icy tracks of sleighs. He pulled all his horses off to the side to let their sleigh go by, but when Henry saw who it was he stopped the sleigh alongside him and leaned around Martha and said, "Orville, I guess you're working, but you ought to come up to Stanley's for the skating."

The man's chapped face was wreathed round by a knitted wool scarf tied under his chin. He peered out from the thick muffler and said, "Hey Henry, hey El," and touched his gloved fingers to his forehead and said, "Miss Lessen," as if they had met, though she didn't remember it. "I'm going up to the divide," he said, "but I'd sure rather be at Stanley's. You fellows keep a good thought for me. I'll be eating out of the government nosebag for the next few days, and I imagine you'll be eating peach pie and pork chops."

Martha remembered him then, and she looked again at the horses he was towing behind him, their muzzles hanging close to the ground, the heavy fog of their breath stirring the dry snow. They were bone-thin, those horses; she guessed they would have been sold for glue if they weren't here with Orville Tippett, who was the Biological Survey man and who spent his winters trapping coyotes and all kinds of cats—bobcats, cougars, lynx—and any wolves that might be left in the county, anything that might be expected to sneak down from the mountains to take a calf or a lamb. Sheepmen and some of the ranchers supplied him with old horses he took up into the mountains and shot for bait. Martha had met him at church with the Blisses or at the Woodruffs' party, she couldn't recall which, and people had told her what he did for a living.

Henry said cheerfully, "We will eat up your share, Orville, you can count on it," and he kissed to the sleigh horses to go ahead. The clay-colored horse Orville Tippett was riding turned yellow eyes toward them and made a deep throaty mare sound, which encouraged one of the Belgians to nicker and shift hindquarters toward her as they were stepping out. When they were a ways down the road, Henry said, "Orville works out of the Portland office, I guess, but he spends pretty much of the winter up here in the reserve, doing away with varmints."

This seemed meant for Martha so she said, "I heard that was what he did." After a minute or two, she said, "Did you think one of those bait horses had a little Belgian in him, judging from the feathering on his legs?"

"He looked like it to me," Henry said, and El Bayard

looked at both of them and said, "They was plugs," in a tone of disgusted astonishment, and which they didn't argue with.

When they were still a couple of miles away from the lake, a column of smoke began to show itself, rising straight up above the crowns of the trees. Henry shook his head and said, "I guess they've got a bonfire going," and El made a slight sound that might have been amusement and said, "It's a good thing they're not hiding out from the law," which was only about the second thing he had said all day. El had a dry sense of humor that not everybody appreciated, but Henry laughed, which was a bit of a surprise to Martha. There was something between El and Henry, she had noticed, a guardedness that left them often silent in each other's company. She had taken this for coolness, an unresolved argument, but in truth, it had all to do with the car wreck that had crippled Pearl and killed Henry's brother—each of them overcareful and shy about saying anything that might bring up that old shared sorrow in the other man's mind.

As soon as they cleared the trees north of the lake Henry pulled up the team, which he said was to breathe the horses but it may have been to let everybody, including the horses, take in the view. It was the kind of view that could make your heart turn over, the long lake nestled in a bowl with the craggy peaks of the Whitehorn Range rising steeply all around. An old glacial moraine, rocky under the snow, bound the shore in a hairpin ridge along the south and west, and a spur of the Whitehorns, dense with trees, came steeply down on the east side. The lake glittered in the sun, an immense sheet of platinum mottled with thin floats of pure white ice. At the outlet the Little Bird Woman River spilled out across a wide plain of rocks and, almost full-grown, shot off through the trees to the northeast.

Stanley had put up his livery and corrals on a small hook of land that jutted out into the lake, and built the cabins at the prettiest point in the meadow east of the river. Will's friends had laid down floorboards and put up two walled tents, one to house their kitchen and one to house the men, just north of the lodging cabins. The snow had been shoveled out and trampled down around the tents and the cabins, and a maze of beaten paths crossed each other going down to the lakeshore and across the meadow to the skating rink and off into the trees where several sleighs were parked on the snow. Eight or ten horses stood nosing through trampled hay in a corral beside the livery.

Some of Will's party were out on the skating rink but the rest were at the camp, going in through the pinned-back door of the cook tent and carrying out tin plates, or they were already sitting on stones or logs upwind from the smoke of the big bonfire and balancing plates on their knees. When Henry veered the Belgians toward the livery somebody from the crowd around the bonfire shouted out, "There's still some flapjacks left but you'd better get over here at the double or they'll be gone!" which brought general laughter.

At the livery, before he had even stepped down from the sleigh, Henry turned to Martha and said, "I don't know if they were joking or not but you ought to get yourself some coffee and cakes before they eat everything up. El and me will get some help with the horses and the unpacking."

To head off and eat before the horses were put away wasn't something she ever did when she was a hired hand; but she had made up her mind to behave like the other girls today. Two young men she didn't know were already walking over to the sleigh, their jaws still working on a last bite of breakfast, and all the girls were sitting, eating their flapjacks. So Martha crossed the beaten-down snow to the cook tent and found a boy inside cooking on a cast-iron griddle on the lid of a sheepherder's stove. She didn't know if he was one of Will's friends or someone who worked for Stanley Cambridge; he was pink-faced and distracted and he barely glanced at her.

The tent smelled strongly of coffee, which brought back in her a needful craving, and she found an empty cup and poured it full from the big dented pot on the edge of the stove, coffee very dark and oily and just under the boiling point. If there was cream anywhere in the tent she didn't see it. When the boy handed her a plate of cakes, she found the huckleberry jam and smeared some over, and then went out and sat on the end of a log and bent her head to the food. She was glad she didn't have Dolly with her, who would have been alarmed by the size of the bonfire.

Half a dozen people were still eating their breakfast. She knew some of them—Roger Newbry and Mary Lee she remembered from the Odd Fellows Christmas party—but most she didn't recognize. She thoughtWill and Lizzie must be out skating on the flooded pond. There were probably twenty people altogether on the rink and around the fire, quite a few more than she'd been expecting. She was afraid even the ones she had met at the party might not remember her, or might be unfriendly. Every so often, she looked over toward Henry and El to see whether they were finished yet with unloading the boxes and turning out the horses, but otherwise kept her head down and plied her fork with frowning concentration, which gave people the idea she wasn't interested in friendship.

She would have gone back for more flapjacks if she had seen other girls doing it, but after her plate was wiped clean she went on sitting where she was, drinking down the bitter coffee slowly. She had thought Henry and El might sit with her to eat their flapjacks but when they came over from the livery they got swept up by their friends. She could hear Henry every little while, laughing or saying something that made other people laugh, but she kept from looking in his direction. It was a surprise, then, when he suddenly lowered himself on her log and handed over a cup of coffee whitened with cream and said, "I dumped in a bunch of sugar. You like things sweet, if I remember right."

"I don't have to have it," she said, which was meant

to be a remark about sugar being in short supply. The words came out stiff, which was from general embarrassment. She glanced at Henry. "Anyway, I didn't see that they had any sugar."

"I brought along a secret stash of that black beet sugar, and it doesn't seem to mind a bit, going into black coffee." His grin had a way of flattening the end of his nose, stretching the skin tight across the line of bone high up where his nose had been broken. He took a couple of swallows from his own cup, which was as milky as hers.

She said, "I didn't see the cream either."

"Well, I had to hunt for it, they're keeping it out of the hands of the unworthy." He was still smiling, looking down at his gloved thumbs where they fidgeted on either side of the coffee cup.

Martha drank down the sweet coffee gratefully.

"Have they got lakes up there around Pendleton?" Henry asked in a meditative sort of way but without notice or warning. There weren't any lakes to speak of around Pendleton, just sinks and sloughs and watering holes and the canals and ditches dug by irrigation cooperatives, but she didn't want him to think she was a brush-popper who had never seen a body of water. She said, "We don't have a lake but we've got the Umatilla River that runs through the whole valley."

"I remember seeing that river. It's got quite a bit more water in it than the Little Bird Woman. Where's that river start from? Is it the Wallowas?"

"I don't know if it's the Wallowas or maybe the

Blues." She was flustered, caught without solid knowledge of her own home territory.

"I've heard that's pretty country over there," he said, without making clear if he meant Pendleton or one of the mountain ranges. Martha thought Elwha County had Umatilla County beat all hollow in terms of scenery, but before she could say so, Henry said, looking out at Lewis Lake in its cup of mountains, "But I guess I never have seen any place prettier than this. I wasn't but seventeen or so when I came here to Elwha County, and I never have wanted to leave."

In the front room of the Woodruff house was a painting she had admired, of a tree-lined canal in autumn and a pair of lovers holding hands, walking through dry leaves on a path beside the bank, and in the far back of the painting a stone bridge arching over the water. It was a scene outside anything in her own experience but she felt strongly that it was in France. She knew a boy in Pendleton who had gone into the army "to get out of the sticks and see that pretty French countryside," and when she had seen the Woodruffs' painting she had understood what he must have meant. She didn't know why Henry Frazer was staying put in Elwha County while so many other men had joined up and were on their way to see the Eiffel Tower and the French countryside, or if his remark about not leaving the valley had anything to do with that. She didn't know him well enough to ask. What popped into her head now was that the countryside in the Woodruffs' painting wasn't a scene a soldier was likely to see—not while the war was going on.

After a few minutes Henry said, squinting over toward the river, "I guess the Little Bird Woman is named for an Indian girl by that name who used to live around here. Indians used to come up here and spend the summer fishing and berry picking. I guess some of them would still be coming here but people complained, and the county passed a rule that keeps them out."

Martha tried to see the snowy meadow as it must have looked in those summers, in the days before Stanley Cambridge built his cabins: a cluster of tepees standing on long, golden grass at the edge of the lake. She didn't know why Elwha County had decided to keep the Indians out, if it might have had to do with some reservation Indians driving off the government agents who tried to register them for the draft. But she wouldn't have minded if they were here right now. During the Round-Up, when Indians came over to Pendleton from the reservation and made a kind of encampment on the fairgrounds, she liked seeing their tepees. For those few days she almost felt like she was living in the old times before everything was so overrun with people, so settled and modern. She was thinking of saying something like that to Henry when he said, "There's some pictures they painted, up there on the rocks," and he made an incomplete gesture that seemed to take in the mountains all around them, "which've got to be pretty old, so I imagine Indians must have been coming up here every summer for a long time. Before any of us showed up—any white men, I mean."

She turned her head and peered at Henry. "What kinds of things did they draw?"

"Oh, horses and deer, things like that, and some that don't appear to be anything but lines and marks." He glanced at Martha. "It's a climb, but I could show you."

She straightened up slightly and said, "All right." She didn't mind having to walk in the snow, so she hoped he meant right now and not some indefinite time that might never happen. He didn't say which it was, but stood and took her plate and both cups from her and headed off with them to the cook tent, and she waited where she was because she still didn't know if he meant to show her the picture rocks now or later or if he had meant his remark only to be polite. As he was walking back up to her he looked at her feet and grinned and said, "Good thing we've both got our boots on," and then she knew.

He led her a short way up the edge of the lake along a path that had already been beaten through the snow and then he left the lake trail and began to break a way uphill into the trees, the snow not even a foot deep in most places, so their boots took most of the wet and their trousers grew dark only around the turned-up cuffs. He and Martha both began huffing a bit as they climbed, and he looked back at her a couple of times but didn't slow down or say anything. The sounds of the skating party became thin and birdlike below them.

She wanted to tell him she could take her turn breaking trail but since she didn't know where they were going she didn't say it. Every so often, with all the snowed-over rocks looking the same, he stopped to get his bearings in the timber and then he went on. Once he silently pointed out to her a row of small craters in the snow that could have been made by deer or elk or maybe sheep. The ground began to be cut with steep-walled ravines and narrow brushy draws where snowmelt would run in the spring. He zigzagged up the face of a sidehill until coming onto the high ridge-line, which they followed up, and after fifteen or twenty minutes they came out of the trees and were standing at the foot of a high, upthrust cliff. A line of smooth rock twelve or fifteen feet tall ran along the bottom beneath a jutting brow of basalt.

Henry turned to her, grinning, pleased as a child. "Well, I wasn't sure I remembered how to get up here, but here it is, like I knew what I was doing."

Martha got her breath and squinted her eyes to make out what he had brought her to see: small, dim figures chipped and carved into the dark stone, the details and outlines worn away smooth in places. She could make out a handful of riderless horses, some animals with branched racks—they might have been elk or some kind of deer—and stick-figure men in stiff poses holding sticks or bows, and several boxy or swirled shapes that looked like the meaningless things toddlers draw when you give them a pencil. None of the figures looked real to her, they were childishly simple, strung out across the rock in an uneven line at eye level like a ragged single-file troop. She had been drawing horses as long as she could remember and almost never was happy with how her drawings came out, the proportions never exactly right, and these horses weren't drawn right either; but she felt, looking at them, exactly as she did when she saw the tepees at the Pendleton Round-Up: a dim thrill of yearning.

"Do you think it was one person who drew all of these pictures?" she said to Henry after they had stood looking for several minutes. A kind of nostalgia had taken hold of her, a regret for something she couldn't have named. She liked thinking the drawings had all been made by one person, someone who came up here year after year to carve a new horse or another deer, someone who had made up a secret language and then started writing down a story no one else could read. One person who kept this place secret, or only told the secret to one friend.

Henry said, studying the pictures, "It could have been. I don't know. Or it could have been the whole tribe taking turns and this was where they wrote down what happened every year. An almanac, something like that."

With a finger of his gloved hand he traced one of the shapes. "I always figured this one meant *summer.*" It wasn't a rayed circle, as she would have drawn the sun, but she could see what Henry meant: that the little boxy shape could have been someone's idea of what the sun looked like. He touched a spiral shape. "And this one, *winter.*"

She had wanted to say something to him earlier having to do with the Indians—that a vital, inexpressible meaning had gone out of the land when the Indians were driven off—but by now the words had become jumbled and wouldn't come out the way she wanted to say them. "I used to wish I was an Indian," she said.

He didn't smile. "Did you? Well, I guess I know what you mean. I always wanted to be one of Lewis's men, old Lewis and Clark. I wanted to see what they saw back then, the way it was, all this country out here before any buildings got put up, and those big herds of antelope and wild horses and so on, like they saw." He dropped his chin and glanced over at Martha and suddenly broke into a smile. "If you were an Indian and I was with Lewis, maybe we'd have run into each other."

Her cheeks were hot. She tried to think of something clever to say, to keep up the imaginary story that had sprung into his mind and hers, but nothing came. What she hadn't said to him was that in her childhood daydreams she was always a boy, a noble Indian boy with long black braids streaming out behind her when she galloped bareback across the wild plain on a painted pony. She looked over at Henry and tried to guess what he was thinking, but when he looked back she lowered her eyes.

They stood a while longer without saying anything.

Then, bending his head back to peer up at the rimrock, he said, "There's a ranger lookout cabin up there somewhere. They built it a couple of years ago. They man it in the summer to watch out for fire on the reserve. Or anyway they did before the war got going good. I don't know who they'll get to man it now, probably some old coot whose eyes are bad." He looked at her and smiled.

She didn't know if he was thinking they might go on up to the top and look for the lookout cabin. "How far is it?"

"I don't know. I haven't ever been up there. But I imagine it's a ways. I'd hate to be the one hauling groceries up to it, unless there's a trail where you could pack things in on a mule. Well, I guess there must be a trail, now I think about it, or how'd they get the wood and windows and stove up there to build the cabin."

"There must be a good view from there."

"I bet there is." He looked up at the mountain again. "We could try to find it if I knew where the trail was, but I sure don't. And I guess the others will start wondering where we are if we don't show up down at the lake pretty soon."

He had evidently gotten the idea that she wanted to go up, so she said, shifting her feet, "I wouldn't want to go up that high in the snow anyway. It's already about as high as our boots."

He looked at her and then away. "Well, if you're still working somewhere around here by next summer, we can go up there and look for it, when we've got a chance of finding it."

A slow heat filled her chest. "Yes," she said.

Going down, they followed their own broken tracks in the snow. Martha struck out ahead of Henry and then was sorry she'd taken the lead, suddenly conscious of being watched from behind and conscious of the way she must look hiking down the hill in men's trousers—not just unwomanly but mannish. When they got down to the lakeshore Henry came up and walked alongside her, and she ought to have felt better about that, but didn't.

"I guess Will and Lizzie must be out there skating," she said, and peered over toward the rink, which was in the low swale of the meadow. The sun was bright, glaring off the ice. People skated back and forth in little groups of two or three but it was impossible to make out their faces.

Henry looked at her and smiled. "I thought I might get you good and tired out and not have to do any skating, but you don't look a bit of it. And I guess that's what we came up here for. I'll get the skates." He cut across the snow to where the sleigh was parked and he came back carrying two pairs of skates.

While they sat at the edge of the ice lacing them up, he said, "Those you're putting on are Emma Adelaide's. Or Aileen's." The skates had been sharpened and oiled and the laces mended.

"They fit me all right," she said. She liked thinking she wore the same boot size as the sisters.

"Mine are pretty old." He held one up to show her or just to admire it. "They belonged to the old man, old Mr. Woodruff, their dad." He had the other skate on, but didn't say if it fit him or not. His unshod foot in a wool sock looked broad and blunt across the toes.

Will and Lizzie went flying past them, their faces flushed with cold or with general happiness, their arms crossed in front and clasped exactly as Martha had seen in book illustrations. Will grinned as they went by and called, "Hey!" over the loud scrape of their skates on the ice. Lizzie's thick wool skirt belled out gracefully around her ankles when they made the curve at the edge of the rink.

Martha had learned to skate from her mother's mother, whose family had come originally from Sweden or Norway—one of those cold northern countries. Gramma Andresen had been a child in Minnesota where there were half a dozen frozen ponds to skate on within a mile of her house; when she settled in Umatilla County and discovered the lack of lakes, she took to carrying water out to a low spot in the pasture as soon as the ground froze every winter. She had two pairs of old skates and all her grandkids took turns sharing them. When it wasn't their turn to wear the skates, they glided around the rink on the flat soles of their worn-out shoes. Skating was one of those things Martha had been cut off from years before when a squabble between her dad and her grandmother flared into outright war.

Martha went out on the ice ahead of Henry and wobbled a bit, then got her balance and began to skate slowly and deliberately along the edge of the rink, staying out of the path of other people skating faster around the long irregular oval. When Henry didn't catch up with her—he skated cautiously, had told her he'd been skating only a handful of times in his life— she made a careful turn and went back to him, grinning. He windmilled his arms once and didn't fall, but he laughed and said, "You'd better hold me up," and she let him take her hand because they were both steadier skating together.

When Will and Lizzie went past them again, Henry said, "We could try that," and Martha thought he meant tearing along over the ice, breakneck, nimble-footed, but then he fumbled to take her outside hand in his inside hand, and she did the same, and they glided along slowly in silence, arms crossed and gloved hands clasped. Other couples skated past them, and Martha again became aware of herself as a big coarse girl wearing a man's loose wool trousers, and she imagined the picture she made skating with Henry wasn't anything close to a photograph or drawing in a novel.

"I heard you had something to do with getting Al Logerwell fired," Henry said to her.

She said flatly, lifting her chin, "He was beating my horses."

They weren't her horses but he knew what she meant and didn't call her on it. He said, "I guess I'm not surprised. I guess that's his whip mark on York?"

238

"Yes it is."

He staggered suddenly, the toe of his skate catching the ice, and he tightened his hands on hers and she braced against him and they didn't fall, either of them. They concentrated on their feet and the surface of the ice and the rhythm of their steady skating. Around them the skate blades cutting the ice made a boisterous clashing noise under the chatter and laughter of other skaters. After a while Henry said, "I heard Logerwell got himself hired by Gordon Allen, up at the JD Ranch."

She shouldn't have been surprised to hear Logerwell had landed work so quickly, but she felt this news as a rebuke of her judgment.

"Gordon is pretty hard on animals himself, so I guess the two of them'll get along all right," Henry said, and he smiled dryly.

Martha thought he could be saying something else— *you can see how much good it did you to get him fired*—and she wanted him to know she never had thought, not even for a minute, that she could protect all the horses in the countryside from men who would beat them. She said stiffly, repeating something she had heard the Woodruff sisters say, "Well, there are plenty of men who will beat a horse. But they'd just better not do it in front of me is all." The bright color in her face wasn't all from the cold and the exercise. She turned her head clear away from Henry, toward the livery barn and the horses standing inside the log rails of the corral. He wasn't sure what he had said to set her off.

"I heard Irwin—is that his name?—hired Ralph Birkmeier's oldest girl to work for him," he said. "I don't know what she knows about farming, but I imagine she won't be beating up the horses, at least."

Martha had met Hilda Birkmeier the day before at the Irwin corral, a girl built like a Shetland pony, short and solid with large callused hands. She wore old overalls she had fixed up herself, sewn double in the knees and the seat, which made Martha think well of her—that and the pony build. Ralph and Mildred Birkmeier lived with their twelve children crowded into a three-room house at the east edge of Opportunity, and since Mrs. Birkmeier often had a baby at the breast, another one weaning, and a third clinging to her skirts, the strain and work of the household had frequently passed down to Hilda. The girl was happy to get away from that, to work outside, and to have a whole house of her own to live in. She had already taken some of Irwin's barn cats to live with her in the cabin that had been Logerwell's.

"When I saw her, she was marking off some holes to set trees into when the ground thaws," Martha said to Henry. "I guess Mr. Irwin bought some orchard stock from a traveling salesman, and he plans to grow fruit."

Henry had a generally poor opinion of all the late-arriving farmers who had been plowing up the dry slopes of Elwha County the past few years. There were just too many of them for the land to support, and they came in with great excitement and plans for growing sunflowers or soybeans or tobacco, but their excitement usually dried up with the dry summers. Where the ridgetops and uplands and sidehills near the homesteads were shorn of grass and tilled, the creeks ran brown with mud every spring, and there were dust devils all over the hills later on in the summer. The bunch-grass pasture was best left to cattle and horses was his belief. He said, "He'd better have a plan for irrigating. I know the sisters never could get apples to grow unless they kept up their watering all summer."

Martha didn't know if Walter Irwin had a plan for watering his trees. She said, "Hilda's not afraid of hard work," which she knew wasn't anywhere near Henry's point—he hadn't said anything against Hilda Birkmeier—but she felt called on at that moment to state her opinion.

"I guess he's lucky to get her then," Henry said. And he told her, "They're a German family," to let her know why a hardworking girl like Hilda Birkmeier hadn't already been snapped up by somebody else.

Martha didn't think she needed to reply to that, but after a moment she said, "They're Americans more than German, I guess. She told me two of her brothers have gone into the army and they're learning to be soldiers."

He smiled at Martha and didn't weigh whether he ought to say what came into his mind—it just popped out. "Well, I hope they can keep from getting into fights like your two brothers and breaking the sergeant's nose before they get over there." She returned him a look that was partly just surprise, but she saw he was teasing her and she crooked her mouth slightly to hide her own smile.

They took a few more turns around the ice, and then she said, "My dad whipped us kids pretty hard," as if this was what they'd been discussing. When Henry glanced at her, she said, "So I guess that's where my brothers get it from." He waited to see if she would say more, now that she had started to tell him something deeper. She looked over toward the lake, which from here had the color of sheet metal against the darkness of the evergreens. "But he's hard on animals, too. He likes to beat horses just about more than anything else."

He listened and then he said, "Is that right? Well, I guess the apple fell a long way from the tree, then."

She turned back to him with another surprised look, a half-laugh. "I guess it did." She dipped her chin slightly to study the toes of her own skates and Henry's skates moving together across the ice, the slow, deliberate, harsh-sounding strokes not quite synchronous.

"He has the arthritis and he got pretty crippled just about the time I got big enough and strong enough I could stop him beating the little kids. And I'd get between him and a horse. But he'd just wait and do it when I wasn't there. He beat a horse of mine this fall, for no good reason except I wasn't there to stop him, beat him so bad he died." She looked at Henry as if she couldn't believe it herself, that her dad would kill a

242

horse for no reason but that. Then she turned her head and looked toward the horses standing in the livery corral. "So I took my other ones, Dolly and T.M. and Rory, and I left there and came down here." She said this last bit with an edge on it, a hard edge, which at first made Henry think she was expecting an argument out of him or was ready to fight him over something; but after he'd let it sink in, he knew she wasn't arguing with him at all—that he wasn't the one she was ready to fight.

After a minute Henry said, "My dad got sick and died early, but my stepdad is a pretty good hand with horses. I learned some from him, and then I went out and learned about cows from George Bliss. I guess I must have been about seventeen when I went to work for Bliss."

She glanced at him and said, "Why did you go over to the Woodruff sisters, then, after being with Mr. Bliss for so long? I know they needed help, but why didn't El go, or somebody else?"

"Oh, I've always liked the sisters. And they're still growing cows, whereas half of Bliss's pastures are in wheat now. And I guess Bliss and me are too much like a dad and his son." He began to smile. "After his two boys left home, he began calling me his foreman, but I don't think he'll ever get over thinking I'm seventeen. The sisters, they let me do what needs doing without telling me how to do it." He waited a bit and then he said, "I had a brother who died last year, and I guess I kind of wanted to get away from Mrs. Bliss, too, who seemed to think I needed her to feel sorry for me."

Martha had five brothers who were all living; she had never had to get over the death of anybody she cared about, except some horses. She'd never had anybody feeling sorry for her in the way Henry meant, so she didn't know for sure if she would want that or not. But she thought she understood what he was saying. She hesitated and then said, "I know it's not the same thing, but whenever I've been bunged up from a fall off a horse I've mostly just wanted to be left alone, not have anybody make a fuss over it, which just makes things hurt worse than otherwise."

He nodded. "Well, it's pretty much the same thing." After a short silence he began to smile. "Anyway, I've got that foreman's house all to myself over at the Split Rock, and I had to listen to El snoring like a freight train when I was working for Bliss."

Martha dipped her chin, smiling too. "I guess I won't ever be a foreman with a house to myself but at least in the barn I don't have to listen to anybody but horses." Henry wondered if she was making a point about wanting to always live alone but then she laughed lightly and said, glancing at him, "I've had horses that snored worse than anybody but they've never kept me awake," and he took these last words as an encouragement.

23

TOWARD THE END of January Tom Kandel began having trouble sleeping at night. He would sit up in the darkness, his legs hanging over the side of the bed, and restlessly rock back and forth above his knees for hours at a time. Ruth at first sat up with him too; she asked him over and over if he was hurting, and she stroked his arm or his forehead as she tried to persuade him to lie down again. But she began gradually to understand or to believe that his restlessness had more to do with fear of dying in the night than with pain, and when nothing she said or did seemed of any use to him she gave up trying to coax him back to sleep. When he sat up in the night she went on lying on the bed pretending he hadn't wakened her, only shifting her body to press an arm or a leg against the small of his back so he would know he was not entirely alone in the darkness.

One day in the last week of the month, just before dawn, he sat up in bed not in the way she had grown used to, but in terrible agony, and began to pace back and forth beside the bed, moaning as an animal moans, a low heavy thrumming from deep in his belly. Ruth sat up in alarm and spoke to him but he hardly seemed to hear her, and when she got out of bed and touched his shoulder he twisted away from her and went out to the front room and began to stalk a path between the dim shapes of the kitchen table and the sofa. Ruth followed him but before long gave up trying to get him to settle or even speak to her, and she went into Fred's little bedroom.

In recent weeks Fred had been staying away from his father as much as he could. The war had caused the price of furs to rise, and the boy had set out a trapline that caught mostly river rats but once in a while a slough muskrat that brought two dollars from Meryl Briggs at the drugstore. After school and on Saturdays he walked the trapline and took care of the chickens and came into the house late in the evenings. Ruth and Tom both understood: it wasn't his father he was staying away from but his father's dying, and they said little about it, wanting to spare their son as much worry as possible. But now Ruth scarcely had the energy to feel concern for the boy—the shine of his eyes wide open in the early-morning twilight, the stiffness of his body lying on the bed. She told him bleakly, "Fred, I want you to go over to the Rocker V and borrow a horse from Mr. Varden and ride into Bingham for the doctor." He began immediately to pull on his clothes as she stood over him. Both of them could hear Tom's low, terrible purr from the dark front room of the house. "Don't kill the horse or yourself from riding too hard," she said after a moment, and briefly rested her hand on her son's thin arm. He went on lacing up his boots in silence.

The fire in the stove had gone out long since, and the house was very cold. Ruth went into their bedroom and lit a lamp and put on a wrapper over her nightgown and found her slippers and Tom's slippers and then she took the lamp and one of Tom's flannel shirts and went to where he was standing in his underwear swaying and groaning in the front room. She intended to make him put on the slippers and the shirt—she was afraid he might take a chill—but when she brought the lamp close to him she could see he was sweating and flushed, the cancer a roaring furnace in his body. She said, "Oh Tom!" and broke into tears. He hardly seemed to see or hear her. His brows were drawn down to the edges of his eyes in a wild, frowning grimace.

In the next hour, as darkness thinned along the edge of the mountains to the southeast, Ruth did little but follow Tom from the bedroom to the front room and back. She tried to persuade him to drink a glass of water or submit to a cool washrag on his face, but he shrugged away from her with a bare and impatient motion and did not answer her at all. Sometimes, briefly, he would sit down—on the edge of the bed, the edge of the sofa, a kitchen chair—and rested his elbows on his knees, hands clenching and unclenching, his head hanging between his shoulders; but if she laid her palm on his undershirt between the jutting wing bones of his back he flinched and groaned and stood again and returned to his agonized prowling. After a while she stopped trying to talk to him, stopped trying to comfort him. She sat in a kitchen chair and watched him pace the house and waited for Fred to bring the doctor. It occurred to her that the chickens hadn't been fed or watered and were still cooped up in their shed, but she could hardly think about that now or do a thing about it. She wasn't willing to leave Tom alone in the house. Waiting with him and watching him stalk through the rooms was all she could do.

In the first days after learning Tom would die she had cried and cried and everything she thought of was painful. But she had not cried in recent days, had slipped into an unfeeling state of mind, removed and closed up. She had been dreading what lay ahead, the unimaginable details of Tom's slow dying, almost more than she dreaded being left alone, and lately she had found her mind skipping over the next few weeks and lighting on the details of rearranging her life once Tom was gone, with the same unemotional attention she might have given to spring housecleaning. She had hoped—had even prayed—that if Tom was dying it could happen soon and be over with. When Tom whispered to her one night that he wished he had the courage to take a gun and shoot himself—*If I'm dying, I might as well get it over with*—she had been startled but had said almost nothing in reply. It was something she herself had thought of, had even wished for, in moments of cold consideration. She was grimly aware this made her a heartless, soulless, unloving wife.

But now that Tom was suddenly sicker—now that she was sitting in a kitchen chair watching him circle and circle the house in feverish agony—that thin, unemotional husk fell easily away, and behind her breastbone was such fear and pain that she had to gasp for breath in harsh, repeated sighs. She was terrified he might be dying—that this was his last death agony—and she wished madly that he should go on living as long as possible, even if it meant going on suffering as he was this morning. The incredibleness of what was happening, the inevitability of it, the finality of it, came flooding into her body in a physical way, and all the meaning she had found in the world, the shape she had cast on it, began to wash away in the undertow.

Every little while she looked out through the kitchen window for Dr. McDonough. The sky had begun to clear—Ruth could make out the dust of a few dim stars against the darkness in the west—and she glimpsed against the wolf-gray light a colorless image that was her own reflection in the glass, though at first she took it for Tom's face, thin brows drawn down to the edges of her eyes in a wild grimace.

The morning went on brightening and lengthening without bringing any sign of Fred or the doctor. Dr. McDonough had always come to the house in a car and Ruth wondered if the snow was too deep for his automobile to get through—if he might have slid off the road into a ditch. It crossed her mind that Fred might have fallen or been bucked off the borrowed horse and might be lying dead in the snow right now, which was an idea too huge and absurd to hold on to. When sometime in the late morning she heard a horse jangling its harness and blowing air right outside the front door, her heart leaped with relief. She went quickly out to the front porch but found it wasn't Fred or the doctor but Martha Lessen. The girl usually would wait at the fence for Ruth to come out and take the mail and the groceries from her, but today Martha had been so startled and alarmed to find the yard bare of chickens that she'd ridden right up to the house, her face stiff with dread. And when Ruth saw who it was, the look that came into her own face was desperate disappointment. She said, "I thought you might be Fred, bringing the doctor," and immediately turned back to the house.

Martha had been afraid to hear her say, *Mr. Kandel has passed away,* but there was nothing in Ruth's words to cheer about. She called to her, "Mrs. Kandel, what can I do to help out?" Ruth stopped a moment and leaned her forehead tiredly on the frame of the door. Then she said, "The chickens, I guess," before stepping inside.

Martha stood down in the slushy snow and led the horse outside the fenced chicken yard and dropped the reins and went back into the yard and across to the chicken house. She opened the coops to let the daylight in, and she found the scratch feed and scattered it on the snow and on the ground inside the coop. The roosters began to make their cautious way out into the cold, and then the hens, though they were all uncannily silent.

When she'd finished, Martha went up to the house again and knocked and said, "Mrs. Kandel?" and after a moment, not hearing anything from inside, she made up her mind to just open the door and step in without waiting to be asked. The house was cold and dim. Ruth

Kandel sat in a kitchen chair with her arms stretched out on the table in front of her. The sleeves of her wrapper were ruched up almost to the elbows, and her forearms lying on the table had a greenish pale cast, the skin stippled with cold. She was staring out the kitchen window but her body seemed pitched toward the sound coming from the bedroom, which was a terrible low grunting, something like the groan a horse makes when it's down on the ground with colic.

Martha's heart quickened. She didn't want to go on standing there by the door, so she said, "Should I stir up a fire in the stove?" and made a move toward the wood.

Ruth looked over at her and said, her voice rough and cracking from tiredness or strain, "He's burning hot, I don't want to heat up the house, I'm afraid it'll make him worse." Her eyes drifted past Martha and fixed on the shelf of books hanging on the wall behind her. She said, "He's in terrible pain," and tightened her mouth in a bad likeness of a smile. Her hair had been done up in a night braid but by now was straggling loose from it. She turned back to the window and after a moment opened her mouth and took in a loud, labored breath, a sigh.

Martha came immediately to the edge of tears. She said, "I'm so sorry, Mrs. Kandel," which she knew was no comfort at all and she wasn't surprised when Ruth went on looking out the window without bothering to answer.

It wasn't clear to Martha how she could be any help

to the Kandels, either of them, but she didn't feel it would be right to leave. She stood a moment trying to think what else she could offer to do, and when her mind failed her she said, "I'll just sit down with you, if that's all right, until the doctor gets here." She didn't wait for Ruth to tell her if it was all right or not, but went over and sat down on a kitchen chair; she took off her hat and placed it carefully on the floor next to her. There wasn't a single thing she could think of to say, and Ruth went on staring out the window in silence, which wasn't silence, not with that low animal moaning carrying on in the bedroom. After a while, Martha became aware that some of the Kandels' roosters had begun to crow, probably had been crowing for minutes. She began to think about the horse she'd left ground-tied outside the fence, a black horse named Sherman that belonged to the Rocker V, and to wonder whether he'd still be standing where she'd left him when she took up the circle again. Cows had begun calving in the past week and she had been riding through snow littered with silvery discarded placentas; she didn't know why she thought of that now, and of the dead mother cow she had come upon earlier in the morning, undelivered of its crosswise calf.

Martha had imagined Tom Kandel to be prostrate on his deathbed, so when he came walking jerkily out from the bedroom she was deeply startled. She hardly recognized him, he was so thin and pale, his face a stiff, wrenched mask. His underwear hanging loosely on his bony frame was dark in patches from sweat. He didn't seem to see his wife or Martha, but circled the room once, closing and unclosing his hands reflexively, and then abruptly he sat on the edge of the sofa and began to hug and rock himself with a low panting sound, a succession of breathless grunts.

Martha looked away in stunned, wordless fear, but Ruth lifted her chin and turned to watch her husband silently. After a while she said, "It was still dark out when I sent Fred for the doctor. What do you suppose is keeping them?"

Martha didn't know if Ruth intended this question for her, or if it was a question at all; but she discovered that she had a cowardly wish to escape back out into the cold morning, which is why she said, "Mrs. Kandel, should I go into Bingham and see what's holding them up?"

Just at that moment they began to hear a car motor and wheels bumping up the lane, and Ruth stood without a word and went out to the porch and waited for the doctor, who drove up to the fence line in a Hudson car with Fred on the seat beside him. When Fred got down from the car to open the gate and let the car through, Ruth called to him, "Fred, you'd better go see to the chickens." Of course Martha had already seen to this work but Ruth didn't remember asking her to do it; what she remembered was that the chicken house had become one of her son's hiding places, one of his refuges from his father's dying. Fred gave her a desperate look of relief and as soon as the car passed by him into the yard he closed the gate and walked off to the chicken house.

The doctor, when he stepped from the running board into the snow, smiled faintly and said to Ruth, "How are you, Mrs. Kandel?" to which she could think of no reply. He came onto the porch and she silently held the door open for him to pass through. He was used to seeing anxious relatives and friends hovering around the edges of sickness, so he barely noted that a girl was standing at the kitchen table, her hands gripping the back of a chair, and he didn't speak to her, but set his hat and bag on the parlor table beside the door and said matter-of-factly to Tom, as if they were merely two people passing the time of day, "Tom, how have things been going for you?" Tom was rocking on the edge of the sofa, his stare fixed on a spot on their little Turkish rug, his eyes pinched nearly closed in his drawn face. The doctor began taking things out of his bag, getting together a hypodermic of morphine and hyoscine, without giving his patient more than a cursory glance.

Ruth watched Dr. McDonough a moment—she hadn't said a word to him—and then went again to sit at the kitchen table. She laid her forehead down on her crossed arms and shut her eyes, which mildly aggravated the doctor. Fred Kandel had been sitting on Dr. McDonough's office stoop when he drove in from an all-night call—thirty miles into Owl Creek Canyon and thirty miles back again, attending to a Hungarian man who had been struck in the forehead by a mule—and they'd set out for the Kandel farm as soon as he refueled the car. The doctor hadn't slept more than two or three hours in the past two days. His chin was stubbled, his mouth sagging with exhaustion. It had been his opinion that Ruth Kandel was a strong-minded woman, even to his way of thinking somewhat too independent and forward. He had expected her to hold up better than this when the first crisis came.

The only sounds in the room were the ticking of a clock and Tom's deep, measured groan. Dr. McDonough went over to him and pulled up the damp undershirt and gave him the morphine and then stood over him, watching in silence for several minutes until Tom's eyes glazed and his moaning ebbed off. The dose was enough to kill a healthy man. It always amazed the doctor, how pain absorbed morphine like a sponge.

"Tom, come on now, let's get you into bed." He helped the man stand and walked with him back to the bedroom. A piss pot sat empty and clean beside the rumpled bed so he held it up and coaxed Tom into passing a little water into it. Then he neatened the quilts and turned them back and helped the man down onto the mattress. Tom turned his head past the doctor and stared off toward a bare corner of the room. His brown hair fell lank against the pillow. He had never been stocky but he was quite thin now, his cheekbones very sharp, his collarbones and the washboard of his ribs visible through the undershirt above the swelling of the tumor. Cancer was rare in those days—Tom Kandel's was only the second case Dr. McDonough had seen in his forty years of treating patients. His other cancer patient had died a terrible slow death, and he expected the same thing for Tom. There was little he knew to do to cut down on the man's suffering, short of killing him with an overdose of morphine.

While Tom went on looking at something invisible in the middle distance, Dr. McDonough listened to the man's pulse and his heart, then pulled the quilts up and stood watching. Finally Tom released a slight sound, a sigh, and closed his eyes. His eyelids were thin and veined, his lashes casting faint shadows on the bones of his cheeks.

The doctor picked up the pot of dark urine and carried it outside and stepped off the porch to fling it away from the house. There was now a path through the snow to the privy, broken with boot prints, and the ground around the chicken house had been shoveled out and stomped down, but there was no sign of the boy, Fred. The doctor took the chill air into his lungs and tipped his head back a moment to look at the sky, which by now was nearly clear.

Ruth and Martha were sitting at the kitchen table when he came back into the house, and they turned their faces to him in perfect synchrony, which he might have found amusing under other circumstances. He said, not unkindly, "Ruth, how are you holding up?"

Ruth turned from him to the window, seeming to lean slightly toward the sky above the edge of the near hills; her mouth, in the image he glimpsed on the wavery window glass, began to twist until it became an unattractive rictus of grief. "There was nothing I could think to do. He wouldn't let me help him."

"You did the only thing you could do, which was sending the boy."

She put her hands to her face and began rubbing her fingertips up and down the sides of her nose and across her mouth and chin, which was a way of hiding nervousness. "He hasn't been right," she said, the words muffled behind her hands. He knew what she meant. Over the last couple of days he had seen a marked change in Tom—slurring of words, dullness, a vacant expression. *Not right in his mind,* was what she meant. *Not himself, not Tom.* She looked at him sidelong, almost a shy look. "Is that from the morphine?"

"Well, it could be the morphine. He's been getting a lot of it, and it does work a change on the brain. Or the disease could be doing it. I've read it affects the mind in some manner, or at least in some cases."

She looked away from him again. "Will he be like this?" she asked him hoarsely. *From now on,* she meant. *Until he dies.*

He said bluntly, "Yes, I expect he will." In fact, he knew it would be worse before the end, quite a bit worse, so perhaps the kindness was in not saying so.

She began to sob tiredly, hiding her face behind her hands. Martha, who had been watching all this with a worried frown, immediately teared up too, and put a hand on Ruth's arm. Dr. McDonough didn't know Martha Lessen and had not, until this minute, taken in that the girl was dressed like a man, which he found curious and a provocation. He watched the two of them a moment and then began to pack up his instruments and bottles. By the time he was ready to leave, Ruth Kandel had more or less finished with her crying. She sat with her chin propped on her two hands, the long fingers pressed into her flushed cheeks, and looked out the window. Sunlight glaring off the snow made of the glass an opaque square of brightness. The girl sitting with Ruth had pulled her own hands into her lap and now stared down into them with a look of distress.

Dr. McDonough said, lifting the handles of his bag, "I imagine he'll sleep quite a while now. I'll come back later today and give him another hypodermic. From now on, he'll need two or three every day. I'll have to show you how to do it yourself. I don't know that I'll always be able to be here when he needs it." Ruth's mouth began to twist with the effort not to resume crying, but she said nothing. The doctor picked up his hat and his bag.

Martha didn't want to go on sitting there with Ruth Kandel—she was desperate to get out of the house and helpless to know how to manage it—and maybe Ruth already knew this. Before the doctor had crossed the porch to his motor, she turned her tired face to the girl and said, "Miss Lessen, I don't know where Fred has gone off to, so I wonder if you'd open the gate for the doctor's car before you go on with your circle ride." Martha gave her a look almost the twin to Fred's—wild with guilty relief.

While the doctor waited for Martha to open the gate and let him out of the yard, he looked at his watch— just past eleven. In earlier days he used to fall asleep behind a team of horses, would wrap the reins around the whip post and then around his wrist so if he dropped the reins they would slide down the post and jerk his wrist and wake him. Now that he had the Hudson he was able to get over the roads more quickly, but he had lost the benefit of sleeping as he drove. Eleven o'clock. The day stretched ahead of him, patients waiting to be seen. It would be hours yet before he could expect to climb into bed.

24

ANOTHER TRICK the old wrangler Roy Barrow had taught Martha Lessen was to put a half-hobble on a front foot, tie a loop in the rope and throw the rope over the horse's back, then draw it up through the loop to pull the front foot up. The horse would generally buck like crazy at that point but shortly he'd get tired and stand still and Martha would tell him what a good horse he was and give him a carrot or a piece of an apple. When he'd been done this way enough times, he wouldn't care if his foot was lifted up and he'd learn to stop whatever he was doing and just stand still when he felt pressure on his legs, so later if he stepped into wire hidden in brush or grass he'd naturally stop before he got tangled. And of course that also took care of any shoeing problems, because a horse done that way would lift his foot and stand for the shoer.

When Martha began to feel she had a little time to spare—the horses giving her less and less trouble—she started in with this foot work. She went after one horse at a time, repeating the lesson four or five days in a row at whatever corral the horse was in, until he got the idea. Some of the horses, having been brought along so far, hardly objected when she lifted their foot, and as soon as she knew they wouldn't give a farrier any inconvenience, she went on to another horse.

In the late part of February she left the Bliss place early in the morning riding Chuck, one of the Varden horses, and when she got to the Romers' she put a half-hobble on him and pulled his foot up. It was the third time he'd been done that way, and when he turned his head toward her and heaved a sigh she said to him, "I guess you've got it figured out," and she lowered his foot again and gave him a carrot. Maude and Big Brownie, both of them the Woodruffs' horses, watched this business with great interest, their heads up and ears pricked. "You'll get a turn," Martha said to them, though she knew they might have been interested only in the carrot.

She was tacking up Maude when Dorothy Romer came down from the house, her face pale and her hair unpinned. When Martha saw the state she was in, she first guessed Mr. Romer had gone into whiskey again and then thought it must be Dorothy who was drunk, her eyelids drooping, her voice slurred as she called in a weak way, "Helen and Clifford are both sick."

Martha said without stopping what she was doing, "I'm sorry to hear it."

Dorothy touched her forehead with trembly fingers and sat down suddenly in the mud, which didn't surprise or alarm Martha, who had experience of serious drinkers. But after a moment of considering, she left the palomino standing in the corral with the cinch not yet tightened, and she went unhurriedly through the rails and over to the woman and squatted down next to her. "Mrs. Romer, are you sick? Do you want me to go for the doctor?" She didn't smell anything on Dorothy's breath except a sickly sourness. She took hold of one of her hands.

"I'm afraid it's the ptomaine poisoning," Dorothy said, and started in with a kind of dry weeping. Her cold hand lay weakly in Martha's. "I don't know where Reuben is. Will you take us to the hospital?"

Martha's heart began to beat loudly in her ears. She said, "I'll have to go and get the wagon." Dorothy swallowed slowly and put her hands down in the mud and pushed to get up; Martha helped her stand again and would have helped her back to the house except Dorothy pulled away and said, "Go on," and made an impatient fluttery gesture toward the pasture where Reuben kept his horses.

She brought in the horses by calling and whistling and holding out a piece of apple, and she harnessed the two who looked to be the most cooperative and hitched them to the Romers' wagon and drove around to the front porch of the house. Dorothy was sitting on the porch steps leaning against an upright, the baby, Alice, lying across her haunches. "I don't know where Reuben is," she said again, with the same tired, tearless, terrible sobbing. Martha was afraid to look too closely at Alice, lying still and pale in the lap of Dorothy's dress.

She went into the house and found Helen and Clifford in a single bed, their limbs flaccid on the tangled sheets. Their eyes followed Martha with a desperate, half-lidded concentration but they didn't lift their hands up to her or speak to her. They were breathing shallowly through open mouths. She carried them out one at a time and laid them down in the back of the wagon, wrapped in the blankets she had stripped from the bed. Then she helped Dorothy climb into the back and lie down with her children. She found a tarp and put it over them all like a tent in case it began to rain, and she drove out of the yard and down the rutted farm lane. At the outskirts of Shelby she stopped a man to ask where the hospital was and he told her there was just one hospital in the valley and it was in Bingham, so she drove on the five more miles. She drove carefully, not to bump their heads on the floorboards. It began to rain lightly, ticking against the tarp and against her hat.

She passed W.G. Boyd's little place at the edge of town and shortly after that she came on his grandson, Joey, on his way home from town. Joey had lately been spending his afternoons and Saturdays ranging the hills collecting the shed antlers of bull elk and buck deer, which brought a few cents a pound from Graham Ellis at the hardware store, and he was walking back from the store and jingling the money in his pocket when Martha saw him. He ran up to the wagon and ran alongside, grinning and splashing his galoshes in the puddles, and he called to her, "Hey, Martha, whose wagon are you driving?"

"Joey, where is the hospital?" she said, and at once he became grave and frightened and told her where it was and then stopped and stood in the road, watching the wagon go away from him.

The Bingham Hospital occupied a brick building that had been the Bingham High School before a bigger school was built closer to the center of town. It was a private hospital owned by Dr. McDonough and Dr. Kelly and an investor who also owned an automobile parts and supply store. The staff kept cows and chickens in a field behind the hospital and had to interrupt their nursing duties to go into the basement and stoke the furnace, but ptomaine poisoning from poorly canned food was a serious matter they were familiar with, and the man Martha had asked for directions in Shelby had telephoned ahead; several hospital people came out and down the wet stone steps as soon as she pulled up in front, and they carried the Romer children inside and walked Dorothy up the steps between two minders, and no one paid a bit of attention to Martha.

It was unclear to her what she ought to do next. She

got down and led the horses out of the driveway and unhitched them from the wagon. They had not even broken a sweat but she hunted up a gunnysack and wiped them down thoroughly and walked them back and forth as if they had run hell-for-leather every mile of the way from the Romers' to Bingham. Then she turned them out on the weeds and grass of the vacant lot next door and sat down on the tailgate of the wagon and waited. The rain quit and then started again and then quit.

She was glad to see W.G. Boyd walking up the hill from town. W.G., from the first she met him, had reminded her of Roy Barrow, the L Bar L wrangler who had got her started with breaking horses; it was not only his arthritic limp but the touch he had with animals, which was a natural gift but also a learned kindness. Martha held W.G. very dear and envied Joey his childhood in company with the old man.

She walked down to meet him, and he called up to her, "What's happened, child?" Walking to the hospital, he had prepared himself to hear that it was Tom Kandel, dead of cancer—that Martha had been a witness to Tom's terrible last suffering.

"It might be ptomaine poisoning," she said, and fought not to begin crying. W.G. frowned and shook his head without understanding what she had said, and then she realized she had not said who was sick. "It's Mrs. Romer and her children."

He didn't know them, which was a relief to him. He took Martha by the hand and said, "Joe was pretty worried," and they walked back up the hill and sat down together on the tailgate. She swung her boots nervously, which set her stiff leather chaps creaking.

"Have you been breaking one of their horses?" he asked her.

"Yes sir. It's the one called Mata Hari."

He nodded as if this cleared up matters for him. After a few minutes, he said, "I'll just go inside and ask how things are going," and she gave him a grateful look.

He was gone half an hour or better. When he came out again he patted Martha's arm and said, "I'm afraid the baby is gone."

"Oh!" Tears sprang in her eyes. She turned her head from him.

"It might be a good long while," he said, without saying a good long while to what. "Why don't you come on home with me and have a bite to eat. There isn't anything you can do anyway."

She had by now remembered Maude standing in the corral and she shook her head. "I'd better get back. I left Maude standing there half dressed." W.G. lifted his eyebrows in surprise, and after a moment she caught on to what she'd said. "Maude's a horse," she said, frowning, and W.G. made a slight dry sound of enlightenment.

"I should look for Mr. Romer, too," Martha said while she was hitching up the horses again. "He should know about his family."

She drove the eight or nine miles back to the Romer

place, every inch of it remembering why she didn't like driving a big old farm wagon, and trying not to think about Dorothy and her children, and trying not to think she might find Maude with her hind foot caught in a loose cinch or down on her knees in the mud, tangled in trailing reins. But the mare was standing indignantly in the corral, her head lifted high to keep from stepping on the reins, and the loose McClelland saddle askew on her back so the cantle hung off her shoulder; she whinnied a shrill complaint when Martha drove into the yard. Martha unharnessed the Romers' draft horses and turned them into the pasture and she stripped the tack off Maude and gave her a carrot and a ration of grain and then she saddled Big Brownie, who hadn't had to stand rooted to his reins all day, and rode back to Shelby.

Elwha was a dry county, so she didn't know where Reuben would have gone to find his liquor or how to go about finding him. She stopped in at the power and light office because she knew he had a contract with them to supply wood, and then she just went along the street inquiring at likely shops and stores if they knew Reuben Romer or where he might be, and she told them his family was sick and needed him. When she'd been at this for quite a while, a man in a barbershop studied her in the mirror and said, "You might try that store down there at Eightmile Crossing." This was a place she had never been to, a roadhouse and store eight miles down Lewis Pass on the road to Canyon City and just over the Grant County line. She knew she

266

might spend the rest of the day riding down there and back without finding him, but no one else had given her any idea where to look.

The Little Bird Woman River sauntered across the valley floor between the Whitehorns and the Clarks Range at an agile but dignified clip, and then at the east end of the valley picked up speed and made a dash downhill, cutting a steep gorge through cliffs and terraces and talus slopes of dark basalt blotched and streaked with red iron oxide, which was the Lewis Pass. The road had been put through in the heyday when the canyon had been settled end to end by the farms of people coming late to the game, claiming homesteads in that marginal land along the river where they could graze a few head of stock on the small handkerchiefs of grass at the bottom and plant alfalfa hay on the patches of flat benchland. In those early days the road had carried a lot of wagon traffic, but the farms had quickly starved out and now the canyon was owned, by and large, by the mule deer and the whitebark pines; the grassland benches were summer range for a few ranches whose winter headquarters were down around Long Creek.

The road, twisting along the bottom of the river gorge, crossed the river and crossed it again—six bridges in fifteen miles—and never out of range of the ringing, boisterous cannon-racket of water pouring downhill between stone walls. The road was almost entirely built on bald scabs of rock so in rainy weather it was a puddled track but muddy only where springs or small creeks brought dirt down from the brushy draws.

The two cars that passed Martha, bumping and jarring over the rough, ridged rock, weren't having any trouble getting through the stream wash. A hardware salesman headed up from Canyon City to his customers in Elwha County stopped his car and shouted over the rattle of the engine, no, he hadn't stopped at Eightmile Crossing, didn't know if a Mr. Romer was in the roadhouse there. In the second car a young couple fully decked out in dusters and goggles and gloves smiled and waved jauntily as they went by, but did not slow to talk. Martha turned Big Brownie to the side of the road each time, and spoke to the horse approvingly as he tolerated the noise of the passing cars, their rattle and throb briefly outshouting the noise of the river.

About the time Martha reached the third bridge the sun broke clear, which threw all the west side of the gorge into shadow and flooded the east side with bright, straw-colored light. She was carrying in her coat pocket a lunch that Louise Bliss had packed in the morning, and she finally gave in to hunger and sat on a rock at the edge of the sunlight and ate her sandwiches while the horse cropped the skimpy grass that sloped down from the road to the river, and then she went on.

At five miles into the canyon, on the steep downgrade between the third and fourth bridge, Martha came around a hairpin curve in the road and found a car whining toward her backward, which wasn't a surprise, as in those days quite a few automobiles would back up the steep hills in reverse to keep the gas running into the carburetor. There was hardly room for her to move over at that particular place, the road caught between a dark wall of basalt and a steep talus slope that dropped down to the river, but she moved Brownie close to the wall and put her hand along his neck to console him while they waited for the car to get by. There were two men in the car, the driver peering back over his shoulder and steering with one hand while his mouth steadily moved in discourse with his passenger, words she couldn't hear over the noise of the river and the high howl of the reverse gear. When he saw Martha he gave her a startled look and must have said something that caused the other man in the car to turn and look, and she saw that this second man was Reuben Romer.

His left eye was droopy and watering—he had spent the day far gone in drink, which was no more than Martha expected—and he was a bit late to recognize her, but then he gave her a lazy, lit-up smile. She raised herself in the stirrups to shout to him, but by then he was turning from her, leaning across the other man to press a horn button bolted to the side of the steering column, a Klaxon horn that blared out suddenly, cutting across the rumbling of the river, and Big Brownie flung his head back in startled fear and backed his rump into the wall and then lunged forward. If she'd been deeper in her seat it wouldn't have unbalanced her, but she half-fell across his shoulder and lost the left stirrup, and when Reuben blew the horn again the horse seemed to just rise up in the air. Martha twisted her fist in his mane to keep aboard without being able to stop him or turn him, and he cleared the road, cleared the car, and hurled himself right off the edge of the road, right out into the sunlight, and she let go her grip without realizing she'd decided to, landed hard in a shower of gravel and rock dust, and in the stunned moment afterward heard the car going on up the road, the horn bellowing twice more to approve the entertainment, and then the whine of the motor swallowed by the curve of rock wall.

She didn't sit up but went on lying where she was, waiting for the sky to settle and come into focus; and then she turned her head to look down the steep, shingly drop to the river, the gravel still sliding and rattling down to where Brownie was gaining his feet, moaning with fear, his hide muddy and scraped, his reins caught up in the dense thickets along the river-bank. She was amazed he wasn't dead. She sat, and her left arm flared in startlingly bright pain, a pain she recognized—she had broken bones three or four times before—and she began to sob, not only from pain but from despair: the horses she was breaking weren't all the way finished yet and she was afraid she might not be able to finish them with her arm in plaster.

She waited until she felt able to stop crying and then she lifted the broken arm carefully with her right hand and guided it into the pocket of her coat and clamped her left elbow against her ribs and waited until she could breathe and then she looked down at Brownie again, considering grimly all the difficulties of getting him out of that steep gorge without breaking more bones—her own or the horse's. The gravelly bank was loose and slippery and damn near standing on its end. If she managed to get down to him from here, she didn't see how she could lead him back up the same way, even if it turned out he wasn't knee-sprung or torn up.

After a while she got carefully onto her feet and recovered her hat from where it was lying in the weeds and she walked down the road a couple of hundred yards until the dropoff flattened somewhat and became a shelving bench, and she stepped down carefully through the rocks and brush to the river and spent the better part of half an hour getting back upstream, picking her way through shrubwood, wading carefully out into the rocky river margins, to reach the place where the horse was stranded.

Brownie was trembling from fear and shock, his hide covered with lather and sweat plastered over with rock dust. His head hung almost to his knees and a yellow froth had dried around his mouth. His off front foot was tangled in a coil of rusted barbed wire some farmer had tossed down into the ravine and blood ran down his leg onto the ground. The saddle was muddy and scraped and one stirrup had torn partway off. Martha said quietly to the horse, "Hey there, Big Brownie," and took her time easing up to him, but when she could she rubbed her face tenderly against his cheek and breathed into his nostrils, and he breathed into hers. She sobbed two or three times. "I'm sorry," she said, which could have been meant for just about anybody but was meant for the horse.

She untangled his reins from the thicket and ran her right hand carefully over his trembling hide and said to him, "I don't discover any broken bones," to encourage them both. Then she found a flat rock and put it under a likely place in the barbed wire and picked up another rock and began carefully and slowly to pound and grind the wire between the two, and when the wire broke she bent the ends back out of the way—all of this done awkwardly with her right hand—and then picked another place in the wire to work on. It was a slow process one-handed, and her right hand not the one she would have liked to be using. She had to cut through the coil at four places before Brownie could step free. Then she spent a slow hour coaxing him back through the brush downstream to the place where they could climb up to the road, which was empty of traffic and likely to remain so, and she started out leading the horse uphill toward Shelby. Brownie was favoring his off shoulder, bringing his leg forward with a peculiar dragging motion; but he set the foot down all right, so she didn't think the damage was to his leg. The foreleg that had been caught in wire had stopped bleeding and she didn't think it was a crippling cut.

A few cow camps were scattered in the breaks of the canyon, used as overnight stops by cowboys trailing cattle between winter and summer ranges. Briggs Newton, who came upon Martha Lessen and her horse an hour or so after they started walking back up the hill, had been headed up to one of the camps. It was late February but the weather had been mild and the recent rains had greened the timbered uplands—some penstemon and wild iris were already blooming in sheltered places on the slopes of the canyon—and he was riding up to take a look at the grassland benches and make up his mind if it might be all right to move some of his cattle. He was deeply astonished and alarmed to see a young girl dressed like Calamity Jane limping up the middle of the road, cradling an arm he guessed to be broken and leading a big lame horse that was all scraped up and muddied, with his mane full of burrs and broken-off twigs.

The river made a hell of a noise going through that canyon and he didn't want to scare her, coming up behind her, so he coughed a couple of times in a loud way and when she half-turned toward him he called out, "Evening," because by then the light was beginning to go out of the canyon. The girl was pale and suffering, he could see, resting her arm gingerly in the pocket of her coat, but she just forced a smile and then turned back around and went on walking along the road.

When he had come up alongside her he said, "You got throwed did you?" which he intended merely as a way into conversation, but thought afterward was a stupid thing to ask.

She said, "Yes sir, more or less," and kept walking along. She seemed to assume Briggs would pass by, go on with his business and let her go on with hers, which he might have done without an argument except she looked to be very close to the age of his daughter Devota. He said, "There's a telephone down at Eightmile at that store. Why don't I put you on this horse and we can go down there. Those folks can telephone for a doctor to see if your arm is broke, and the doctor can set it if it is."

The girl looked over at the horse Briggs was riding, which was a gray gelding he called Teddy, but she kept walking and said, "Thank you, I'd just rather go on back home."

"Where is that? Up at Shelby?"

"Yes sir, near there."

"Well that's a good three- or four-miles hike, is my guess, and pretty much every bit of it uphill. You come on now, and I'll take you down to that store at Eightmile. It ain't but a couple of miles, and you can ring your folks from there."

"Thank you, I'd just rather go on home."

He thought about Devota and what he might want if somebody came upon her walking up the road with a broken arm and a lame horse, and miles from home. "Well all right, then. But you're in no shape to walk home, and that horse of yours is in no shape to be ridden, and I'm heading up to Shelby myself." This last was a lie, but he figured she wouldn't give him any leeway if he told her the truth. "I'm not in no hurry and I'm wearing my broke-in boots and my arm ain't broke, and there's no reason for you to walk when you can ride. So why don't I get down off Teddy and let you be the one riding."

She looked at him and at the horse, and from her look he expected her to give him an argument—to tell him it wasn't her foot that was broke or something along those lines—but what she said was "He's a nice-looking horse. His name's Teddy?"

He had almost saddled a different horse for the ride up into the canyon, a skittery knothead named Adios, and it occurred to him to thank God for small favors. Teddy was the most tame beast he owned, and he had a smooth and level walk for carrying a girl with a broken arm. But he could see he had to get around her pride, so he grinned and said to her, every word of it a lie, "Well here's an idea. I bought this horse for my daughter who hasn't done much riding at all, and I was trying him out tonight to see how he'll do. It'd be a favor to me if you got up on him, because I guess if he's gentle enough for carrying a girl with a broken arm, he'll be gentle enough for a girl who ain't rode much."

Martha looked at Briggs and began to smile, which even in the failing light he could make out the meaning of—his wife had been telling him for thirty-five years he was the world's worst liar and ought to give up trying. The girl said, "I appreciate it, but I'm all right walking, it's not my foot that's broke."

Briggs had to laugh. "Well all right, but I'll just walk along with you for a ways, if you don't mind the company." He got down from the horse and fell into step with the girl.

After a while she said, looking at Teddy with somewhat more attention, "He's got a bright look to his eye and I like the way he moves. I imagine he's a good horse."

"He is," Briggs said, and then he took one last run at her: "He's the most imperturbable horse I ever met, and if you change your mind and decide to try him out, you will discover him to have a smooth and level walk."

She gave the horse another close look, her face shadowed by her big hat so he couldn't quite see her expression, but Briggs wasn't surprised when she slipped his hook. She said, gesturing with the reins of her own horse, "This horse I was riding is still pretty green, but I think he'll turn out as good as any I ever met. He was tangled up in barb wire and he just stayed put, he didn't start jumping around and make it worse. His name is Big Brownie."

Briggs had been watching the horse, how he brought his off front leg forward. "Looks like he's sprained his shoulder," he said.

"Yes sir. But he'll be all right if I can get him fomented and give him some rest."

"I guess that's right."

Briggs went on talking to her about various things, not to distract the girl from her broken arm but to distract himself from the boredom of a long slow walk up a darkening road. He spoke of his wife, Oleta, and their four children, the youngest being Devota, who was just a bit younger than Martha, and he described to her the ranch he and his brother ran together, which they had got from their father and enlarged and improved upon. It was the first place you came to after the outfall of the canyon, he said, their land running west to east on the south side of the Whitehorns, with the broad lower reach of the Little Bird Woman River bisecting it near the midpoint. They had about a hundred acres of good bent grass for hay, he told her—two cuttings in a wet year—and plenty of grazing in the fall after the last cutting. There were still some decent patches of bunch grass on the slopes where they turned their cows and horses in the spring and winter, and timber higher up on the mountains for firewood and posts, and some good big logs for building sheds, and an allotment in the gorge for summer grazing. He allowed that some of Grant County wasn't too beautiful or too prosperous—a lot of rock and sagebrush and too dry for growing wheat—but he and his family had a beautiful and prosperous piece of it.

Even in those days the Newton ranch was well along toward overgrazed, and in later years the brothers quarreled and then one of them died and the ranch got broken up and sold; and in the 1930s after Canyon City burned to the ground, the old Newton hay fields were used as dusty holding pens for a stock-feeding operation that shipped steers out in rail cars from John

Day. But Martha had formed a picture of Briggs Newton's ranch as a paradise straight out of a Western romance, and she said on an impulse, "Maybe I'll come down to Grant County in the fall if you've got any horses need breaking to saddle." This offer sprang out of her old plan, the idea that once she got away from her parents' house she would live a footloose cowboy life, going all around the countryside looking for horses to break. It didn't much matter that in recent weeks she had been thinking she might want to stay a while longer in Elwha County, hire on with the Woodruffs or the Thiedes or the Blisses after the circle ride was finished. Briggs Newton didn't offer her any work, and from his silence Martha understood that breaking bones wasn't much of a credential for somebody who was breaking horses.

When they topped out of the canyon, Walter Irwin's was the first farm they came to. Lights were still burning in his house and in the little house Hilda Birkmeier was staying in, and Martha told Briggs these were folks she knew and that Mr. Irwin had a telephone. Standing there at the turnoff to Irwin's farm, she thanked Briggs for keeping her company and he said, "Don't mention it. You take care of that arm and that there lame horse." After a moment he also said, purely out of politeness, "And you come see me when you get to Grant County, maybe I'll put you to work." She offered Briggs her unbroken hand, which he took gingerly but didn't pump, and then he climbed up on Teddy and turned him back down the road to hunt up his cow camp in the moonlight. Martha hadn't ever believed him when he said he was going all the way to Shelby, and by now they had both forgotten his telling her that.

Hilda came to the door in pajamas with her hands full of sewing and an anxious look on her face—it wasn't usual for somebody to stop by the farm after dark—but she put down the sewing and pulled on a coat over her pajamas and stuck her feet in yard boots and came right outside when Martha told her she had a lame horse and a broken arm. Hilda knew how to keep a hot poultice on a sprain, she said to Martha's question, and she knew how to make liniment and how to clean a cut, so Martha left Brownie with her and walked up the hill to Irwin's to ask the use of his telephone.

She was desperate to call the hospital in Bingham to inquire about Dorothy and the children, and then she intended to ring up the Blisses and beg a ride back to the ranch—she had the idea she might get by with tightly wrapping her arm and not seeing a doctor at all. But Irwin, alarmed at the sight of Martha arriving pale and filthy on his porch, forced her to sit in a chair while he made the telephone calls himself; he didn't take it seriously when she said she didn't want her arm put in plaster. She had to wait, at the point of tears from tiredness and pain and nervous strain, while he called Shelby to locate a doctor, someone available at this hour to receive a girl with a broken arm, and then rang up the Blisses with the news about their injured broncobuster, and went back and forth with them until it was settled that Irwin himself would bring Martha into Shelby to the doctor's, and the Blisses would come for her after her arm was set. When Irwin finally called the hospital to ask about the Romers and then hung up the telephone and turned to tell her the children and their mother were still sick but evidently had stepped away from death's door, Martha was too far gone to hold back the crying. Irwin stood across the room from her without a single idea how he should handle the case of this crying girl in front of him, and in a few moments she was able to tighten her mouth and stop the tears.

"I don't usually cry, Mr. Irwin," she said to him in embarrassment. "I'm just so glad they're still hanging on."

Irwin, who had seen her come close to tears the day he had fired Alfred Logerwell, by now believed it *was* her usual habit to cry. He said generously, "Well, in these cases I suppose a girl ought to cry, and a man ought not to," and he smiled slightly to emphasize the point—that he himself was not the crying kind. The girls Martha knew, girls from farms and ranches, weren't much given to crying, or no more so than the men, and she might have told him so, except she had hardly taken in what he said. She closed her eyes and leaned her head back in the chair and immediately saw in the reddish darkness Reuben Romer's face as he turned toward her in the car, and her own hand grabbing hold of Big Brownie's coarse mane, and the blurred camelback trunk of the car sliding past her on the rock-ribbed road.

After a few minutes she opened her eyes again and discovered Irwin still standing there, leaning forward watching her with an anxious expression, his hands thrust into his pockets. She didn't know how long he had been looking at her, and this startled and embarrassed her.

"I ought to go down and see how Hilda is coming along with Brownie," she said without really wishing to, and that woke Mr. Irwin to the matter at hand. He had to crank up his auto-truck so he could take Martha into Shelby, he said, and while he was down there putting water in the radiator he'd find out from Hilda how that lame horse was doing. He put on his coat and hat and went out, and it was a great relief to Martha that for the next ten or fifteen minutes she was able to sit in the house alone without needing to move and without anybody studying her.

Later on, after Dr. Padham had set the arm, and the Blisses had driven her back to the ranch, and Louise had made Martha go up to Miriam's unused bedroom to spend the night on a decent bed, Louise telephoned the Woodruff sisters to let them know what had happened to the girl, or as much of the story as they had been able to pry out of her, though of course the person who was meant to receive this information was Henry Frazer.

On the Sunday following Will Wright's skating party, Henry had borrowed the Woodruff sleigh a second time and driven Martha up the narrowing valley of Blue Stem Creek into the foothills of the Clarks Range to see a pile of rocks some people claimed was an Indian grave or sacred site, and they walked around and found a few old arrowheads and had a picnic on the snow; and the next Sunday, with the snow gone and the sky clearing, they went on horseback to the two-lane bowling alley in Opportunity and shared a piece of pie afterward at a luncheonette and when they walked back to the stable to get their horses Henry asked if it would be all right if he held her hand, and she said it was.

Then cows began calving in the fields near the ranch house and Henry was at work from daybreak until after dark without much of a break, and even though the sisters were taking the night shift, he had been getting up at midnight to see if they needed him to help out with anything and sometimes they did. With Henry busy all the time, Martha had gone back to riding the circle on Sundays and they had seen each other only a few times in the past couple of weeks, occasions when he happened to be at the barns or the corrals fooling around with an orphan calf as Martha rode up to change horses.

Louise and the Woodruffs had been watching with great satisfaction this business between Henry and Martha—all of them tickled to death that Henry, after two or three near-misses, girls entirely the wrong sort for him, was finally courting a girl who suited him to a tee, and all of them amazed and gratified that Martha appeared willing to be courted. Louise had said on the telephone it wasn't a bad break, and ordinarily none of them would have considered a broken arm a matter of great concern; but at the breakfast table in the morning, after the sisters had passed on to Henry what they knew, they prevailed on him to go over to the Bliss ranch and bring back an eyewitness account of how badly Martha was stove up. They told him they could handle things, for heaven's sake, for the two or three hours he'd be gone.

Henry didn't give the sisters much of an argument. He hadn't seen Martha at all in the past few days, and the calving had started to taper off, and he wanted to hear for himself exactly what had happened. Henry Frazer possessed a somewhat warm temper, and he was already thinking he might want to call on Reuben Romer and was already sorting out what he might want to say to him at that visit.

Martha was sitting in the front room of the Bliss house drinking coffee and reading the newspaper when Henry showed up, and her face colored when she saw him. Louise had extracted from her a promise that she wouldn't lift a finger for a good twenty-four hours, so she was sitting there in Louise's borrowed kimono, which was embarrassing on several counts, not least because she didn't want Henry to think she was lazy or frail. But he laughed when he saw her lounging and said, "I heard you figured out how to get a few days off," and his teasing took some of the heat out of her embarrassment. Henry hadn't really been worried about Martha but now that he was with her and could see for himself that she was in good shape, his jaw loosened right up.

Louise left the two of them alone in the front room—she busied herself making a certain amount of noise in the kitchen—so they were able to talk together quietly. Martha wouldn't tell him more than the bare story about the accident down in Lewis Pass and played down Reuben's part in it, and wouldn't blame Brownie either. She should have had a better seat, she told him stubbornly, and it was her fault she hadn't accustomed any of the horses to the sound of a car horn. She was more interested in praising Brownie for what he did right. "That horse just stood there so good, with his foot all tangled in the barb wire," she said. "I was so proud of him." And when Henry said, "He had a good teacher," she ducked her chin to try to hide her smile.

It wasn't until late that day that Jeanne and Frank McWilliams, stopping by the Romer farm to offer their condolences over the death of baby Alice, discovered Reuben Romer dead in the house. He had come home and eaten the same canned string beans that had sickened his family, and had died alone without ever knowing what had happened to his wife and children, or that his youngest child had died the day before while he was drinking whiskey at the roadhouse at Eightmile Crossing.

25

LATE IN THE NIGHT near the end of February Ruth Kandel woke abruptly without memory of the dream that had set her heart racing. She sat up carefully in the bed and when Tom didn't stir she put on a sweater over her nightdress, went out to the front room, and pulled a chair close to the little bit of remaining heat in the stove and took her knitting into her lap. This was something she had begun doing—knitting or taking up embroidery for half an hour or so—to quiet her mind and body before trying again to sleep beside her husband now that both she and Tom had become such restless sleepers. She had turned the heel of the sock the night before and was knitting toward the toe, every stitch pulled tight against the next one, loop and pull, loop and pull, the khaki wool yarn hard and smooth in her hands. She counted stitches, and in the hypnotic rhythm of the counting was not able to think about much of anything consequential.

What she had felt lately, watching over Tom, was a terrible kind of aloneness—not the feeling that her friends had abandoned her, but that she couldn't possibly expect them to know what was happening to Tom, and to her, and to Fred, and could never expect to find the words to tell them. After that terrible night when she had had to send Fred for Dr. McDonough, the morphine Tom was getting or the progress of the cancer had made him by turns vacant or belligerent, inclined toward inexplicable behavior and repetitive restlessness. He hardly spoke to her at all now, was not able to follow a train of thought or a conversation, and he no longer slept for very long but stirred awake all through the day and night and then walked the house, or sat with his elbows on his knees, rocking and frowning, not answering when she spoke to him. He was so weak and unsteady on his feet that when he stood to urinate in the night jar or went out to the privy she was afraid he would fall and crack his head or break a bone. He swayed and repeatedly had to stop himself from buckling at the knees, but he was oddly prudish or stubborn about his body, obstinate and silent in refusing to let her steady him, help him with his toileting, help him dress, bathe, comb his hair. She could no longer leave him alone in the house for fear he might wander into trouble—take all the books off their shelves and scatter them in random piles on the floor, or stoke the stove until she worried the chimney would catch fire and burn the house down. When he woke in the night she had to get up with him now, had to tiredly cajole and persuade to keep him from heading out to the road in the freezing cold or in a downpour in his underwear. When he finally slept, his legs and arms twitched and jerked and shifted cease-lessly under the quilts and kept Ruth from sleeping herself; in any case she tried not to let herself fall into a deep sleep: if he got out of bed without waking her, she was afraid he might do himself some kind of harm.

Dr. McDonough had lately been after her to put Tom into the hospital in Bingham but she was determined to keep him at home as long as possible. She didn't trust the hospital staff—quite a few of the trained nurses had gone off to war—and she didn't want Tom to die surrounded by strangers. The terrible truth was that Tom himself had become a stranger to her, which to her mind was almost the worst thing. Lavinia Horne, whose husband had frozen to death a year earlier hiking back from Owl Creek Canyon after going down there to buy himself some moonshine, had told Ruth to count her blessings: at least Tom's death wouldn't be a shock, she would know it was coming, could be prepared for it and able to say goodbye properly. But Ruth had been thunderstruck by Tom's sudden worsening—his mind going out of him before his soul—and she felt cheated of the chance to say goodbye, almost as much as if he'd dropped dead from apoplexy on the kitchen floor. She felt she hadn't told Tom what she ought to have told him—had been holding back on the important things, expecting to say them when the end drew near, and now there was no one to say them to. She had lost him already, weeks before she expected him to die.

The regular counting of the knitted stitches kept her from thinking of any boy's foot inside the sock she was making, any foot that had flesh and nails, calluses, blisters, a real foot that might be torn away by a bomb blast or a falling fuse. She didn't think about Tom either, or not directly, nothing beyond the wordless relief of escaping from their little bedroom and his restless movements in the bed. The light in the front room was poor but she didn't think about the oil lamp on the table beside her, how the wick needed trimming; she didn't think about the mud Fred had tracked in on the floors earlier in the day or the dust on all the tables deep enough to sweep a finger through—how she never could stay ahead of her housework now, not any of it, not even the dusting. The entirety of her tired mind was bent on pulling the stitches over and then under the needle, one by one.

She hadn't been knitting more than ten minutes when she heard Tom stirring around in the bedroom, and her stomach tightened as it used to when Fred was a colicky baby and his first faint whimpering at night was almost always a signal of hours of inconsolable wailing. She let down her knitting into her lap but didn't immediately go into the other room to start the wearying work of persuading her husband back to bed; she first had to gather up her will. Her tiredness, now that Tom was so sick, was an inexpressible heaviness in all her limbs, a tiredness not only of the body. She often prayed not for Tom but for relief from what was happening—just a few hours without the strain of caring for him.

The springs creaked and he suddenly appeared in the front room, though she hadn't heard his feet shuffling over the floorboards. He stood in the dim light, his fleshless bones loose in the union suit, and blinked at her with a curiously puzzled expression.

"Ruth, what are you doing out here in the middle of the night?" he said. This was so much like Tom, her Tom, that her eyes burned suddenly with tears.

"I couldn't sleep," she said, "so I've been knitting."

"You're crying. Why are you crying?" He continued to look at her in frowning bewilderment. "Something's wrong, I feel it. What's happening? Tell me what's wrong."

There was such vehemence in his voice, intensity in his face, that it frightened her. What he was asking was ambiguous, undefined, but she thought she knew what it was. "I couldn't sleep," she said with a kind of desperation, and then, "You're dying. Do you remember?"

He looked at her in stunned silence. "I'm dying?" His eyes welled with tears. "Why am I dying?"

"Oh Tom, you have a cancer." She began to cry in earnest, and his face twisted into grief. He came blindly across the room to her and knelt at her chair, took her into his arms in a fierce grasp, and they clung together crying. "I'm sorry, I'm sorry," he said, with his mouth in his wife's tangled hair.

Fred by then had come staggering out of his little bedroom, his face flushed with sleep and terror. He cried out, "What! What's happening?" and they tried to stop their sobbing for his sake but could not. Tom put out his hand wordlessly to the boy and Fred fell onto them both, twining his arms around them, his thin body racked by coughs of grief.

It was a gift of grace, this last lucid evening of Tom

Kandel's life. In the morning he was dim and silent and vacant again, and before he died—a week, less than a week—he would worsen, become bedridden, agitated night and day with terrible pain or an unknowable anxiety. But that night after they had cried themselves out Tom sat on the floor, his bony spine resting against his wife's knees, one hand cupping his son's head to his shoulder and the other gripping his wife's hand as she leaned over him and rested her cheek against the top of his hair, and he said every important thing that had gone unsaid. He told them how much he loved them both, and how much he loved their life together, and how proud he was of Fred. He told them he would miss seeing his son a man and married, would miss meeting and holding his grandchildren, but—a dim smile—"if your mother is right in her beliefs of a life beyond the grave, then when you hear the floor creak at night it will be me looking in on you." He talked to them about the farm: if they had to sell the place after he was gone they should remember that it was possible to make a good life anywhere. He asked both of them, but especially Fred, to read Montaigne and Walt Whitman and to pay attention to what those men had to say about dying and about death and about happiness. He told Ruth that he would miss seeing her grow to be an old woman, which surprised her—such an odd and deeply loving thing to say—and which made her cry again. He asked her to put their wedding photograph and a Kodak picture of Fred in the pocket of the suit he would be buried in, "just in case you've been right in your church-belief all these years, and when I'm in heaven I'm able to take the pictures out and look at them." And he said to Ruth that she was a strong-minded woman, as strong as any woman he had ever known, and he expected her to get back on her feet in no time.

There were long silences between the things he said to them. Neither Ruth nor Fred spoke very much. Ruth would remember afterward that she had meant to say certain things herself and that she had not said them. She and Fred murmured "yes" over and over, and breathed in the warm scent of Tom, the realness, the aliveness of him, while they waited for what he would say next. Afterward their memories differed in small ways. Fred thought he heard his father say that happiness was not a state of mind, that it was moments here and there in a life, and the important thing was just to try to be well content. Ruth remembered Tom telling them they'd eventually become happy again after he was gone, that happiness was the natural and desirable state and they shouldn't feel guilty or selfish about that, but look for and relish the coming moments of joy.

When Tom died a few days later Ruth was out of the room, had gone into the kitchen to reheat the pot of black coffee for the third time, and when she came in again and found he was gone she sat down at the edge of the bed. She felt a choking in her throat, a need to gasp, to catch her breath again and again as if his death had been unexpected. She picked up his hand and held it, stroked his forearm over and over, smoothing the fine hair flat with her palm. *It was only just those few minutes I was gone! Couldn't you have waited?* She was so very tired, it was hard to sort out what she felt; it was hard afterward to remember if she had even cried, and if she had, what the tears were about. Later she would realize that these were the first minutes of his unending absence and of her beginning to experience a kind of meaninglessness in the world, a nullity that she would be years overcoming, but she didn't realize that just yet.

Before she went to wake up Fred, before she told him his father had died, she bathed Tom's body right there in their bed. She sluiced the washcloth, the warm soapy water, very gently over his bony ribs and shoulders, over his skin grown so thin and tender. She laved the water in slow strokes over his long, pale limbs, lifting one after the other his flaccid arms, his legs. He had lost so much weight she thought he would be easy to move, but his body was leaden, unwieldy. She turned him partway onto his side, propped against the pillows, in order to wash his back and his nether parts. Afterward she swabbed out his mouth, his ears, soaped and rinsed his lank and greasy hair and gave him a haircut with scissors; she cleaned and trimmed his fingernails, scraped the whiskers from his slack cheeks with a razor and soap. His eyes behind the half-closed lids did not watch her. He was still warm under her hands, his body as familiar to her, as intimately known, as her own.

26

MOST OF THE MEN in those days belonged to fraternal clubs. Every up-and-coming town had a Sons of the Pioneers, an Odd Fellows Lodge, a Knights of Pythias, or Woodmen of the World—two or three brotherhoods whose purpose was to give men a reason to get together. Women had their own secret societies and organized sisterhoods but in general didn't need to look for excuses to gather. In Elwha County groups of women were always coming together to finish a quilt for a family that had been burned out or to embroider a burial dress and coverlet for a poor dead baby whose mother was still sick in bed with eclampsia. And when the war came on, women found plenty of purpose and reason to congregate, knitting socks for soldiers and sailors or preparing comfort kits for the Red Cross to ship overseas.

Before the war and during it, Louise Bliss was a member of several needlework circles, none of which was formal enough to require a name or a fixed meeting date. She wasn't the sort to belong to Eastern Star or that kind of sorority but she was a founding member of a study club of women who called themselves the Elwha Valley Literary Society, which met in the Shelby Grange Hall every first Thursday of the month with the stated purpose of keeping up with current events and the issues of the day and discussing the

293

great works of literature. Louise had been a young woman with young children when the club first began to meet, and in those early years of the new century when almost everything seemed to be going well and people still had faith in themselves and in this country's right conduct, debate and discussion in the Literary Society had often given way to the staging of scenes from classic paintings or novels. Keeping up with current affairs had meant, at least for some women, having an opinion about the craze for a certain kind of hat or one of the new dances, and literary discussion more often than not involved the recitation and praise of various members' overwrought nature poetry.

It was after the war broke out in Europe that the Literary Society became, for a few years, a serious discussion group. Members were reading daily about the starving children in Flanders, and some had sons or brothers who had gone to Canada to enlist in the Royal Navy; they argued and discussed whether newspaper reports of atrocities—INFANTS SPITTED ON GERMAN SWORDS!—ought to be taken at face value or whether, as some people said, this sort of thing was warmongering propaganda. Before long the society began mounting formal debates on the question of whether Americans ought to get involved in Europe's war; this led to formal and informal argument over other matters, for instance whether Margaret Sanger in Brooklyn ought to have been arrested for handing out birth control information and whether Jeannette

Rankin over in Montana would cause a riot when she arrived in Washington D.C. as the first woman elected to Congress. In a women's club devoted to the topics of the day, there was no shortage of matters for discussion.

That was all in the three years while war raged in Europe but before the United States of America joined the fighting. After that most people seemed to feel there was less reason or room for engaging in debate. If their government declared war, people felt their one duty was to help the country win it; to act otherwise would be treasonable. Women in the Elwha Valley Literary Society sat together knitting sweaters and socks while visiting speechmakers urged the virtues of wartime sacrifice. There weren't any debates about whether the Committee of Public Information was censoring the news and issuing propaganda; it was generally believed, if these things were happening, they were in the best interests of the war effort and "for the sake of the boys." In January, after the defeat of the national women's suffrage bill, it was not suffragism that came up for discussion but questions about the responsibilities of patriotism. Angry suffragists had marched in numbers on the Capitol and the White House, and some angry women in the Literary Society made it clear they thought protest marches at this particular time, with American boys beginning to die overseas, was out-and-out insurrection. When Bruno Walter was suspended as conductor of the Chicago Symphony Orchestra it was a widely held opinion in the study club that the symphony had done the right thing—Walter was German, after all, and hadn't bothered to apply for American citizenship.

Louise Bliss, who had always disliked argument and discord, had kept out of the early debates about war and sedition, and after the start of the U.S. war her patriotism took the form of steadfast knitting and a Liberty Garden. While George pored over the war news out of a terrible compulsion, Louise avoided the newspapers: their son Jack was over there and she couldn't bear to read the details of battles or the names of the dead soldiers, who by January were dying at the rate of five or six every day, and by February sometimes as many as a dozen. Of course by June it would be twenty-five or thirty and, by October, two hundred a day, but all of that was still waiting offshore, like lightning over the water, and in February Louise was still of the opinion that ten or twelve was a great many.

She was deeply distressed by the unpleasantness that the war had brought to the Elwha Valley Literary Society, rifts that had left some of the women not speaking to others. Sometime in the winter months Mary Remlinger and Jessie Klages, whose children were American-born but who were themselves Rhinelanders, had dropped out of the society, and Irene Thiede began staying away from any meetings billed as patriotic in subject matter. Louise had never warmed to Mary Remlinger but she liked Jessie Klages and was particularly fond of Irene Thiede and wished they hadn't been made to feel unwelcome.

That was the winter Louise took it into her head that Shelby ought to have a library. After quizzing Martha about the lending library in Pendleton, she brought the idea to her study club. It was a difficult time for fundraising, what with everybody putting their savings into Liberty Bonds, but Louise argued that creating a library was more a matter of raising books than raising money and she swung the vote in favor of the project. She hadn't said so, but her unspoken hope was that this undertaking might distract the members from matters and arguments related to war.

A Shelby Reading Room Committee was formed and promptly named Louise Bliss chairwoman; members of the committee began petitioning the owners of buildings in Shelby to donate space for the new library. In the meantime, books collected from members' own shelves and the closets and shelves of their importuned neighbors went to the Bliss ranch. Louise or George, or occasionally whichever hired hand happened to be there, carried the books upstairs to Miriam Bliss's old bedroom, where they stood in loose piles and stacks against the walls or in boxes set down on the bare mattress.

"I don't know whether you know it," George said to Louise one day early in March after he had carried up three or four armloads of books, "but I'm getting too old to make that trip up the stairs more than forty or fifty times a day."

He was standing on the back porch with his hands tucked into the bib of his overalls, and Louise was on her knees in the garden pulling up weeds around her rhubarb plants. She hadn't gone out there intending to start weeding but while she'd been standing in the yard chatting with Pauline Ashe—it was Pauline's books George was teasing her about—her eye had gone to a particularly flagrant burdock that had raised its coarse head above the rhubarb patch, and one thing had led to another. "George, I'm too tired to find that amusing," she said, and was more than half-serious about it. It had been a clear mild day, so springlike that she had dragged the carpets outside one by one and beaten them clean of their winter dirt. Her arms and her back ached; she didn't know why she was now out in the garden pulling up weeds.

George watched her silently for a while and then took out his pouch of Bull Durham and made a cigarette and smoked it, leaning against one of the porch uprights. It had been an unusually open winter, and from that porch on a clear day you could see all the way across the valley to the Whitehorns, their jagged peaks rising dramatically from the valley floor without much in the way of preliminary foothills. This was late in the day and the sky didn't have a cloud in it, and a reddish light, streaked and veined, had climbed up the mountains so they seemed garishly painted against the blue. George was used to the sight and hardly took notice of it. "What did your library ladies decide to do about those German books?" he said.

The library project, as it turned out, had brought on new problems without easing any of the old ones. A box of German-language books, left anonymously on the porch of the Grange Hall, had raised a terrible furor, as quite a few women thought the books had been left there by a Bohemian or Rhinelander as a deliberate insult to the society. Anyone would know, went the argument, that such books were absolutely unwanted by this or any library in the nation. And there had been bitter disagreement over what to do with English translations of books by famous German writers—Goethe, for instance. Four or five women of a literary bent had been firm in their opinion that the books were innocent and ought to be accepted, but more than a few others wanted them carried straight out to the town dump; this arguing had caused two more women to stop coming to the meetings.

"They're not my ladies," Louise said crossly, "and I'm just about at the point of quitting the whole thing." She had been suffering from a sour stomach for days, which she blamed on this business of the German books.

George didn't know if she meant quitting the Elwha Valley Literary Society or quitting the Library Committee and he didn't think her tone allowed him to ask. He said cheerfully, "Well I'm just about at the point of buying myself an automobile plow." He hadn't planned to say this to Louise yet, but the tractor was what popped out of his mouth when he opened it. He'd been thinking about buying a Fordson for a while now and lining up arguments in favor of the idea, the boiled-down version being that the world needed more wheat, and banks had become generous about loaning money to the farmers growing it, and the new Ford tractors were small and surefooted. Up until three or four years before, the only plowing George ever did was turning over Louise's garden, but with a lot of his pasture grass now given over to growing wheat, plowing was a hateful chore that took up more and more of his time right when he ought to be getting ready to brand the calf crop. If he still had three or four men working for him he wouldn't worry so much about getting it all done, but Will Wright had gone off with the last batch of enlistees and now it was down to just himself and El Bayard. He didn't know how the two of them would ever get the wheat fields plowed and planted before it came roundup time.

Louise said, "Who have you been talking to?" which sounded to George like an accusation of some kind. He knew she meant the various equipment salesmen who regularly visited the ranches, or their own son Orie, who had picked up from his friend Ray a belief in the future of gasoline power. It seemed to George an odd contradiction that fellows studying veterinary medicine, and whose future livelihood depended on the continued use of horses and mules for farm work, should tout the benefits of machinery, but neither Orie nor Ray seemed to see the rub.

Louise's manner put George's back up a little. He had wanted to give her something new to stew about other than the German library books but now that he had riled her up he was feeling fairly riled up himself.

"I've been talking to myself is who I've been talking to, and what I've been saying is that I might buy myself an automobile plow that won't need horses having to be harnessed up every morning and fed twice a day and given half of every damn day off to rest up."

Louise said irritably, "Every gasoline engine you've got is always breaking down, I notice, or needing fooling with, and at least we can grow the feed for the horses whereas gasoline is steep. And anyway we didn't get much of a wheat crop the past two years so I don't know why you'd want to go into debt to grow more of it." She stood up from the rhubarb and brushed her dirty hands together and looked over at her husband. "But I imagine you've got your mind made up already and you're not asking my opinion."

The truth was, she looked favorably on the progress of technology—it was Louise who had pressed her husband to buy an automobile. And it was also true that just about everybody she knew had been stepped on or kicked or thrown or run away with or had bones broken by horses. As if proof were needed, even Martha Lessen, who was clever as could be around horses, was wearing plaster on her arm right now. Louise had known neighbors killed by horses and one who'd been kicked in the head and afterward never had more than the mind of a child. If, as people were already saying, horses on all the farms and ranches would soon be replaced by machinery she wouldn't be sorry about it or silly enough for nostalgia.

But she was in an argumentative mood or just irritated that George had brought up the matter of the German books when he ought to have known how it would upset her. Or it was the funerals weighing on her. They had been to a string of funerals in recent weeks, starting with the Romers, people they hardly knew except to nod to when they passed on the road, but for Martha's sake they had gone to the burial of that poor baby and the baby's father, the two of them laid to rest in the same grave. It had just about killed her to see the watchful, bewildered way Dorothy Romer's two older children clung to their mother and the stunned look in that woman's face. Then at the end of February there had been a service for the first Elwha County boy killed and buried over there in France. He had been the son of a Basque sheep rancher in Owl Creek Canyon, a stranger to the cattle ranchers living in the valley but nevertheless a local boy, and the whole county had taken the news hard. And the very next day Tom Kandel had died of cancer, which wasn't a shock but had saddened Louise beyond all reason. Tom was an exception among the newcomer homesteaders, someone with a practical mind and the follow-through to carry out a plan. She had often bought eggs from Tom when her own hens weren't laying enough to supply the table and had gone to him for a stock of new chicks after a coyote tore up her henhouse. Louise liked Tom, everybody did. Then Old Karl Thiede, who hadn't been out of bed since he broke his pelvis in the autumn, took pneumonia and died. Karl wasn't as old as all that—he might have been sixty or sixty-five—and the others who died had all been young. She wished George could realize how all this was weighing on her. At Tom Kandel's funeral, when poetry had been read in addition to Scripture, George had bent to her and asked irritably in a whisper what the hell part of the Bible those verses came from, which had distressed Louise. She wished George could understand how she had found herself deeply moved by the poems and by knowing that Tom, in his last days, had asked for them to be read at his funeral.

"Since you're not the one doing the plowing, I don't see exactly how your opinion comes into it," George said now, and he stepped down off the porch and headed for the bunkhouse. His dog came scrambling out from under the porch to follow him.

Louise hadn't really thought she and George were arguing but when he walked off she realized they were. They didn't argue very often and neither of them liked it when they did. George was usually the one who walked away, and his habit was to spend an hour or so playing cards with his hired hands and then come back to the house whistling and cheerful, pretending he and Louise hadn't had a disagreement. Louise's habit was to go over and over the argument and rework it until she had all the words lined up in the order and manner she ought to have said them. In the first years of their marriage she used to wait tensely for George to come back to the house so she could tell him what she'd thought of to say; but then his relentless good humor would surprise and charm her and she wouldn't be able to find an opening to bring it up again. After all these years—they'd been married when Louise was barely sixteen—they were both set in these habits, and though Louise still liked to go over an argument in her mind, she knew she wouldn't say any of it to George, or not until he brought it up again himself. Lying in bed tonight, for instance, he might ask her whether she thought a Fordson automobile plow was a good idea, as if he hadn't ever mentioned it before; and after they talked about the tractor for a while she might begin to tell him her deepening worries about the Literary Society and how the recent funerals had brought her very low in her mind.

Watching George cross the yard to the bunkhouse, Louise was suddenly sorry she'd been so cross. In recent months his shoulders had become stooped, or they had been stooped for a while and she had only just realized it, and he often walked around like a tired old man, his boots scuffing the dirt. He wasn't old yet, only fifty-one, but she knew his hips and knees hurt him most of the time and he'd begun to have trouble with his bowels. She hoped what she felt just now—a little stab of fear or foreboding—wasn't any sort of premonition. Her mother had always believed in such things, believed she had "second sight," and that a chill along her spine or the creeping of her flesh was a portent or warning of imminent suffering. Once when Louise was about twelve her mother standing at the sink had suddenly turned an ashen face to Louise and said, "It's Harry," in a horrified way. Harry was Louise's uncle, her mother's eldest brother. It was more than a year later that Harry drowned in the Columbia River coming back from a trip to The Dalles, but Louise's mother always believed she'd had a genuine forewarning of it that day a year earlier, standing in her kitchen.

Louise left the weeds lying in a wilting pile in the garden and went into the house to start the supper, and sure enough when George and El came in for supper George was determinedly cheerful and he started right in telling Louise a doubtless corrupted version of the moving picture he had watched the last time he gave his Liberty Bond speech at the Shelby theater. Louise had stopped going with him to the movies on account of the newsreels of all the soldiers, their heartbreaking grins as they marched past the camera, but he knew she liked to hear about the picture show just so long as it wasn't anything to do with war. She poured coffee for him and for El sitting at the table, and then while she went on getting the supper ready she listened to the story George was telling her, a three-reel jungle story that involved lions and elephants and a heroine in breeches and sun helmet, and she made a point of interrupting him to question certain confusing parts of the plot so he would know she was listening. Just about the time he finished recounting the movie Martha came in tired and hungry from her circle ride and Louise brought the potato soup to the table.

She had made an unsatisfactory Liberty Bread earlier in the day from oats and almost no wheat flour and felt she ought to apologize for it. "Evidently patriotism now requires a lot of chewing," she said sourly, and George, who had had to stand up to get the leverage to saw slabs off the loaf, winked across the table at her and said, "If we start complaining I guess you can feed it to the horses, but I don't hear any of us complaining." Of course there never were any complaints about the food she put on the table, which she knew had more to do with how hungry and hard-worked they all were than with the excellence of her cooking. Even their girl broncobuster, after breaking her arm and watching a child die of spoiled food, always ate up every bit of what was on her plate and could always be persuaded to finish off whatever was left on any platter. The cast on her arm the past couple of weeks just caused her to eat more slowly, as she had trouble carving bites of roast, trouble pressing down a knife or a fork with her left hand.

Louise ate lightly—her stomach was bothering her—and began doing up the dishes while the others were still sitting around the table. They'd all been talking about the mild weather and this had led to George telling a story about the March weather several years earlier when he had lost fifty-three cows and their calves all at once, trapped by deep snow on the banks of Ax Handle Creek. They had calved out at the ranch and then he had moved them along the creek where there was good shelter and good pasture, but a late spring storm had dropped a couple of feet of snow, which the wind had blown into high drifts. Water in the Ax Handle rose and rose, and the cows and calves, trapped between the drifts and the flooded creek, were too cold and weak to swim out of trouble. Louise had heard this old story several times before—he had told it to her with tears standing in his eyes the night he came back from finding all those drowned and frozen animals—but El had only heard it once and Martha never had; they listened to the boss in grave silence, leaning over the table on their elbows.

Louise was struck suddenly by the disconcerting likeness: El with his rigidly crooked arm from that old break and Martha, her wrist fixed straight in a plaster cast. The edge of it that showed below her shirt cuff was already filthy and chipped, and Louise almost opened her mouth to say something about it before deciding there wouldn't be any point. She had seen enough broken bones over the years so as not to be distressed unless a break was grievous; but no one had had a bit of luck trying to persuade the girl to give up her circle ride after that first day, and only the Lord knew what would happen if she was bucked off and landed on that arm. Dr. Padham wasn't the best doctor in the world and Martha hadn't let him run the plaster as far up and down the arm as he had wanted to—she needed to be able to use that arm, she said, and couldn't be budged from her stubborn stand. It would be a wonder if the girl didn't wind up like El Bayard, who could handle ranch work but could hardly comb his own hair or shave his whiskers on account of the poor job that had been done setting his bad break.

As soon as Louise finished cleaning up the supper dishes she went upstairs and left the rest of them still talking. She heard the telephone ring a little while later, their own ring, which made her sour stomach clench: it would be somebody on the Reading Room Committee wanting to put in her two cents' worth about the German books. She could hear George's voice downstairs, a murmur of wordless sounds. Louise was already in her nightdress and in bed by then, which George would surely know, and she didn't expect him to come up the stairs to get her, just to listen to one more complaint about something to do with the library. But he did come up, making a slow climb of it, and stood in the dark doorway a moment, his silhouette black against the dim light leaking up from the kitchen, and then he came over and sat on the edge of the bed beside her and she knew what it was before he even got the words out.

"Honey, don't cry now, he's not dead, but Jack's got hurt over there."

She didn't cry, but a high surf arose loud in her ears and her throat almost closed shut, and it took her a while to get enough voice to ask him to tell her everything he knew, which wasn't much. Jack had lost a leg, that was what it came down to, although George tried hard not to say it in just those words. They both fell into silence. Finally George stood up and went downstairs and she heard him talking to Martha and El briefly and then heard the hands go out of the house. After a minute or two George turned down the lamps and came back upstairs and undressed in the darkness and climbed into bed next to her. He was lying on his back, and she turned onto her side and folded herself over him, one of her legs thrown across his haunches and her breasts crushed to his ribs. She put the flat of her hand on his chest, the heavy thumping of his heart. He was hairy front and back—for years she had teased him about shedding in the spring—and the feel of him under her hand, that animal's pelt, was familiar and warm. After a moment she closed her fingers in it.

She was thinking Jack could still die. It was a terrible wound and there could be infection; they'd have to get him back across the Atlantic Ocean in a ship that could be blown to bits like the Lusitania by a German U-boat. But she didn't say this to George. She said, "Jack can still ranch. If he can drive horses, he can ranch. Bud Adey drove a twelve-horse freight wagon and trailer after he lost his leg."

George didn't answer her. Louise's head was tucked under his chin and he could feel her words huffing warm against his breastbone. He reached over and put his hand on the back of her nightdress between the shoulder blades and pressed her against him but he didn't speak. Jack didn't lose his leg was what he was thinking; he had the damn thing blasted off. Later on he happened to think about the automobile plow, how in most respects it was nothing more than a big motorcar built heavy for towing and for running over soft ground, and how Bud Adey never had been able to drive a motorcar—he just couldn't manage the pedals with one leg.

27

IN THOSE YEARS the plots of movies weren't far removed from the dime novels that had been popular since the Civil War. There were stories about brave and true Mounties and Texas Rangers, frontiersmen in coonskin caps, heroes with swords and plumed hats, Kit Carson–style scouts; titillating stories of girls dressed up in breeches and pith helmets, cave girls in fur tunics, brown-skinned girls in grass or leather skirts, innocent girls in jeopardy from mustache-twirling villains. Quite a few movies made a point of the barbaric and the unusual—Eskimo people in the Far North, for instance, building their ice-block igloos. The movies brought a lot of people their first glimpse of a seaside bathing beach, a woman smoking, colored people in a jazz band, men in swallowtail tuxedos, a woman in a negligee. Charlie Chaplin was popular, and Buster Keaton, unlucky young men coping with the mysteries of modern life; it was from those picture shows that most people in the West had their first moving images of electric streetcars, ocean liners, airplanes. And in the war years there rained down a storm of movies about boys in uniform, boys who were the pride of their fathers and the envy of their younger brothers.

It wasn't a war movie that Henry Frazer and Martha Lessen saw early in April but it was the next thing to it: a picture called *Fear Has Said Its Prayers*, in which a shallow, self-absorbed mother dissuades her son from joining the army and the boy goes downhill from there, stripped of his right to virile manhood, his right to give his life for his country.

During the reel changes a Four Minute Man named John Johnson, who owned a stone quarry at the edge of Shelby, stood up and urged the audience to sign food pledge cards promising to eat less meat, sugar, wheat, and pork, and to buy Liberty Bonds as a way of "doing your bit" for the soldiers who were on their way to France to fight for a democratic world.

"We here in America are not sleeping in mud tonight, eating crackers and cold bacon," Mr. Johnson said in a nervous high tenor. "We are not lying in caves with the murderous thunder and lightning above; not standing gun in hand with death lurking all around and above. Unlike those boys over there, we are not privileged to give our all for America, we are privileged only to do the best we can" and so forth, straight out of the pamphlet he held in his hand.

Martha had not been to the movies since coming into Elwha County in November, and the last Four Minute Speech she'd heard was the one George Bliss had delivered at the dinner table on Christmas Day. But by this point in the war it was hard to walk down a street or open a newspaper without seeing or hearing about spies hiding in the ranks of your neighbors, about the evils of extravagance and the virtues of wearing half-soled shoes and mended trousers, so the messages in John Johnson's speeches were familiar to her and to pretty much everybody in the theater. They had all signed food pledge cards and were wearing Liberty Buttons to confirm their patriotism. While the cameraman hurried to change the reels and John Johnson delivered his invocations—"Who'll help? Who'll speak to his neighbors about saving the waste of food? Who? Hands up! Hands up!"—more people chatted with their friends or walked up the aisles to stretch their legs than shouted affirmations to the Four Minute Man.

Henry Frazer had ridden over to the Bliss ranch to collect Martha and El, and the three of them had ridden into Shelby on horseback and met the others in front of the movie theater—El's sister Pearl and two of her friends, and also Chuck McGee and his wife, Nancy. Henry and Chuck had known each other for years, they were both the sons of Scotsmen and had come into Elwha County around the same time and gone to work for neighboring ranches. Henry had come in 1904 as a seventeen-year-old wrangler for the railroad and stayed in the valley after delivering a carload of horses to George Bliss; Chuck had come a few months later from a farm in Kansas, a green boy looking for his chance to be a cowboy. After he was hired to drive dairy cows through the Ipsoot Pass to one of the first homestead farms in the valley, he found work on the Split Rock Ranch, where old man

Woodruff in the last year of his life taught him how to be a cowboy; now Chuck was foreman on the Burnt Creek Company Ranch at the west end of the county. He and Nancy had driven to town in a Maxwell car that belonged to the company.

While the reels were being changed, the three men in the party talked about the roundup and branding that was about to start and about the calving season just ended; the girls talked about people they knew in common, people Martha mostly didn't know—a girl who had come down with TB and another who had moved to Portland and was guarding a livestock yard two evenings a week. Sitting between Henry and one of Pearl's friends, Martha listened more to what the men said than to the women and sometimes chimed in when she could think of something to say. She had helped out with moving cattle and with branding since she was thirteen years old and had worked the calving season one year for a small ranch near Hermiston; but she had mostly worked on haying crews or with horses, so her practical knowledge of cows felt meager; she listened to the men to pick up bits of their know-how.

From time to time she caught Henry stealing a look at her, and she thought he must be sizing up whether she was feeling lonesome or left out. She wasn't, particularly, and tried to let him know it by thinking of more to say. She wished the movie they were watching had been about the frozen North or the jungles of Africa, because she'd read *The Call of the Wild* recently and *Tarzan of the Apes*, and could have joined any talk that arose about wolves and sled dogs, or lions and alligators.

Once she'd been to a movie palace in Pendleton where a nine-piece orchestra had accompanied the action in the moving picture, but in Shelby it was just a woman playing a piano. While Martha listened to the men talk about cattle she studied the piano player's hair, which was a short, straight curtain trimmed off just below her ears. At the third reel change Nancy, who had noticed what Martha was looking at, leaned across her husband and said to her, "Are you thinking of cutting your hair short? I was thinking of doing it but Chuck wants me to keep it long." Nancy had a thick mane of red hair bundled into a Psyche knot.

Chuck put his arm across his wife's shoulders and grinned at her and said, "Honey, I married a girl, not a boy, and I want to keep it that way." Then one of Pearl's friends, an unmarried girl, jumped in warmly to say that a husband's opinion shouldn't come into it, and a loud and laughing discussion began that saved Martha from answering Nancy's question.

She had been thinking of cutting her hair short ever since she broke her arm. It had become a hard and awkward business just getting a comb through her hair using only her right hand, hard and painful trying to wash her hair or tie it back now that her arm was in a plaster cast. And she liked the idea of being able to put on her hat in the morning without giving a moment's thought to her hair—as free as any man. She thought

Pearl's friend Eula had only been teasing Chuck, not making a serious point, but she felt, herself, that a married woman should have as much right as a single girl to make her own decisions. What Henry's friend had said, about not wanting to be married to a boy, was enough to make her think twice, though. For this trip to the movies she had borrowed one of Louise's pintucked shirtwaists and had traded her cowboy hat for her grandmother's old velvet-trimmed hat and swapped her canvas coat for a light corduroy jacket that was another of Louise's hand-me-downs; but she had ridden into town tonight on horseback, dressed in pants and boots, while every one of the other girls was in a skirt. Any one of them could have cut her hair without being mistaken for a boy, but Martha had already marched out to the limits of decency by going around corsetless and wearing men's pegged trousers and boots when she was on horseback, which was most of the time. She didn't want Henry or anybody else to think she wanted to be a man or be taken for one.

Henry grinned and kept still through all the lively talk about whether a married woman should let her husband decide on the length of her hair, but when the lights went down for the third reel he leaned close to Martha and said, "I wouldn't mind it." He had said almost the same thing once before, about her being tall, which she hadn't ever forgotten. This time he might have meant that he wouldn't mind short hair or that he wouldn't mind being a husband who made all the decisions; Martha didn't know for sure which it was, but either way her face grew warm.

When they left the theater they walked in a crowd up the sidewalk, all of them dawdling along so Pearl on her canes could keep up, and they went into the Crystal Café and ordered a whole dried-peach pie and sat around it, dueling with their forks. They talked a little about *Fear Has Said Its Prayers*, getting into particular mothers they knew or had heard about, mothers dead set against their sons going to war but who weren't very much like the mother in the picture show; and then they went on to other war talk, the battle at the Somme River being fought just then. The newspapers had been saying the Germans were trying to end the war before too many American troops could arrive at the front, and things were going badly for the Allies.

Nobody at the table knew if Will Wright was anywhere near the Somme. The Blisses had had three or four letters from him, which they'd made a practice of passing on to El and Martha at the supper table, but in those letters there had been only a good many descriptions of the weather and the countryside, jokes about army food, and sometimes a sentence about dead Heinies seen along a road or in a shell hole—nothing about any battles, and no names of particular towns or rivers, which the censors would have snipped out anyway.

El Bayard and Will Wright had worked together at the Bliss ranch for almost two years without becoming particular friends, for the reason that Will was still a young kid who hadn't seen much of anything, and El was forty and had seen more than he wanted to; so El had been surprised, just a few days before, to get a letter from him. What Will had written was that the war wasn't any bit the Great Adventure he'd expected; that there were long stretches of unrelieved monotony and discomfort, and then short, terrifying bombardments or fusillades; that he had seen men die in gruesome ways; that most of his time was spent in dull boredom and misery, crouching in a trench or a dugout waiting to be killed.

El hadn't shared the letter with anybody at the Bliss ranch but he had shown it to Pearl, whose fiancé, Jim, would have been a conscientious objector if he had lived long enough to be drafted. Conscientious objectors were being jailed and beaten all over the country, their houses and cars stoned. While the others at the table talked about the battle of the Somme, and about the great number of soldiers who had lately shipped east through Umatilla County and Pendleton—more than thirty thousand in a two-week stretch—El met Pearl's look and then studied his fork as he took a last stab at the pie. Pearl had told him that Lizzie Wright, Will's new bride, was expecting a child in the autumn.

Earlier in the week a fire had burned the barn and livery out at Stanley's Camp and the talk around the table was soon on to that; then someone asked Martha about her horses and she told them the horses were mostly finished; they were as gentle and tame as could be, and they knew much of what they would need to know in their working lives. Pearl and her friends were town girls who couldn't be expected to be very interested in horses, so she didn't say more than that. But there were things she planned to say later to Henry, who she knew would be interested: things to do with ending the circle ride and parting company with certain horses she had grown fond of.

She had taken Dandy, the Kandels' blue roan horse, over to the Kandel farm earlier in the day—it was Fred's thirteenth birthday, and Mrs. Kandel had asked Martha to wait until that day to deliver the horse to Fred. At Tom's funeral in February the boy had come up to Martha and told her fiercely, "I won't ever sell Dandy, I'll keep him no matter what," which Martha had thought must be part of something he and Mrs. Kandel had been talking, or arguing, about. She imagined it had to do with whether Ruth Kandel planned to keep the farm or sell it, now that she was a widow. At the time Martha hadn't heard either way, but just the other morning when she and Ruth were talking out by the fence and Martha asked how she was getting along, Ruth had smiled dryly, her chin puckering up, and said, "I'm afraid Tom was right. I'm as tough as one of these old hens," which Martha took to mean she intended to stay put.

Fred was an inexperienced rider; he was quick to jerk at the reins, and he bumped the horse with his heels to get him moving even after Martha told him a light squeeze with the knees would do the job. But he was just a boy and she could see he loved the horse already by the way he put his face right up to the prickle of Dandy's whiskers and by the way he kissed the velvet skin at the corner of the horse's mouth when he thought no one was looking. He might get to be a good rider or anyway a decent one eventually—she had seen plenty of dull colts that turned out to be serviceable horses and thought it must be the same with boys. And Dandy was a patient sort.

She had spent some of her circle wages to buy the horse called Mata Hari from Dorothy Romer before Dorothy and Helen and Clifford packed up and moved back to Wisconsin. Dorothy had said she wanted to sell all of Reuben's horses, and Martha had helped her find buyers for the others, the four heavy pulling horses and a gray gelding saddle horse that had a hard mouth and a habit of bolting his food; but she liked Mata Hari and was afraid if somebody else bought her and treated her the least bit rough, she'd go back to biting and bucking. It was interesting to Martha that when she put Mattie in with Dolly the two took to each other right away, and that it was Mattie who seemed to rule the roost, Dolly completely beguiled by the pretty little Dutch spy. Martha hadn't expected that. She was surprised, too, that Dorothy Romer seemed to be grieving for her worthless husband as much as for the baby, Alice. One morning Dorothy had gone on for half an hour about Reuben's many gifts and charms— had broken down and sobbed as she said she didn't know what she would do without him.

W.G. Boyd's horse, Skip, who had been so afraid of

everything, had calmed down a great deal but never had become entirely trustworthy. Martha hadn't been able to get him over his fear of things lying on the ground, things with a certain heft or shape, not only thick limbs of wood or fence posts but a bucket tipped on its side, a big stone, a calf curled up asleep. She knew W.G. had been planning to sell the horse, but she hated to see Skip passed on to someone who might not understand why he was afraid—somebody who might think the way to get him to behave was to beat the fear out of him. She had toyed with the idea of buying him herself, but she didn't have use for a horse that wasn't trustworthy; and she had four horses to feed now that she had Mata Hari. When she told W.G. what she was worried about, and what Skip was like, he didn't bat an eye. He said, well then, he'd just send the horse into retirement. His pasture didn't have much of anything on the ground that might scare the horse, he told Martha, and maybe Skip would enjoy the company of a donkey somebody had recently given him.

As it happened, in later years Skip turned out to be entirely trustworthy. After the war was over, whenever Joe and his dad came down from Pendleton to visit W.G., Joe would climb onto Skip and ride him everywhere bareback and if Joe turned him loose to crop the grass while he went off to visit with some of his old schoolmates the horse would walk back on his own and wait for W.G. to let him into the pasture. It was the company of that old donkey that did it, or at least that's what Martha thought, just the steady company of a friend who wasn't afraid of a single thing in the world.

When their crowd had finished off the pie, they sat talking for a while more, and then El walked back with Pearl and her friends to the apartment building where the girls all lived. He planned to stay over, to sleep on the floor in Pearl's place so he could go with her on the train the next morning to Pendleton and then on to Portland, where they were seeing a doctor who they hoped could do Pearl some good. If Pearl wound up having an operation, El might be leaving George Bliss shorthanded for as much as a couple of months; but the calving was all finished and the branding not started yet, and since word had come to them about Jack being wounded, George had seemed to lose all interest in planting wheat. He had leased out the wheat fields to a corporation up in Umatilla County, and that outfit had brought in a big crew of what looked to be fifty-year-old tramps and a few normal-school girls, along with a hundred horses, and got the fields plowed and drilled in less than a week. Now that the calving was finished, the only ranch work comprised corralling the two-year-old steers to be sold and taking bulls and heifers up to summer pasture; there had been some talk that if Martha decided to stay on in the county she could help George move his cattle.

After El and the girls left the café, Henry and Martha and the McGees stayed a few more minutes, drinking coffee to wash down the pie and talking about cows, of course, and horses, and about Emma Adelaide Woodruff, who had been stepped on by a cow and was hobbling around with a broken toe. When Chuck and Nancy drove off in the Maxwell, Henry and Martha walked up the street to get their horses from Bert Widner's stables.

There were street lights on the main street of the town and on the crossroad that went up the valley to Bingham but the lights had been left off to conserve those hundreds of cords of wood for the war, and the sidewalks were mostly dark and empty. Henry took her right hand, the one that wasn't in a cast, and after a moment leaned over and kissed her quickly on the mouth. They hadn't stopped walking, and the motion caused his teeth to scrape across her bottom lip. When he thought he tasted blood on his tongue he said, "Did I cut your lip?" She ran her tongue over the scrape and said, "No, it's all right," and then touched her mouth with her finger. There was something endearing in that gesture, Henry thought, and he stopped her from walking and pulled her to him and kissed her again lightly, his tongue touching the place on her lip where she was cut.

This wasn't the first time they had kissed, or the second, but there hadn't been enough times for Martha to grow casual about it. She had seen plenty of horses and cattle coupling, she had known about that rough urgency, that brute coming together, but not this other: his callused hand cupping the nape of her neck to bring her close to him, and the salty taste of him, the smell of him, his warm male breath, the stubble of his chin against her cheek. She was conscious of bright heat and a feeling like pins and needles inside the unfamiliar clothes she'd borrowed from Louise Bliss, her breasts in the shirtwaist seeming to yearn toward Henry's barrel chest. None of it, or almost none of it, was what she had imagined would happen between a man and a woman.

He kissed her twice more slowly and then couldn't prevent himself from pulling her hair back and exploring the shell of her ear lightly with his lips and his tongue. Her breath caught and she bent her head back and he kissed her open throat and the ridgeline of her jaw and then down along her collarbone. He put his hands at her waist and held her hard against him and he kissed her over and over until they were both panting as if they'd been running, as if they were running from something and afraid to stop, and he was hardly aware when his hands moved down to stroke her hips. She was by then trembling under his touch, his mouth, and when he became aware of it—it was a little while—he made himself stop what he was doing, what his mouth and hands were doing, and he pulled away slightly and held her by the shoulders without kissing her, his cheek resting against the side of her hair, and both of them now shaking slightly.

Henry had been close to engaged once, to a girl who worked at the Elwha County courthouse, a modern girl acquainted with rubber condoms—she had laughed, calling them *"capotes,* my little French darlings"— and she had shown Henry how they should be used. He had used them more than once or twice but not so often as to feel like a top horse. Martha wasn't anything like the girl from the courthouse and when he kissed her he tried to be aware of where his hands were, and was intensely aware of where he wanted them to be. The times with that other girl had been more than three years before, but now with Martha, when the heat flamed up in his body, his body knew exactly what should happen next. He had pulled back because he was afraid the power over what happened next was more his than hers and because she wasn't anything like the girl who worked at the courthouse.

When some boys passed them on the sidewalk they stepped apart, looking at the ground in shamefaced embarrassment, and when the boys had gone by Martha reached for his hand again and they went on walking toward the stables. After a minute, Henry said hoarsely, "We could go for a walk before we head back. We could walk down by the river." He wasn't inviting her to lie down with him on the ground—he hoped she knew that; it was just that he wasn't ready to quit walking with her in the soft night, the darkness.

The weather had been wet the past couple of weeks, and Martha thought the ground by the river might still be muddy for walking—it didn't cross her mind that Henry might have been asking her to lie down with him—but she said, "All right," because she didn't want to head back yet either. They couldn't go on kissing if they were on horseback, and she wanted him to go on kissing her.

They turned off the sidewalk and found the path that

fishermen used, working their way up and down the riverbank. The water was black with bright coins of light scattered on it from a few houses lit up along the other bank. Henry held her hand and they walked slowly. The ground was soft but not as wet or muddy as all that, and they walked clear out to the farthest edge of town and stood there in the darkness looking out at the river.

"I want to ask you something," Henry said after a few minutes. He had been worrying in recent weeks, as Martha's circle ride got closer to finished, that if he didn't say something soon she might just ride on out of the county like all the other itinerant wranglers he'd known—ride off looking for more horses to break. But he hadn't planned to say it just now, and he frowned out at the black weight of water moving without cease in front of them. The river was at spring flood already, and the low booming sound it made was like far-off continuous thunder.

Martha said, "What?" almost dreamily, caught up in something, and when she turned toward him, the bare shape of her face in the night took on the look of a girl about twelve years old, a child so innocent and absolutely devoid of guile that he thought suddenly she was too young to even know what he was asking of her, what he meant to ask of her, and that he ought to let her grow up first, without a man's hands, his hands, despoiling her. But then she smiled and said, "What?" again, and leaned into him and kissed him on the mouth. The child had gone out of her face, and she was Martha whom he loved, and he would have taken her down on the ground right then if it had been possible to do it and still go on living with himself.

He said huskily, "I want to ask you if you'd think about marrying me."

So there it was. Her eyes widened but she wasn't surprised. She had expected that Henry might want to marry her, and for weeks had gone over and over her answer in her mind. She said slowly, gravely, "I would think about it," which he might have taken as a good start except she had begun to frown, looking at him, and he thought he knew what was coming next, and his heart started beating loudly in his ears. But it was just that she had made up her mind to say several things if Henry proposed, and her own heart was thudding so loudly it took her a minute, standing there frowning, to get them lined up so she could remember and say them all.

"I'd want you to know, first, that I would still want to go on breaking horses and working outside," she said. She raised her eyebrows, half-questioning him, but then went on with the rest quickly before he could begin to answer. "So I guess I'd want somebody else hired in to do the housework and the cooking, or else I guess you would have to get used to living with things being dirty, and eating sandwiches. And when I'm not working with horses I'd want to help you and work with the cows; that's something I could learn to do, and I'd want to. And when there are children, they'd have to get used to riding on the front of the saddle like Young Karl, because I wouldn't want to stay in the house like women usually do." Then, because the last thing was the hardest for her to say, she began to blush, which she thought he couldn't see in the darkness, and the only reason she didn't drop her eyes from him was because he was almost invisible to her against the black river. She said, her voice beginning to shake, "And I wouldn't want to have as many babies as my mother had, six children in six years." She was twenty years old. She didn't have any idea how to keep from having a child every year except by leaving her husband alone in his bed, and she thought that was what she was saying to him. She took a breath, to give herself a moment more to think. Her big mouth pursed slightly. "I don't know if you would mind having a wife like that," she said, and just for a moment she was a child again, her voice catching on the last words.

He couldn't have been more astonished. He stared at her and had to think what to say. There wasn't any way in the world he could talk to her about condoms. Finally he said, "You know I'm just a hired hand and I don't know as I'll ever be able to have a house or land that's mine, or afford my own hired help." He tried to smile. "I don't know if you'd mind having a husband like that."

She seemed not to know what he was getting at and went on looking at him and frowning. They were standing a little apart, not touching—she had dropped his hand when he first asked her about marriage—and she was standing on the high ground, taller even than usual, and looking down on him a bit. He thought some more and finally he said, "I guess if we can't afford to hire help there's other ways around it. I'm already used to doing for myself, washing and cleaning. I can make eggs and pancakes, so I guess we wouldn't always have to eat sandwiches."

Then she understood what he was saying and she tried to hide a smile, as if she was twelve again and shy, but when he reached for her hand she came up to him and pressed herself to him and wanted him to kiss her, and he did.

In those days it wasn't legal to ship condoms across state lines, and Henry didn't know if it was legal to buy and sell them in Elwha County. He didn't know where that girl at the courthouse had gotten her French darlings. He wondered if Chuck might know, or Emil Thiede.

28

PATRIOTISM RAN WILD in those days, like a plague of fever. People clamored for war protesters to be kicked out of the country, and laws aimed at German spies were used to send conscientious objectors to jail, and pacifist ministers, journalists who wrote antiwar editorials, soldiers who complained of bad conditions in the army, teachers who spoke out in favor of German literature.

Elwha County had a Home Guard without much to

guard, so after the barn at Stanley's Camp burned down, members of the Guard went around to three or four German settlers in that part of the valley and turned over their furniture looking for a reason to say they'd set the fire. One thing led to another and one of the farmhouses got burned down and a man named Kurt Schweiger was stabbed with a guardsman's sword, which didn't kill him, but after he came out of the hospital he and his family packed up and moved out of the valley.

Early in April, about a week after Kurt Schweiger was stabbed, Millard Rankin, the chairman of the Liberty Bond committee and also a volunteer with the Home Guard, stopped by the Thiede place with a Kodak box camera and walked around the yard taking pictures of the house and the barns and the horses standing in the pasture. Irene watched him for a few minutes from the kitchen window and then went out and asked him what he was doing and he gave her a high-handed explanation—that he planned to use the pictures at the next patriotic meeting to show folks how preposterous it was that the well-off Thiedes had purchased only two hundred dollars in Liberty Bonds. She gave Millard a check for two hundred more, which she knew was giving in to extortion, and when Emil got home he said in a fury that he would go to the bank in the morning and stop the check; then he stormed out to the barn without touching his supper.

Irene put Young Karl to bed and went into the room that had been Old Karl's, which she now used for sewing, and she sewed a while, piecing the quilt she had begun from scraps of her father-in-law's shirts, the ones too worn out to be worth mending for her husband to wear. Quite a bit later Emil came into the house, came back to the bedroom where she was sewing and stood in the doorway behind her. She didn't think she would be able to stop herself from crying if she turned to look at him, so she went on sewing, and finally he said, "It won't kill us to have four hundred dollars in bonds."

She inhaled sharply and said, "We had a good calf crop," as if he had disputed it, and as if that was the only point that mattered.

Emil watched her another minute. "It's all right, honey," he said quietly. "Come on out and warm me up some supper." And then he came across the room and put his hands on her shoulders and waited until she could quit her crying.

Neither of them said anything about Kurt Schweiger being stabbed. Neither of them knew if Millard Rankin's visit had anything to do with the fire at Stanley's Camp—the Home Guard feeling its oats—or if the Liberty Bond committee had just decided to squeeze a few more dollars out of some of the old-time ranchers. But they figured they knew which it was.

29

THE WAR HAD MADE cloth and buttons scarce and high-priced, so Louise Bliss and the women in her sewing group got together and made Martha's wedding trousseau from several cast-off dresses collected from their own closets. They picked out the stitches and resewed the bodices and sleeves to fit Martha and to resemble styles they had seen advertised in the *Ladies Home Journal*, and in two or three days put together the pieces that would make it possible for Martha to live as a married woman: a muslin nightgown trimmed with ribbon, a brown suit that would do for the wedding and the wedding trip, and two housedresses, one a blue-and-white check and one a pale green with a cream-colored bodice. Louise doubted Martha would wear either of the dresses, but felt she should have them anyway.

Late in April, after the roundup and branding was finished on the ranches and after the cast had come off Martha Lessen's arm, Henry and Martha were married in the Woodruffs' big log living room. They spent their wedding night in the foreman's house on the Split Rock Ranch, and the next day Henry took her on the train over to Haines in the Baker Valley, where his mother and stepfather and his two sisters lived.

Martha and Henry took the spur line up to Pendleton and changed trains there. They had a couple of hours between trains and the weather was soft, the way it can be in April, and not raining, and Martha wanted to see her brothers, the younger ones still at home, so they walked from the station out to her dad's place, which was a fair walk.

Her dad when he came to the door looked pretty surprised to see her, and he shook Henry's hand and said, "Jesus Christ, I never figured this. I figured her for an old maid."

Martha turned red, but Henry just said in a flat way, "You figured wrong."

Martha's mother heard them talking and came in from the kitchen, wiping her hands. She said, "Hello, Martha," and after she heard that Henry and Martha were married she asked when, and they told her just the day before and that this was their wedding trip, and she said, "Well, all right," and nodded, but that was all, and then she went back into the kitchen.

They didn't stay long—they had that long walk to get back to catch the train—and it turned out two of her brothers were away, digging irrigation ditches for a wheat ranch over in the Stanfield Project. But they went out to the barn where Mike, who was the youngest, was repairing an old drill. Martha and her brothers had grown up in a house where people didn't touch, so when Mike lifted his head and saw her there, they both just stood and looked at each other, smiling. He had grown about half a foot since she'd seen him, or it appeared that way to her.

"Hey, Martha."

"Hey, Mike." Her hand was inside the bend of Henry's elbow. "This is Henry."

Henry went over and shook Mike's hand as if they were two men—well, Mike was almost a man, fourteen, nearly fifteen. He peered at Henry and seemed about to ask him something but then he looked at Martha and asked it. "Is he your husband?"

Martha started to blush. "Yes," she said.

They visited a few minutes, talking about horses more than anything else, and when they left, Mike walked with them as far as the lane. He said, "I sure wish Bert and Stevie were here. They're working over in Stanfield."

"I know, Dad told me. When you see them, you tell them how much I miss you all." She couldn't stop from feeling teary. "Maybe you could all come down to see me in Elwha County. You could think about moving down there. There's plenty of work."

"Oh yeah?" He ducked his head, casting a look back toward the house. "I don't know. Dad's pretty stove up." He touched the sleeve of Martha's suit and said, "I'm not used to seeing you in a skirt," and they didn't talk any more about the boys moving down to the valley.

Haines was right on the Union Pacific line, a shipping point for grain and livestock grown in the south part of Union County; Ernest Bailey—that was Henry's stepfather's name—worked as a switchman for the railroad yard there. He was a short, wiry-built man who reminded Martha slightly of Orie's friend

Ray Buford, except for being about sixty years old. Henry's mother was short too and very stout, her bosom a great shelf above a loosely tied corset. She had a ruddy face and a brow bone without much in the way of eyebrows, which was where Henry had come by that look. The two girls, Henry's sisters, had both been married quickly before their husbands shipped over to France, and they had come home to live until the war should end. They looked like their dad, who was Ernest Bailey: they were short and thin and had his sand-colored hair.

They were all easy for Martha to like, although she was uncomfortable with how much Mrs. Bailey and the girls enjoyed hugging her, and kissing her on her forehead or cheeks. They hugged and kissed Henry too, but she didn't mind that so much; she liked watching them together, their easy affection with one another, which didn't make her feel like an outsider but like someone watching a moving picture and caught up in the story. Henry and Jim's father had died when the two boys were four and six, so Ernest Bailey was pretty much the only father Henry remembered. Sometimes Martha looked over and caught Mr. Bailey looking at his wife and his daughters and his stepson with a bemused, charmed smile, and tears standing in his eyes. The whole family was sentimental, every one of them. Henry hadn't been able to hold back a few tears when he spoke his vows at their wedding, and now Martha saw where that came from.

On the fireplace mantelpiece was a large picture in

an ornate cardboard frame, a picture that must have been taken several years back, the two girls and Henry and his brother, Jim, standing behind Mr. and Mrs. Bailey, who were sitting together on an upholstered bench. If she had met him in the street, a stranger, Martha felt she would have known Jim for Henry's brother, they were that much alike, and she had a sudden apprehension of his loss, and the family's loss. In the photograph, all their faces were shining with the seriousness of the moment.

Jane moved her things into her sister Susan's bedroom so there would be a bed for Henry and Martha to sleep in, and sometime after midnight they all settled down to try to sleep. Martha thought Henry would turn his back to her while she undressed and got into the muslin gown—he had done that on their wedding night—but he sat down on the edge of the bed and began unbuttoning his shirt and didn't look away.

"Your parents are just the other side of this wall," she whispered to him, and he smiled and whispered back, "They can't see through the wall."

He took off the rest of his outer clothes while Martha slowly undid some of her buttons, and he folded his clothes neatly and put them down in their suitcase, and then Martha looked away, blushing, while he stepped out of his knit cotton underdrawers and put on the nightshirt he had bought for the wedding trip. She thought he might get into the bed then and finally turn his back to her, but he sat again on the edge of the bed and waited, his eyes on her, while she went on

undressing slowly. The light in the room was dim—
they had brought in just a candle—but when she got
down to her underthings she began to blush fiercely.
From where he sat on the bed, Henry reached out his
hand and caught one of her hands and drew her slowly
to him. He made a long low sound like a deep sigh and
slowly lifted up her undershirt and helped her out of it,
and then her underdrawers. When she was entirely
naked, her skin flaming, he stood up and put his hands
at her waist and whispered into her ear, "I never have
seen anything prettier." But he was as shy as Martha
about anything his parents and his sisters might hear,
all of them being so close by in the small house—he
could hear them talking and moving about, squeaking
the bedsprings, in the other rooms; he knew they
would hear any sound he and Martha made. And he
was afraid if he began touching his wife—his wife!—
there wouldn't be any stopping. So he helped her on
with the muslin gown and then blew out the candle
and they lay down on the bed together in the darkness,
their legs and arms enfolded; and after a while their
hearts quit racing.

There had been a moment, a bright sharp moment as
they stood before the preacher in the Woodruffs' front
room making their wedding promises, when Martha
thought suddenly of Ruth and Tom Kandel—a flash of
insight and of fear—that in marrying Henry she was
throwing herself open to the very thing she had seen in
Ruth's face that terrible morning when Tom was in so
much pain, the morning they had waited together for

the doctor to come. It was a glimpse of the hard truth that loving someone meant living every moment with the knowledge he might die—die in a horrible way—and leave you alone. But Martha was barely twenty years old and this was not something she could hold in her mind for very long. Lying in the darkness with the living heat and weight of her new husband clasped against her breast, she imagined they would go on being happy and young forever.

30

IN THAT SAME MONTH, April of 1918, the month Irene Thiede bought more bonds to keep the Home Guard from tarring and feathering Emil or setting fire to their house or their barn, another kind of fever was set to run through the country. Clyde Boyd, in a letter to his young son, Joe, and his father, W.G., wrote that an influenza was going through the camps in Kansas where he was teaching men to string telephone line; and Will Wright, in a letter to Lizzie, wrote that the flu was going through the men on the front lines, brought over with the last shipload of soldiers from the States.

Over the next months and into the summer of that year, more than half a million people all over the country died of flu, and it killed some people in Elwha County: Alfred Logerwell was one, and also Pearl Bayard. But it fell out that most of the people Martha knew, people who were her friends and her family, made it through the flu epidemic and the war alive.

Both of Henry's brothers-in-law and even Will Wright came home more or less unharmed, although more than a hundred thousand American boys died over there from battle and disease and one of them was Roger Newbry, the friend who had joined up with Will.

Of the four million horses sent over to that war, a million died outright, and of the three million still alive when the end was reached, only a handful made it home alive, horses written up in the newspapers— this or that one brought home by a captain or a colonel whose life had been saved by his horse. After the armistice, with so many farms and fields racked by years of bombs and mustard gas, the three million horses who had survived were butchered for meat to feed all the hungry refugees, something the newspapers failed to mention. Martha wouldn't learn of it until she was a woman of fifty sitting in her living room reading *Life* magazine, dropping the magazine into her lap with a helpless cry.

After the war the spirit of ruthless intolerance and repression that had caused so much trouble in those years carried right over into the peace. In the first months after the war ended, the Ku Klux Klan placed an advertisement in the *Elwha Valley Times-Gazette* calling for new members—"Patriots Who Hold This Country Dear"—to conceal their identities in robes and hoods and march from the Shelby meeting hall to the fairgrounds for a public initiation. Not a single Negro person was living in Elwha County in those days, and the Chinese were all in Grant County or Baker County working the mines, and the Indians were penned up in other parts of the state; but there was a Jewish family running a dry-goods store in Shelby and some Basques and Mexicans down in Owl Creek Canyon and plenty of Catholics of all stripes; and that was where the local Klan planned to focus its attention. That, and patriotic vigilance to keep the Negroes and Chinese and Indians and various undesirable immigrants from moving in and overrunning the valley.

This was around the time the League of Nations was defeated in the Senate, and Jack Bliss, sitting in his wheelchair at the kitchen table with the newspaper spread open on his lap, told George and Louise heatedly that America's reputation around the world as a peaceful and democratic nation, a country with a mission for good, was dead now, had died with that vote. Louise said in dismay, "Oh Jack, I hate to think so." When George looked over at Louise, he wasn't surprised to see her mouth looking drawn-down and thin. He and Louise both worried a good deal over Jack, who was in pain much of the time and suffered from night terrors, dreams his parents couldn't imagine and therefore never spoke of. George didn't feel he had room in his life just now for worrying about what the rest of the world thought of the United States of America.

Not much more than a year after the war ended, Jack Bliss married one of the Glasser sisters and opened a business selling carpet sweepers and other household appliances; in the 1920s, George and Louise moved to town and gave over the running of the ranch to their son-in-law, Howard Hubertine. In those years just before the start of the Great Depression, a couple of money men from Pendleton bought Stanley's Camp and macadamized the road going up to the lake; on the ashes of the livery barn they built a two-lane bowling alley and a dance hall and a hotel, which for a few prosperous years brought crowds of townspeople from as far as Prineville and La Grande and Baker City for summer holidays. When things went downhill in the thirties, the government claimed the property and redrew the boundaries of the forest reserve to take in Stanley's Camp. And sometime in the late thirties a WPA crew built a dam at the outlet of the lake for power and to hold the spring runoff on the Little Bird Woman River, which served to irrigate a few farms in the upper valley and also quickly put an end to the fish runs. Stanley's cabins had been log-built with the bark left on, which made a sentimental picture, but they were run up from the bare ground without any sort of foundation, and the gaps between the logs stuffed with newspaper and pebble dash. After the hotel was built Stanley's little cabins were left vacant and went quickly to ruin, and by the time the dam went up, not much was left of those old cabins but crumbled heaps of litter in the bare outline of logs.

In 1938, after George died, Miriam Hubertine persuaded her mother to write a history of Elwha County, from Indian days to the end of the Great War. Louise's thin little book was called *The Wonderful Country* and dedicated "To My Dear Family and Friends," and it was published by the *Times-Gazette* in celebration of the county's fiftieth anniversary of incorporation. By then, Emil Thiede had twice been elected to the Board of County Commissioners, and Louise's chapter about the war years—the way the Thiedes among others had been made to feel isolated and despised—struck most people as a quaint and improbable fiction. Within a couple of years there would be an internment camp in the county, and a few hundred Japanese Americans living in made-over livestock barns, but not many people saw this as having anything to do with Louise's story about that earlier war.

In later years when Martha was an old woman—as old as the Woodruff sisters had been when Martha first came into Elwha County—one of her granddaughters pointed out to her that her life had overlapped with the lives of the famous Apache Indian Geronimo and the famous Western gunslinger John Wesley Hardin; that she had seen Buffalo Bill, in his fringed and beaded leathers and shock of white hair, when he came through Pendleton and set up his Wild West Show on the fairgrounds; and that when she was sixty years old and she and Henry were living on a ranch in northern Nevada she had stood out on her porch and watched that other show, the mushroom cloud from an A-bomb they were testing over there in the desert. And wasn't that just amazing to think about?

Martha was taken aback. All her childhood dreams went flying through her mind in a moment. She remembered how, in her dreams, she had galloped bareback across fenceless prairies through grass as high as the horse's belly. She had dreamed of living like the Indians, intimate with animals, intimate with the earth. Sometimes in those dreams, just as in the Western romances, she had no name, no family. For a while she had taken as her heroes the cowboys of those novels—lone horsemen, symbols of independence and freedom—who were not a bit like the cowboys she knew in her life, men whose only freedom was the right to quit at the drop of a hat and look for work on down the road.

It occurred to her now that the West of her dreams was not—never could be—the testing ground for atomic bombs; and she wondered how it had happened. She said to her granddaughter, without planning to say it, "You know, honey, I guess we brought about the end of our cowboy dreams ourselves." It was a startling thing to hear herself say, but then she thought: Here I am in my old age and just at the beginning of figuring out what that means, or what to do about it.

ACKNOWLEDGMENTS

This book grew slowly from a seed planted years ago by Teresa Jordan in her oral history *Cowgirls: Women of the American West*. It's been a long germination, but I would now like to thank Teresa, and to thank "the rancher's daughter" Marie Bell, whose words recorded by Teresa quietly took root in my mind. This is not Marie's story, of course, but I have borrowed Marie's seed words almost verbatim for the opening lines of the novel.

I'm grateful to Soapstone and Fishtrap for residencies in support of this writing, and to the Harris family of Soda Springs, Idaho, for time spent on horseback and for stories around the supper table, especially McGee Harris's story about stranded cows and the horse that righted himself after drowning.

And thanks to Russ Johnson of Georgetown, Idaho; Corine Elser of Crane, Oregon; Gigi Meyer of Alfalfa, Oregon; Linda and Martin Birnbaum of Summerville, Oregon; Stella and John Lillicrop of Mitchell, Oregon; Samantha Waltz of Portland, Oregon; Becky Sheridan of Lakeview, Oregon; and especially Lesley Neuman of Rescue, California: for schooling me in the art and the hearts of horses.

Center Point Publishing
600 Brooks Road ● PO Box 1
Thorndike ME 04986-0001 USA

(207) 568-3717

US & Canada:
1 800 929-9108
www.centerpointlargeprint.com